For Mum, Dad and Lizzie

Special wishes to

Jemima, Sophia, Emilia, Max, Toby and Jack

To

Everyone who has inspired my writing

& the reader who picks up a book and steps into a new world.

Cover design Liz Mullin

A FREEDOM WARRIOR BOOK

First Published 2017

Copyright @ Katherine Mullin 2017

The Lost King

By

Kate Mullin

When your dreams seem furthest away,

That is when they are the closest to you.

Remember, time is important for dreams to prevail.

Dreams will follow patience,

their lengthy-making is always underestimated.

Chapter 1. A Boy

As the afternoon disappeared, the evening stood with grey light spread across the night's sky. Horses and their riders, Dexy and Jee Hanna trotted along with purpose and supplies to take to The Silver Mountains.

Dexy slowed, he had seen a mound by the side of the path. Was it a body? "Stop the horses, I'm gonna see what that is over there!" said Dexy slowing down his horse to a stop and jumping down. He was calm but urgent in his approach. "What is it?" said Jee Hanna.
"I don't know. I think I know what it might be...' Dexy whispered seriously.
"You think it's a body?" asked Jee Hanna.
"Only one way to find out," said Dexy. It looked more like a human the closer he got.

His charm, never far away was wasted on Jee Hanna, a spider fairy, young enough to be his daughter. He had taken her in and raised her since most spider fairies had been 'erased' in the Great War ten years ago. They lived far in the mountains now, with other 'outsiders', who liked it that way, or have no choice.

As Dexy walked over from the dusty track, he wondered who was lying so awkwardly, lifeless and still, was it a trick or someone in need? As Dexy approached, he realised this was not the body of a man, but a boy.

Jee Hanna took the reins and walked both horses together as they looked at the boy lying at the edge of the woods in front of them. Her dark whispery spider hair covered her face and body like a beautiful cloak. She was pretty; most spider fairies were. She had that glittery outline which made them look magical in any light. Her silver specs of dust lined the end of each hair making her glow.

For now, the sun shone and the clouds now drifting over leaving the small boy to cool and shiver.

"Bring some water and a blanket," Dexy instructed Jee Hanna.

She passed them, knowing the next few moments would tell a lot for the person who lay in front of them. A boy. He looked small but that might have been because he was curled up she thought.

Dexy poured water out onto his own hands and then carefully over the boy's face. "Will he be ok?" she asked.

"He is breathing, though it's light," he said.

Dexy had seen many wounded soldiers in his time. He knew the boy would live, but he needed to wake him from his unconscious danger. Dexy moved the boy's body round so that he could see his face, and stretched out his legs to give him room to breathe and get air back into him.

"Someone's given him a good licking. Not his lucky day!" said Dexy trying to get him awake.

Dexy worked on the boy keeping him warm and getting him to wake up. He knew how to treat wounds; he had seen to his own enough times. He knew how to clean an open wound and check for broken bones. He knew that keeping the boy hydrated and conscious would be the key to keeping him alive. The watery blood trickled away from his wounds, as he washed the dirty smashed face. He became clearer to them, a young boy not older than twelve at most. His face started to show more features, and the dirt and blood moved reluctantly from his face, with each dab of Dexy's clean cloth.

"Can we get him to the horse? Take him to the mountains?" asked Jee Hanna, as she gazed at the small boy in front of her. "We can care for him there and he can get better," she added hopefully.

"No we need to get him awake. Then we take him home. He won't be far from home and he will have a family waiting for him, starting to worry as to why he has not come home for his next meal," he snapped.

Dexy did not need a boy to mend in the mountains; he had other business there. Jee Hanna on the other hand, enjoyed the thought of a person to look after; she could nurse, make better and befriend. He looked nice, the boy. He looked kind. She liked him already, even though he was lying in front of her in a pool of blood and dust.

"Can you hear me?" Dexy tried. "Can you hear me?"

He shook carefully, trying to stir the boy into some sort of consciousness. The boy's body like a rag swaying with each shake, again and again. Jee Hanna watched knowing that if anyone could help wake the boy it was Dexy. The minutes passed. The boy be twitched. A strange sound came from him.

"Ahhhnn, aaahhhmmmm," he whimpered trying to wake.

"Boy can you hear me?" Dexy tried again, relieved at some noise no matter how pain-filled it sounded.

A sweat had begun to drip out of the boy and Dexy tried to comfort him with more water, his only 'medicine' for now.

"Try to drink," Dexy encouraged as he held water to the boy's lips.

"Boy, you're ok. You are good. Can you hear me? I am going to get you home. Can you hear me?" Dexy persevered.

"He's waking up, isn't he?" cried Jee Hanna.

"He's in a lot of pain, but he'll be ok," Dexy assured her. "We need to clean his wounds. Bring some more cloths from the bags. Let's get his face cleaned up and have a look at him, whoever he is. He's only a young one that's for sure."

"Lucc..." Luca tried. "Lucca..."

Jee Hanna noticed as she passed the towels over, "he's trying to speak."

"Luccaa" Luca tried again.

"He's saying something. Luca. Is that your name? Luca, we're gonna help you," she said reassuringly.

"Can you hear me, boy?" Dexy shook him again, gently but assured.

"Luca," said the boy, he was determined to speak now some thoughts had returned.

The grey sky, darker than the one he had walked along to this morning in glorious sunshine hours earlier. He could see the outline of the strangers in front of him, they were becoming clearer with every moment, but so was the pain. It flooded back to him with a frightening jolt, his body's aching kept him quiet again and his eyes shut once more.

"He's saying, Luca...! Luca! You're going to be safe Luca. You will be ok," Jee Hanna was thrilled to learn his name- it had sent her heart leaping!

She was as any young girl and fell quickly 'in love' with new acquaintances, though she knew to remain sensible in front of Dexy, who would not approve if she gave herself away.

"Luca, we need to get you home. Can you tell us where you live?" Dexy mopped his wounds and the boy's face and injuries both became clearer with each sweep. He looked better by the second, the congealed blood moving away to show smaller wounds, which would heal. He opened his eyes and squinted for a second time at Dexy. He felt that he was safe and tried to speak but no words came out.

"Where do you live, Luca? We can take you home," said Dexy.

"The Daccorian region... the village by the White Lake," Luca managed. He wanted to get home with an urgency that was overwhelming him. He spoke with all his might, getting more used to the constant tornadoes of pain which lashed around his body.

"Save your energy boy. We'll get you home. It's not that far," Dexy was a master of comfort and protection. He was well known for this amongst his friends and now Luca was fortunate enough to be in his care.

His luck maybe had not run all the way out on him today after all.

"Jee Hanna, can you help me get him onto one of the horses?" Dexy spoke relieved and happier.

The three set off. A saddled horse carried Luca home.

Little did they know, that this was a beginning like no other...
Their lives would become entwined forever. The boy knew nothing of Dexy and who he was; but Dexy was about to discover a truth about the boy that would change their lives forever.

Not since ten years ago after the Great War had changed everything...

But as everything changed, so it must change again. This meeting would be the catalyst for a change beyond all that had become known...The stars know this and now so do you...They of course knew nothing.

Time knew...oh she knew... she was a keeper.

Chapter 2. Discovery

"Time is as important as anything in order for dreams to prevail."

Dexy led the horses keeping a steady pace with the boy on one, Jee Hanna holding him steady, sat behind him so he didn't fall.
"We need to head North, the track should lead us to the lake the boy spoke of," said Dexy. He seemed to have no doubt that they would get Luca home.

Jee Hanna knew of 'The White Lake' that Luca had mentioned... It was said, that you could see creatures and people who have died. The lake has given messages from the dead on many occasions. She wondered if they could stop for some rest there and she could take her time to see if her family would come. Of course she knew they had to get Luca home, but she thought she would ask Dexy to think about it on the way home. She hoped he would let her. She daydreamed of her brothers and sisters, Margo and Dylan, Jemmy and Dally. Her family! Then she turned to think of the boy she was keeping steady in front of her. She could sense he was in pain. She wondered what his family would be like, who was missing him and if they cared. They took him to his home.

Luca had only a mother.

Ava Lockharth was worrying. With each thought, another dreadful scenario of what might have happened to her son entered her head. She could not help but go to the window every minute to see if her boy was on his way, walking up the path? Her thoughts shifted between worry and anger. How could he put her through this torment? He knew she would worry?

She had warmed a potato and leek soup, the evening meal so many times on the open fire... 'just in time for your tea' she could hear herself saying, as she had imagined him arriving at last. Of course the soup now crusty and dry, bore no impact on her son returning home at the usual time. He was now five hours late and it was becoming dark. She never let him out on his own after dark. She was a protective mother and she never compromised on this. She kept him close at all times. She needed to- he was her only child.

Ava was unable to sit still. She stood at times and then paced at other moments, though the stone cottage. It was unbearable- the not knowing. She had lit so many candles around the small front room, as something to do, their flickering a constant moving shadow on the wall. The light shining on her beautiful face, her features, delicate and light even though she was tense, waiting for news of her son, or better still his arrival home. She had called round at neighbour Roper Stern's home earlier. When she told him that Luca was over two hours late, he had gone out to look for her boy, but she had had no word from him either.

Roper Stern treated Luca as a son. Luca was the best friend of his daughter Ettie. They had played together since they were babies and had strong bond, which was obvious when they were together. Ettie was tucked up in bed unaware of her friend's dreadful ordeal. She would have cried herself to sleep if she had known of his situation.

Ava could do nothing but wait for news. She hoped it would be soon. She sat once more and clenched her weary hands, squeezing her fears through each finger, making them ache. Her house awaited the boy with an amber glow. It stood out in the village where others were blowing out their candles for the night and taking themselves to bed.

The moon was a thin narrow wisp in the air, a lemon peel hanging on a pin. It was surrounded by hopeful stars that could pick out drops of dust and shine themselves in lines of glittering light through the night sky, out onto the lake and the paths. Ava knew the stars could see her boy, wherever he was. She wished she they could speak. Where could he be?

Instead she spoke to the boy's father and her husband in her head. His soft voice she could hear in her head and she could remember him as his voice came to her. The air around her felt softer and her arms prickled as the hair on them brushed forwards with thoughts of her late husband. It was always him that she spoke to in times of worry. He never left her. He had promised her that as he walked down to the battlegrounds on the day his life ended. She could feel his spirit with her. Her husband would always calm her worried mind, just as he had done when he was alive.

She went back to that day.
The day he fell. She went over it many times in her mind. They had been tension at the castle for weeks, they knew an invasion was planned. Messengers had warned resistance was building, that the sluggetts in the Saccorion region would come. Finally, they did.

The sluggett army filed into the castle and lined the City walls.

Marcus had no choice but to place his armour on and prepare for battle. The army ready to defend the city. The outnumbered soldiers fell slowly, there were too many sluggetts, they fought and fell as the day pattered on. It was clear that they were no match for the four thousand sluggetts; at four to one.

Ava knew she would have to get away, to run to a place of safety, even if her husband was still fighting in the fields.

She never forgot leaving him that day. Marcus was her husband. It was like leaving half her mind and taking a muddled confused one in its place. She could not think straight without him.

She had no choice but to leave as the fighting became fierce and the attackers gathered their strength. Her advisors made sure she did. They had to protect the royal queen. They knew that if the Slug King won this battle, she would be the first to be executed. She was a threat to the Slug King's position. He would not risk keeping her alive. She was a greater risk than even he could have imagined- she was carrying a small gift in her stomach. She had to protect it at all costs. The baby boy was born six months later, but his father would never see him. Luca would never know his father. His father was never made it home from the battlefields. He was gone. The King no more. The news of his death hit the queen (Amber then, now Ava) so hard she felt her heart had been ripped from her chest. Her mind thought of him every day and with Luca missing, she imagined him out looking for his son, and by her side, comforting her. Ava drifted back to the present, and cursed the moon that her son was not still home.

Back on the path, with the slither of a moon above the travellers, Luca became more conscious with every horse trot. He did not talk; his energy was gone. He concentrated on keeping himself on the horse. Jee Hanna helped him, steadying him if he swayed one way or the other. He knew it was evening. He felt safe with his new companions, even though he did not know them. Their reassurances of home helped.

Luca knew his mum would be frantic by now. He wished the journey would end as quickly. He looked around to see if he recognised the gravel path and the hooded trees. It was difficult in the dark. The area was still unfamiliar to him. He always worried about his mum. He was a kind boy. He was used to thinking of her feelings, since his father was not around to do it. Ava had always known she had had a sensitive and caring child. His thoughtfulness reminded her of his father, as if he were still alive. Luca could hear his mother's voice in his head willing him home. He tried not to think about it. It was not helping him, but it was better than thoughts of the boys from the attack, which kept jumping into his mind. The gang with the boy's faces kept appearing in front of him. The laughing hung in his head. He tried not to think of the beating, but it was too difficult not too. It was flooding back to him. His thoughts swirled around his head like a wind from the east. He saw the boy reach out and punch him. The tall boy was too big to escape.

Suddenly, the next thought snapped him awake from his memory of the attack. He remembered his bracelet! He checked his wrist quickly to see. It was gone. They had taken it. The bracelet had gone. The boy had taken it. He remembered. He remembered it all too clearly. He groaned with pain. The gift from his father gone. The only thing that meant something to him. His mother had told him to keep it safe and not to wear it outside. She had told him on so many occasions. She even made him promise and now it was gone. How could he have let them take it? How could he have been so stupid, he told himself. His anger ran through his veins like a pumping volcano erupting in his body. His father had been given it by the king, for his services and loyalty. It was inscribed, "For a king." His mother told him how his father had been given it as a great honour.

He let out a loud yell which startled the sleepy Jee Hanna and purposeful Dexy.

"Friggastrons! Ah! Ah!" yelled Luca. It was not a word he used often.

Dexy looked at the boy. He was amused at his outburst as much as relieved that he was making some noise. Jee Hanna was shocked.

"What's wrong? Are you ok?" she asked.

"Baggastons!" cried Luca in even more anger.

Dexy searched his face to see why the anger now. The boy's red eyes glanced at him.

"What is it, boy?" said Dexy, patting the horses to reassure them to keep walking.

"They took something of mine. It was precious to me!" said Luca.

"What did they take?" asked Jee Hanna, intrigued.

"Anything they took they can have. They didn't finish you and that's what matters," said Dexy forcefully.

"My bracelet!" Luca cried, he was angrier and he was not calming down from Dexy's words. "Those pigs took my bracelet!"

"You can get another one I am sure," Jee Hanna tried to offer words of comfort.

"And can my father come back from the dead and give it to me?" snapped Luca.

Dexy cut in,

"That's enough boy, Jee Hanna was only trying to help. We are sorry about your bracelet, but there is no need to speak to the spider fairy like that," Dexy was looking carefully at the boy's face. He could see something familiar about it. Was it the anger he recognised? Or was it something else, he thought.

Jee Hanna had gone quiet after Luca's outburst. They rode on. After a few minutes of silence, Luca spoke again.

"I'm sorry. Thank you for helping me."

"That's ok. You wanna see Dexy when he loses it now that's something," said Jee Hanna making a joke.

"Hey, I never lose it. I am always in control," laughed Dexy, as his thoughts raced back to a time where he had seen this boy's face before.

He was thinking at one million seconds speed. He hardly dared believe the thought, which had just come to him moments earlier. Could this be? Could this be the boy? Could it be that he had found the boy who had only been whispered about by spider fairies and falconettes and freedom warriors? Dexy looked again. He wanted to be sure. He looked into the boy's eyes and he recognised their colours. It was the boy...he was sure. It was what they had been hoping for ten years since the Great War and now he had it all here right in front of him. The boy would be going home but not for long if Dexy got his way!

They continued on their journey, but Dexy was thinking only of revenge and uprising. It was his only thought now he had seen the boy. The boy they had all hoped to find one day~ Luca was that boy! Marcus' son.

Roper Stern was becoming weary. He had eaten last at lunchtime and now the silvery moon reminded him that it was later than he wanted it to be. He cared nothing for his lost meal. His thoughts were on Luca. His hopes of finding the boy were becoming less by the second. The night was black. He wondered where he could possibly be. He wondered about turning back, but how could he return to Ava with no answers? What would he say?

Time was passing slowly. It seemed to suspend in the air, making minutes of worrying feel like an unbearable trickle of torturing seconds. He felt each mile that he covered. His feet were beginning to feel numb. His long sandal straps that tied to his legs, rubbed against his calves and the dirt in between his toes from the path grated like intolerable ants. The shaking of his feet, from time to time, did nothing to ease his discomfort.

He was a dependable man whose face was soft for his age, but showed some signs of worry lines in the places where kindness rests too, making them never harsh. His youth had been full and now in his old age, his statue showed a well-lived life. He was broad and his belly was large and sturdy. His legs showing proud muscles that were round and sculpted. His broad dependable shoulders matched his character.

Roper tried not to think of what could have happened in the hours Luca had been away. Instead he believed Luca, a boy whose character was good, would not come to any harm, he hoped. The boy had never been in much trouble. It was often his own daughter Ettie who would find the trouble and Luca would usually pull them out of it. They were a great couple of friends, 'best and till the end' they always laughed.

The night was black. The stars were small and shone half bright as the night continued, aging like a dark old man. The view became a bland mixture of grey outlines, of hedges and fields, with paths and woodlands nearby woolly shadows. Roper stopped and stretched his hands resting them on his back. His owl-wise eyes scrunched and closed to refresh his troubled mind. He hoped on opening them, he would have a new view, idea, or plan to put into action. But nothing came to him. A plan would be too much to ask for. He was searching in the dark and the boy he was looking for could be anywhere by now. Roper was out of ideas. Should he carry on? He stood again with hand over his thick, whiskery grey moustache. He was stopping more than he was walking- a sign of his weariness and of the night's silent wish for him to sleep. Weary, weary, weary as the colder air filled the night, Roper was losing hope. He turned back. He had gone as far as he could. The boy would not have left the Daccorian region. Surely?

The three travellers were well inside the Daccorian region. They had taken a different route to Roper. The boy had talked of the White Lake and they were almost upon it now. The path led them around the edge, where dragonfly wingtips could still be made out like bits of cotton floating peacefully on the surface. It was steamy, and the magical glow from it sent a ripple of excitement through Jee Hanna, as she gazed across at the beautiful sight. Luca had seen it many times before. He had always hoped his father would come to him, but it had never happened. People had talked of their loved ones giving messages, reflecting in the water, but it was not to be for Luca. He felt abandoned not only by his father but by the Lake too.

Jee Hanna had had exactly the same wish as Luca. She wanted to see her family again, she wished for their appearance at the Lake. She wondered dreamily about the White Lake and its powers. She took her chance to ask Luca more. It would be good to keep him awake now and talk of something of interest to both of them. It would also alert Dexy to her interest in it and make it easier for her to ask him for a visit on the way home.

"Is it true that the Lake brings messages from the dead?" she asked, hoping for lots of stories.

"I have never seen anything in it or had any messages. So I don't know for sure, but there are many stories. The stories say that a white lady appears and speaks. They could be made up, or they could be from people desperate to see something," Luca said.

"...or true," Jee Hanna finished his sentence.

"Yes, or true," he replied.

He tried not to sound too bitter when he talked about the Lake. He had been hurt by it. He felt he had been so let down; to be sent nothing, no word from his father. It struck his heart cruelly every time he thought of it. Yet every story he heard filled him with renewed hope and he would return to the lake, hopeful, no sign from his father. The Lake seemed to have 'chosen ones'. He would never admit that he had spent many hours sat by the water waiting for his father to come. It was Ettie who knew where to find him, on such days, but she kept his secret safe, as she knew he would be embarrassed if anyone knew. Luca used his thoughts to give him strength as he learnt the lesson the Lake was giving him. He learnt not to rely on sympathy from the water. He knew he could not rely on a message being his right to receive. He had to respect that, if no message came, then this was what he had to accept, no matter how much it hurt. He didn't like to feel so desperate, so had made himself keep his lake visits short. The White Lake was not a happy place for Luca anymore.

"Do you think the stories are true?" Jee Hanna probed him further.

"I guess so, yes, yes I do," he concluded, his faith in the Lake never faltered. His hope for his father's appearance did.

Dexy listened to the boy more closely than before. He was taking in his every word. He watched Luca. He looked at his face and his mannerisms. He studied his every move. He was checking that he was not wrong, something about the boy had unsettled him. He wanted to be sure that this was the boy. Who else could it be? He had the bracelet from his father. Dexy knew 'the bracelet' well, as his father had never taken it off when he was alive and now here was his son in front of Dexy, as clear as day. Luca looked like his father. He was the image of him, Dexy thought it to himself. Even the way Luca talked reminded Dexy of the boy's father!

"Yes, I have met creatures who have talked of the White Lady. They say their friends and family who died in The Great War and have spoken to them from the lake," Dexy joined their chatter.

Jee Hanna took her chance to ask,

"Could we come back this way and stop for a while, just to see..."

"Our first priority is to get Luca home and then we will have to make like the wind for home ourselves," Dexy was careful not to say where home was as it would arouse suspicion, even if the boy was in their care.

"If we have time...?" Jee Hanna pleaded. She would not give up so easily.

"We won't have time, you know we won't," Dexy replied, sternly but gently as he knew it mattered to the spider fairy. "One day we shall make time and I will bring you here again, but not this time," he added. His final word!

Jee Hanna didn't reply. She knew her voice would be filled with disappointment, and didn't want either of her travelling companions to hear that. She swallowed a lump in her throat and blinked the tears back from her eyes, which had come from nowhere. She held on to her deep memories of her brothers and sisters and felt the unfairness race through her body like a tornado. Her silence a sign of her sadness.

"I have never seen anything. I always hoped I would see my father, but I never have," Luca added.

Jee Hanna felt sympathy for him. He was brave to tell them she thought. She hoped her fate would be different to his when she had time to look into the White Lake. She hoped she would get an appearance from her lost loved family. She went dreamy at the thought of messages from her family and what they might be, as they trotted on, she replaced the pain in her heart with a wish for that day to come.

Luca, now wanted to see his mother more than anything. He knew they were only a twenty-minute horse walk away. He clung on and counted down the minutes as they rode on. The familiar path filled him with new strength. He explained the shortest route to Dexy. Dexy led them on through the night path. He started to think carefully about what he would say to Luca' mother when they arrived after the initial excitement and relief was out of the way.

Sure enough, soon they were at the cottage. A soft outline of a small thatched roof presented itself in front of them and a short path led to the wooden door, simple and plain. Dexy knocked, but it was opened before his first knuckle had reached the wood. Ava ran out straight to her son. Luca fell off the horse into his mother's arms. She wept as she held him tightly. She carried him in, forgetting to even look at the strangers whom he had arrived with, though the door stayed open to let them in. Luca was placed in a chair by the fire. He slumped into it, flinching at the movement from her carrying him.

"My poor boy. Look at your face!" she said as she saw his wounds for the first time.

"He'll be ok," Dexy spoke.

She looked up, reminded that she had company.

"Yes, yes, I know. Look at him," she said in a motherly tone full of relief and love. She helped him get comfortable. His body hurt. It was not ready for a new position. He wanted to be left. Jee Hanna tied up the horses and Dexy checked they were secure. Then they went inside. Ava's grey dress, touched the ground, made her graceful.

"We found him just south of the woodlands," said Dexy. He watched her, a simple woman, not a queen.

"Do you know what happened?" she asked.

"We think some boys got to him. We found him lying unconscious, in this state," said Dexy. "We think older boys attacked him, lucky we found him."

Jee Hanna remained silent. Her little body cold from the night, was enjoying the warmth from the fire in the room, which made her body tingle as it started to thaw. "Thank you for bringing him home. Please sit down," she offered them small wooden chairs with rounded backs, which were more comfortable than they looked. Luca was in the bigger chair, which had arms to it and cushions. His mum was looking at him checking each cut to see the damage to his face and chest. "Thank you," said Dexy.

Jee Hanna and Dexy sat both happy for warmth. Dexy moved his stool nearer the fire and warmed his hands. Jee Hanna hunched her shoulders to snap up the more heat from the fire's embers. Ava had found a clean cloth. She dipped it in the water to bathe her son's wounds, wiping away crusted blood stains from his skin. She hoped it would all wipe away.

"I will clean him up and put him to bed. He can tell me what happened tomorrow," she said gratefully. "Would you like a drink of raspberry tea?"

"We shall, but don't worry about us, see to your son. May I get some water for the horses?" Dexy was always calm and would know what to say. He found some old pots and filled them. It was not his home, but he didn't want her to fetch for them either.

"Thank you, " gushed Jee Hanna, as she sat. She felt should say something but didn't know what else to say. She would leave the talking to Dexy. She liked the house. She was used to the mountains. She had lived there most of her life. The house seemed so cosy and comfortable in comparison to her mountain cave.

"Is she your daughter?" Ava asked, though continued to see to her son who was sleepy, gritting his teeth as the water stung each cut. She dabbed the places that looked the worst.

"No, she is one of the last spider fairies, aren't you? So I take care of her," he replied.

They all knew what this meant. Since the Great War, in which spider fairies did not do well and most were wiped out. Some were seen from time to time, but it was rare. Jee Hanna smiled. She was used to it.

"Oh, yes, I see now. Gosh, my mind is...well, you know. I was going out of my mind with worry," she said, feeling embarrassed to have not looked properly to see that indeed she was not a girl.

She could only focus on her son. She smiled to see her him even in this state, with a small tear dripping out of the corner of her eye. He was home she thought with tremendous joy. She was relieved beyond belief! She continued to wash him - his face, neck and chest. The clean warm water was working. Luca smiled back at his mother. The smells of home greeted his nostrils, potato and leek soup tones he knew well were drifting through the air. His felt his mum's soft hands near. Her voice never changed though he could tell it was shaken with worry, but he was home. At last, he was home. He closed his eyes. Relief washed over him. His mother caressed him like a baby and his breathing lowered. Sleep was not far away now.

"Home is where a heart will beat safely. It feels like a kind soul welcoming you into her arms, offering peace and comfort like a warm blanket. Home is with you forever. There is always a way back home.

Chapter 3. Disagreement

Back in the mountains tempers were getting short. Waiting for Dexy and Jee Hanna, with the food, which had not arrived, had left Gobbler in a very bad mood. His moods were always controlled by how full his stomach was. An empty stomach equalled a cross troll.

"Where the devil's aunt have they got to?" he said grumpily.

"I am sure they are on their way. They will turn up when they can," said Falentona calmly.

"It's getting late and my stomach is as empty as a squirrel's larder at the end of the winter," complained Gobbler.

The grumbling in his intestines, making Falentona try not to laugh, as she knew it would infuriate her hungry friend. They were all hungry. It had been a long day. They always had their big meal together in the cave, when the fire could keep them warm as well as heating meat and vegetables. Falentona was more worried about the increasing lateness of her friends, but she knew Dexy would have good reason and would keep Jee Hanna safe.

"Why don't you keep busy, mend the leather bags or something?" suggested Jax. Dexy's younger brother.

"I can't work on an empty stomach," snapped Gobbler.

"You find work difficult at the best of times..." chipped in Falentona.

She was a harsh looking falconette, but her wit made her a sharp character. She kept their spirits high at all times and would tell stories of her time spent in the palace, as the head falcon to the Queen Norsa of Monfore. She escaped the difficult queen to live in the mountains. She was the only falconette who had arrived in the mountains, a few years after the War.

"I work best with food in my stomach, yes. I hope you're not implying that I don't pull my own weight," he said with continued grumpiness.

"That would be difficult," said Jax sarcastically.

"Yes, very funny. Very funny! Trolls need to eat," he concluded.

"Of course you work hard, Gobbs! No one's having a go. We're all getting hungry. We will give them a bit longer," said Jax, trying to make amends.

It was a happy group. Their caved home was carved secretly into the largest of the Silver Mountains, as if they ordered it. These were the Silver Mountains, which were south of the Daccorian region. They were deceptively large inside. They ran to the West of the Slug City, almost opposite each other, but thirty miles apart. The cracks and crevices of the largest mountain were wide enough for rooms, each one a different function: kitchen, bedrooms and storage. Clever hooks and shelves had made good use of space and the amount of tools and features they had was something to be admired. Each 'outsider' had their own skills and used them well for the success of the group. The accomplishment of living in such harsh territory had been a challenge, which had made them a close-knit family. They were not family, of course, but bickered enough for it to be almost the same and they had grown to love each other dearly. The loving arguments and lively discussions were never far away, but laughter always won in the end, with a bit of sulking in between.

The 'outsiders' had lived here since the Great War. They did not know when they might return home and some had no homes to go to. And so had made it their business, to make their place of rest a comfortable, homely one. Each had their own tale to tell...

Gobbler had been injured in the Great War. His own pack of trolls did not want him with them. An injured troll was always outcast. They had abandoned him and he had been left to fend for himself in the woods. They would not carry him; it was the way trolls were. (Their heartless rules might seem cruel, to a non-troll.) For weeks, he had managed on tiny meagre rations and nursed himself back to health. He had been in the woods so for two months, when Dexy had stumbled across him. The troll had been happy to share a hearty meal of insects, forest leaves and hedgehog meat, by the fire. They got along instantly. Gobbler had many a tale to tell. His chewed and lived-in, dark green face, would wrinkle with delight, to have a person to listen to his tales. He would talk of the way of the trolls and his old life. Dexy was keen to learn of other creatures and cultures. He found out; it was a great sign of a troll to have many pimples on their noses and cheeks, it showed wisdom. Gobbler had several and had talked of them appearing and his pride at having them. He made it his business to walk that way again and catch up with his friend. They would converse for hours, many times since, sharing what food they had. Their friendship had led to trust. Dexy had sensed Gobbler was a social, sensitive soul who needed friends. Eventually, he had invited him to the mountains to join the group and Gobbler accepted the invitation with great enthusiasm. He was grateful. He had been lonely on his own. He missed company and friendship like a puppy dog, always eager to please. He was clumsy, but supplied the troop with endless laughter and amusement. His laugh so loud and infectious; he had been a great addition to the group.

Dexy had left his family when he was thirteen. His father gave him a miserable life of insults and beatings. The day he left he just ran so far away and decided to never go back, apart from to get his younger brother, he did this three weeks later, when he knew he could make it alone and support them both. His brother Jax was only seven at the time. He went back in the dark of a warm night and took his brother out of his bed and carried quietly to a place of safety. Jax knew his brother would return for him and the three weeks of waiting had seemed like an eternity. The two brothers had had lived together ever since. They built a hut, which was both strong and secure enough for them to live successfully. They hunted together. They practiced fights and running. Each had strong spirits and a lust for life in the outdoors. Jax enjoyed making weapons and tools out of anything he could. Dexy was athletic and competitive. He would go into the town and win fighting tournaments that were put on in the market, which made him a name and some money. This brought him to the attention of King Marcus who ruled in those days. A fair and well-liked king, that was all before the Great War...

Marcus watched Dexy's skills and took him on as a worker to be in charge of training and weapon making. Over the years, he became a loyal friend to the Royal guardsmen, teaching fighting skills to the soldiers and the king himself. He was like gladiator. His military mind and sense of survival was useful to the king, who took Dexy's advice on many occasion. It seemed to come naturally to him, but it all ended when Gerrado, the Slug King had waged war against the kingdom, ten years ago and now ruled in a cruel ruthless way which left villagers and towns creatures in fear, downtrodden and grieving for the days in the peaceful rule of King Marcus. They had lost a bitter battle and the war they never expected had destroyed a once happy kingdom. Most who could had fled to the Daccorian region. The city was unstable and not safe but even out in the countryside, they had to pay heavy taxes to him to remain there. It had been a disaster to lose a war against the Slug King and his army of compassion-less sluggetts. Their number and strength had been too much for the small army. With his King Marcus dead, carried from the battlefield, Dexy could not risk being near the town, where he would be recognised by enemies and killed. Their survival demanded that they left the city. Both Dexy and Jax headed for the Silver mountains, far beyond the Daccorian region out of the village settlements and fled to the mountains for safety. They were the first of the 'outsiders' to live in the mountains.

His other companions had found their way there by accident.

Keto, was human, as far as anyone could tell and no one ever asked him. He was so old and seemed to have lived for at least a hundred years. His long white hair was sleek. He had a wise old face, which twisted into many looks. He was wiry and thin. He mixed potions and herbs to make medicines when they were sick, though he was almost certainly blind in one eye and eyesight failed in the other. He got by, but sometimes it was clear he could not see as well as he pretended to. Maybe that was his reason for staying. He never left the mountain, but would make lists of items he needed for the others to collect and help him make their much needed remedies for every illness. His creams and medicines always worked. Jax had asked if he was like a wizard, but he had replied that there was no magic, only science in his concoctions. He said he did not believe in magic and that wizards were myths from stories, as far as he knew. He didn't seem to have anywhere else to be, and kept his story of where he was from to himself. Everyone respected this, though they would try to question him from time to time, hoping for some information, but it never came. He would tell them of other things, whilst stroking his long beard, which reached the floor and curled round like a large ringlet. His usefulness had been invaluable to the group and they could not imagine being without him.

Samlit was a 'harefoot'. A rabbit man, a fine musician whose floppy ears loved a tune. He sang the days away. His clothes were simple and bright, a little green waistcoat, he never took off, made him look tiny. He was the smallest of the group, but he could make the most noise. He owned a banjo and a pipe, which he never let out of his sight. He hummed and clapped and tapped and scraped, anything he could get his hands on would become an instrument. He kept them jolly on the long cold nights and told poetry with powerful performances.

Jee Hanna had been saved by Dexy. He had found her wondering, aimlessly and tear-sodden, lost amongst the destruction of the war, when she was only five. He could see her family had been slaughtered, (it was him who buried them and others along the way). Jee Hanna was left sitting in an empty field looking for them. He took her with him so that she was not killed by the sluggetts, like the rest of her family. She had survived the terrible war when her family and most spider fairies had not. They were wiped out as a group and no one knew how many now still lived. Jee Hanna would not have survived without Dexy and she saw him as her father figure and knew no different, though she did have memories of her family which would flood back to her in dreams and moments when she closed her eyes.

Falentona, a great falconette. She found the mountain with ease. She had known about the outsiders for a while. After leaving the queen, she would fly above, circling and listening in on their merry chatter. She had been spotted by Dexy. He had smiled at her one day and watched her hover. He left some meat outside to see if she would take it. He called her one clear bright afternoon, as she sawed in the sky. He held out his arm and she flew down to meet him at last. Samlit the harefoot had worried at first, by her arrival, but she promised him no harm and eventually he had believed her. She would sleep above them in a nest outside the cave, as she was happier outside, but she would join meals and daily chores and meetings, with everyone.

"Gobbler is right, it is getting late. I will fly over the Daccorian region to see if there is any sight of them," said Falentona, who could cover miles of ground from above in the sky.

"Good idea," agreed Jax, who was wondering if they were in some sort of trouble. Maybe a sluggett had found them? Had they been recognized and captured? It was always at the back of everyone's minds.

"I will circle, but will be back soon. If they are not in the Daccorian region, then they have wandered further for some unknown reason, but really they should be there," said Falentona.

"Well, it will make us feel better to know you are looking for them. They have probably settled down for the night in the woods," said Jax.

"I will fly by Dexy's old wood hut, worth a shot," exclaimed Falentona.

"Yeah, they are probably tucked up, asleep in there, tummies full and toasty warm," said Gobbler.

"Let's hope so," said Jax.

"See you in a bit," cried Falentona, as she spread her wings and her legs sprang off the side of the mountain's edge and she leapt forward and within seconds was gliding away into the distance. Her wing could be seen, beating round, working hard to fly faster and further, over the largest area she could. Her pointed beak made her look fierce and purposeful. She had every intention of finding them if they were still on foot.

The others wanted to keep busy and their minds needed occupying.

"Shall we have some bread cakes to keep us going? And there is some corn on the cob too," said Gobbler.

"Yeah we need to eat," said Jax.

"Do you want some help, Gobbler?" asked Samlit.

"Can you put another log on the fire? We can toast the bread cakes and boil water for some nettle tea. Any of that mashed pumpkin left?" said Gobbler, excited that the others were now as hungry as he was.

"No, threw it out this morning, was off," said Jax.

"Shame, would have gone well," said Gobbler.

And so as smoke bellowed out of the cave, on the side of the Silver Mountain, the 'outsiders' busied themselves with the evening meal. Their stomachs were all feeling empty and their minds were full of worry. They ate in silence and each locked in their own thoughts. Gobbler noises taking such deep breaths with the food at his lips, made them smile eventually. Happy and glad that they were together, Gobbler's love of food never changing, reassured them, in a strange way that Dexy and Jee Hanna would be fine. Both the troll and the food had boosted their spirits and things seemed bearable in the Silver Mountain. Morning would tell them if their friends were in danger, or just late and sleeping out.

Dexy and Jee Hanna were also eating. The soup, which Luca's mum had finally been able to heat and use, was going down a treat. It was only when they started eating that they realised they were ravenous. Their worry and curiosity for Luca had made them forget their hunger, but now he was safe their bellies were in command again and growling for food. The soft potato and leek, slid down like buttery eels, and the bread was a perfect blend of soft dough inside with a crispy crust to chew heartily.

Luca had been put to bed, unable to stay awake. His mum, now eating, as the knots in her stomach felt better. She wanted to show the two travellers who had helped bring her son home her gratitude. It started with a meal and she offered them soft beds in the loft for the night. After all, it was getting late and they could make their way in the morning. Jee Hanna was relieved. She could relax and revitalise in comfort before tomorrow, her little wings and body were aching now from a long day on the horse. Dexy agreed that they could get back to the Silver Mountains by breakfast if they left at dawn and so it was, that they would stay the night.

"Thank you so much for bringing Luca back here," said Ava.

"We could not leave him," said Dexy.

"Some would," said Ava. She knew people were cruel.

"He will be fine. I have a friend who is a healer. I will get him to make some cream for your son," he said. "He is young and resilient. He will be back to normal after a few days of rest."

"Yes," smiled Ava, as she knew he was right. Her heart was so happy that her son was safe and home.

Dexy liked Ava. Her integrity and quiet pride were admirable. She looked strong, her steely eyes, but her features were fine and gave her a kindness, which was tangible. Her hair was long, it added to her beauty. She was pure and beautiful. Dexy watched her move as if she were a fragile object. She looked back at him.

"Do I know you?" she asked. "I mean, I know it seems strange, but I feel like we have met before."

"Maybe we have," said Dexy smiling but quietly, he noticed Jee Hanna was looking sleepy, as he tapped her arm. (He did not want to give anything away. He knew they had met before, but he was not prepared to say in front of Jee Hanna. Ten years had passed since they had seen each other at the palace. Ava would not want to be discovered. He spoke to Jee Hanna softly, "You look tired. Why don't you get to bed?"

Her little soft brown eyes were closing, her eyelashes, so long they were tangling together, with each attempt to stay open.

"Yes, I am tired," she whispered.

"I will show you to your bed," Ava offered.

"Thank you." She needed no other prompts, for she was as sleepy as a door mouse, more tired since the soup settled in her stomach.

The little spider fairy followed Ava up the wooden, loft stairs and drifted into a perfect sleep, as she scrunched herself up tightly, inside the white clean sheets and grey wool blanket that was laid out. The mattress moulded to her body, providing a soft base to lie on.

As Ava walked down the stairs, back to her visitor, she watched him tidy the dishes and pour some hot tea.

"You shouldn't be doing that. Leave it to me,"

"It is no bother," he said. He didn't mind.

"I can do it. You are a guest," she told him off.

He felt familiar to her again.

"I wanted to talk to you," he said, as he handed her the cup of tea and she sat back by the fire, pulling a blanket around her shoulders.

"It's hot," she smiled as she sipped.

Dexy continued.

"We have met before…" he paused. "A long time ago" he added, as he waited for her reaction.

She looked curious and then worried. He did know her, but it was not a good thing.

"I was one of your husband's aides, before the war," he said.

"My husband is dead. We are poor. I work around the village. You must be mistaken," she had tensed up.

"I am not mistaken, though am I?" he said, persisting.

"Your mind is playing tricks," she said unconvincingly. Taking in some tea to wet her dry throat.

"I recognised your son... It took me a while, but he is just like his father. He is the image of his father. I finally realised when he mentioned the bracelet. The boys took it from him. I know I am not mistaken," Dexy said.

She stopped and looked at his face, trying to gain an idea of what to say to him. Her mouth was quivering as if it was unsure.

"You must be mistaken," she eventually repeated. "There is no bracelet."

"But I am not, am I," he replied, wanting her to admit it. Their eyes never looked away for one moment and they fixed on each other, as if they could not move. "If you admit that there is a bracelet then you are one step closer to being found out- the truth about who you are, or who you were...and who your son is..." he added carefully.

"If you are right, then you must know that you are putting us in danger, by being here," she said, quietly.

"I can also protect you both," he said.

"Any contact with an outsider, would put us in danger. You are a freedom fighter, aren't you? The bracelet, he shouldn't have been wearing it, I told him not too."

"But did you tell him why?" asked Dexy.

"No! I have to protect him," she answered, seeming alarmed by the mention of the bracelet.

"Maybe you should have. He has a right to know the truth about who he is," said Dexy.

"And how would that help him? What good would it do? I have kept 'us' hidden to protect him. We have lived here peacefully for ten years. No one knows who we are, to keep him safe…you understand? Your being here could put him in danger. I don't want you to come here again," she warned.

"I want to teach the boy, prepare him for what might occur, so that he can learn as his father did," Dexy continued.

"Learn how to fight? Learn about taking back the kingdom and risking his own life? I have seen what war can do and I have no appetite for it. You want to use him, as a sign to start the uprising. You want his royal name, but I want him safe. You would risk his life, so that others will follow and worst of all, you would promise him, as their King, like his father," she rambled. Her voice urgent now. "How long do you think it will be before they come looking for him? That bracelet will not go unnoticed by others who know. How long have you got before they find him? A month? Two months? A year? They won't stop till they find him,"

"And what would you suggest I do?" she snapped.

"Let him come with me…to the mountains," he whispered, with conviction.

"Never," she said, so quickly that he had hardly finished.

"It's the only way," he said.

"Never. It is no way," she said.

They reached a silence. After a while, Dexy said,

"I am not your enemy."

"Anyone who puts Luca is danger is my enemy," she replied.

"I have saved him today and I will continue to protect him, as I did his father," he said.

"His father is dead. I think you did a bad job," she said, bitterly and out of character.

"His father was injured, I thought the Loban Masters would get him to safety...I am sorry. I never expected..." Dexy looked sad and troubled.

"I know. You did your best. But I don't want my son involved in your plans," she said.

"But he is involved, whether you like it or not. He is the rightful heir to the throne. You were, still should be the Queen," he insisted.

"Times change. People change," she said.

"The Kingdom has changed. People and creatures alike are all repressed. The Slug Pit King rules as a cruel dictator. Yes things change, but not always for the better,"

"But my son is safe," she replied, unmoved.

"For now. But the time will come. You must know that," he said, trying not to be hard.

"It's late. We should get to bed. You said you were leaving at dawn?" she wanted to end their chat.

Dexy could see he would have to leave it for tonight. They were both tired. It had been a long day. They both had little energy to talk now.

"Yes. We hope to be on the road by then," he said.

"I will be up; to see you away. We shall say no more," she said. "Goodnight."

Dexy nodded, disappointedly. It had gone badly. The conversation, he had planned in his mind with her, as he had ridden to her house, that afternoon. But even though he had nodded, he knew he would not give up. This was not the last they would say. There was so much more to say...

Ava tried to sleep, but for a long time, her mind spun with many worries. She had never told Luca the truth about his roots. She had done it to protect him. Had she done the right thing? She lay awake, the night seemed endless and morning seemed far away. Still in shock from the day; her son in a mess, the freedom fighter who now slept under her roof and the bracelet gone; waiting to be discovered. She had always believed she had taken care of everything, but it seemed her efforts might have been in vain and only time would tell if her worst fears would come back to haunt her...

Eventually, she drifted into a confused and turbulent sleep. Today had brought her son back to her, but new fears and worries would not leave her now. She knew things would never be the same for them again. She wondered if her son would ever be safe? This was the day she had dreaded. She feared it would come, one day she knew her secret would be discovered...their past would be uncovered and their futures uncertain. She wondered if her son would ever be safe again and if their secret would remain. She knew it was unlikely.

Chapter 4 The White Lake.

"A heart never lets go of a loved one, even after death it holds on just as tightly."

The black night was at its darkest, and the moon a thin curl had to work hard to be seen. The stars sleepy as they twinkled like dusty diamonds in the air. Luca and Ava Lockharth were asleep. Dexy had finally fallen too after his conversation with the queen had kept him churning, till he could no longer fight his need for sleep. He had hoped she would want to help gain back their Kingdom, for her son. He had been wrong. He finally drifted into sleep even with the disappointment.

Jee Hanna had slept from the moment she had gone to bed, her little bones and hairs were tired and fragile. She had soundly slept for several hours, but was beginning to stir as she turned over. Her body twisting and she woke wondering for a moment where she was. Then she remembered the day before~ the boy Luca and how they had taken him home. She looked around the loft bedroom where she been sleeping. Luca was over to the side and Dexy in the corner. It was a cosy place with warm tones and wooden beams running through the soft walls and windows of air and breeze, so very different from her cold caved bedroom walls back in the mountains. Her mind drifted to Luca and their conversation of the White Lake and the lady who could come with news of those who had passed. She remembered their journey, past the White Lake, her wish to stay and look into its belly and try and see her family. She could not stop thinking about it for she wanted so much to see the lake and have her chance of a message from the Lady of the Lake.

Jee Hanna began to plan in her head. She did this for what seemed like ages. She imagined herself at the lake, she wondered if she could sneak out without being seen. Could she? She pictured the White Lake again; it wouldn't leave her thoughts... She imagined the white lady rising from it. She could creep out back to the lake on her own. She wondered again, this time with more certainty. It would only be a twenty-minute walk. She would be gone less than an hour and no one would miss her. The reward of seeing her family seemed too great to resist, or turn her back on. It seemed like a perfect chance. The night was dark, but she was motivated by thoughts of her family. She thought no more and swung the feet around and onto the floor from her bed, she sat up and placed them firmly on the floor. She heard the sleepy breaths of the others and she sat up. She was going!

Reaching for her knitted black jumper, she placed it over her head, with each movement she felt a new pang of excitement. She then tied her warm fur black cloak over it, to keep out the cold. As she put it on she moved her hair from under the cloak, so it rested down her back. She was quiet. She looked over to Dexy's bed. She could see he was in the deepest sleep. Luca and Ava were far over in the other side of the loft. They were sleeping too. She reached for her boots, made of leather and fur. She did not put them on yet, but carried them out with her, in her left hand, so as not to risk making any noise.

Slowly, as to not make a sound, she climbed down the ladder and made it onto the kitchen floor. She tiptoed across the cold stone tiles and carefully opened the front door. She balanced in the doorway before stepping out, placed her boots on each foot, a warm relief. She headed past the horses, tied to the garden fence, trying not to disturb them, as she knew they could give her away with one noisy neigh. Thankfully, they were silent.

Once onto the path, she headed towards the lake. Her legs carried her, as her wings were tied back- she was not gonna use them tonight. She almost ran, her walk was so fast. She was conscious of the time she had, desperate to get to the lake. Her heart pounded happily at the hope that was in front of her. The prospect of seeing her family again. Twenty minutes seemed like two. She was there even quicker than she thought possible. The moon guided her, like a night torch.

Once there, her excitement turned to nerves. The lake stood peaceful and mournful, as it reflected the stars and moon in its silvery water. The deep cold chill seemed to sigh around its surface. The dark blue water promised a mirror from the past, to those who would dare to look. She wished that the night sky would lighten a little, so that she could take it in. Darker than she imagined, it's depths endless, made her feel more alone than ever.

She remembered wandering as a baby, on her own, that day when Dexy had found her. She remembered her confusion and the chilling realisation that she was on her own. These thoughts made her spine shiver. She felt the lake was taking her back to that day. The day her family had gone. She felt it all over again, except this time she was older and understood more. The lake was calling to her, warning her too, even in its calmness she knew it was showing her it's power. These feelings were preparing her for what was to come.

Looking down, standing on the edge, toes touching as far as they could. She peered into the water. It rippled, from nowhere, as there was no wind, but it seemed to welcome her with the circling waves, soft at first and then building with every second. The spider fairy made sure she was standing strong. She never took her eye from the spot in front of her. It became like a spinning well, the water circling faster as the lake became alive. Her eyes as widened as she looked into the water... It rippled again and again. Each ripple gave hope. The ripples each time moving the water with more force. Jee Hanna stepped back to steady herself from the flowing moving water, as her ankles became drenched in the water from the ruffling waves. The water's edge and surface had changed, from calm to quick movements. Something was coming...

Steam or smoke, she could not tell. It rose like thickening bundles growing across the water. They travelled forwards towards the little fairy, rising into the air. It smelt sweet and grew thicker as the moments past. Jee Hanna held her breath. A shadowy figure reached out her hand. It was a lady.

The White Lady. She looked like a wispy willow tree, her tall body in a white long dress, with sleeves dripping into the water, draped over her, in her elegant silvery glow. The night sky lit up with her presence. She was like a burning candle, which shone over the whole lake. Her face soft and ghostly, all white apart from eyes as black as the night. Jee Hanna tried to breathe again, but she found it hard to catch her breath. She was being pulled further into the water. She had to stop herself from being pulled over. The lady took her hand. She held her tight and she walked further into the lake. She encouraged her onwards. Further and further they walked. She felt safe. She held her arm and let her balance, with her legs and waist surrounded by water. Then they stopped and a blank circle appeared in the water. Jee Hanna concentrated as the White Lady pointed towards it.

"Spider fairy," the White Lady said. "Who have you come for?"

"I want to see my family again," Jee Hanna managed this sentence.

"They are here. They are all wanting to see you," said the lady. Her face a glowing outline of white, a statue of marble, covered in silk. Her long white hair reached the water's surface, it shone like silky threads of cobweb. Her dark eyes blazed back at Jee Hanna. There was a slight redness around them, but they were black beads of comfort. The eyes of the White Lady were never forgotten once seen.

Jee Hanna looked down and at her feet in the hollow circle became a clear image. This hole melted in front of her as the water moved away to create a space. In this small pool, she saw an outline of her family. They were faint at first, but as the water moved, the image became clearer. They waved to her. They smiled at her and blew kisses. They were there, right in front of her! Each one of her family, as clear as the days before she had been parted from them... Their images in beautiful glowing bubbles.

"They say they watch you every day," the White Lady spoke again. "They miss you so much. They say they watch over you with your friends in the Silver Mountains."

Jee Hanna gasped at this news.

"They tell me, it was a great thing to save the boy today. It will change things forever," she spoke slowly, but with a clear comfort to her voice.

Jee Hanna was mesmerised and watched, in delight. Tears came from nowhere.

She was joyful, but the tears would not stop falling down her dark face. The hairs were wet with her salty tears and she licked her mouth and they tasted so sweet to her. She watched her family waving back at her. They looked happy and real. She was so close to them it made her insides burst with joy. Dylan, her brother, did a handstand. He loved to show off. It was definitely them. They looked so happy. They were happy. The relief that Jee Hanna felt at seeing them happy was overwhelming. She reached out to touch the image in the pool, but her hand disappeared into the water. Her fingers made it ripple again and so distort the image. She waited for it to come back to her. She could not take her eyes off it. She wanted to see them all clearly again. She waited and watched. The water calmed and her family stood in front of her again. The White Lady studied her carefully and smiled. She was pleased to have a worthy visitor. Her smile was so kind and comforting. The moments passed with delicious joy, and happiness reigned in Jee Hanna's heart for each second she had been given. Jee Hanna watched on, wanting to stay there forever with her family flying and skipping happily in the pool. They sprinkled moon dust all around. Their flying was erratic and chaotic. They were carefree and joyful, as spider fairies should be. They played and played. They giggled and jumped. They showed their agility and grace, like a flying dance troop. It was a sight to behold and Jee Hanna watched with a happy heart. She felt her own wings tingle with delight. They were trying to open, from a folded position, as urges to fly raced through the little spider fairy's body. She wanted to fly too, but her wings were clipped down tonight.

The entertainment continued and the White Lady seemed to enjoy these moments as much as Jee Hanna, as she smiled, watching the fairy's joy melt into her lake and onwards. The love flowing between her and her family again as it had been before, so real and they were alive in front of her again as she could never have believed or even hoped to dream.

This enchantment was beautiful, but suddenly her moments of heaven were awakened by a crashing lump of mud, landing by her feet. At first it was hard to see what it was but as more bits that flew past, she could see more lumps of mud and stone flying past her, aiming for her! Jee Hanna was so startled, she couldn't imagine where these lumps could be coming from, was someone throwing them at her? She did not want to turn away for one second from her family to look, but it was impossible, as she was getting hit again. First on the shoulder, then the head and her arm. What was it? Who was it and what did they want? Some lumps landed in the pool and blurred the vision in the water again. The water was disturbed and the bubbles of her family became ruffled and bounced precariously over the disturbed peaceful water. The moment was dying, the lumps were threatening everything. The White Lady was disappearing.

The glow of the White Lady now faint. The water went blacker. Her family became distant as the water was disturbed again. The light that had shone on it changed back to a dull darkness, Jee Hanna felt more pellets. She tried to swat them like flies, since she wanted to keep her eyes on the pool at all costs. Still more and more came. They were too hard and big to keep ignoring. She felt another lump fly past her shoulder. She ducked a little to protect herself. Though she did not know what from. As she did, she watched the White Lady sink back, disappearing entirely into the lake. Her family went with her too. It was too quick. The water swallowed them back into its depths. The whole vision was gone as everything disappeared. The water, unsettled and jumping with each drop of debris that fell into it. She cried out, but no sound came from her mouth. The lake became a muddy speckled pool, as the rocks and mud continued. The mud missiles got bigger and faster!

"Come back," she screamed, but it was too late, they were gone.

She knew they were gone!

Jee Hanna turned finally to see what was attacking her. She looked towards the shore a few feet away to see what or who it could possibly be. She could see two tall dark shapes, yet she didn't know what they were. She tried to work out who they could be, as she ducked again to miss more clumps of mud, which were being thrown. The missiles continued. Her body started to shiver, as the cold of the water hit her. The reality of the dark night and the cold water came to her like a snapping bite from a dog. It was the coldest time of the night and the water stung now. So cold; it attacked her like a frost-bite. She walked back to the lakeside, shivering. She had waded up to her knees. The freezing night air hit her. The night wind hit the back of her legs with a stinging bite. Two thin figures were throwing again.

"Hello?" she called. She thought it would help, but then worried it might be the wrong thing to do.

"Ahhh, a ghost!" one shouted.

"Stay back," shouted the other.

"Kill it!" shouted the first.

"I am trying," replied the other.

"I knew we shouldn't have drunk so much. We're seeing things," said one of them.

"That's real, that. That's not a hallucination, you know," said the other.

Jee Hanna was closer now and finally could see…

Sluggetts! It was two drunken sluggetts. Their helmets were off and they were as ugly as ever. Sluggetts always stood vertically on the end of their tails. They were grey skinned and pale, thin with slumpy bellies half way down, which stuck out. Their sausage-shaped bodies were long and thin and unpleasant. Their complexion always sickly grey, like bland beanpoles. Their gummy mouths with no teeth, constantly dribbled a runny slime. They had no lips; their mouths drooped downwards at the bottom, like bottomless holes. They had small dull eyes, which looked dead inside, a blank grey coloured iris that gave no hope. They were on their way back to The Slug Palace.

Jee Hanna wondered what to do. Did they think she was the ghost of the lake? The pellets of mud kept flying past her.

"I'm not a ghost," she shouted, as she was got nearer,

"Yeah sure. We saw your white mist and we know what a ghost looks like. You're that White Lady, aren't you?" said the shorter of the two sluggetts.

"We know who you are," said the taller one, putting his helmet back on for protection, as Jee Hanna got nearer with every step.

"The White Lady has gone," said Jee Hanna.

"You can't fool us. It's her," cried the shorter one.

"Well, if I am the White Lady, why am I all dressed in black?" she questioned cleverly.

The sluggetts looked dumb- founded. They watched her. Their suspicious minds did not know what to do.

"Don't come any closer," demanded the taller one suddenly, as he took out a bow and arrow.

Jee Hanna stopped still. She knew the sluggett was stupid enough to fire it. Even if he was drunk, she was close enough to be hit.

"That's right. You just stay there," he said, as he tried to hold his arrow in place.

"Don't shoot me. I'm just a spider fairy," Jee Hanna pleaded.

"They were all killed in the Great War. Didn't know they existed. They're all dead," the sluggett without the bow said.

"See what did I tell, you? She's a ghost. One of those spider fairies back from the dead! Back for revenge, for being extinct..ed, like," said the thick sluggett.

The two slimy bodies, wreaked of slug sweat which hit Jee Hanna's nostrils with an unpleasant aroma. Sluggetts were thick, dumb creatures, but this made them dangerous now. Jee Hanna stood as she realised she had nowhere to go. She thought about swimming over to the other side of the lake, but it was cold and dark and the distance too far. She knew she might drown and stood a better chance against the sluggetts. But she knew she was trapped. She stood no chance against the two of them, armed with arrows.

She thought of Dexy and wondered, if she did escape, how cross he would be with her on a scale of one to ten. Probably ten! She laughed to herself at this thought, a nervous and scared; a preposterous reaction to the predicament she now found herself in. Dexy was the least of her worries. Sluggetts were dangerous! She had been told from an early age and she knew of their reputation for mindless misery. They lacked compassion and empathy with other creatures and were one-dimensional slugs by body and nature. They were to be avoided at all costs. Jee Hanna knew she would not get a second chance if they wanted to kill her, they would.

Roper Stern was half an hour from his home. He felt drained and annoyed. He was sure he would have found Luca. His stomach was sick with hunger and disappointment, but at so late an hour, he had no choice but to return home. It would be like looking for a needle in a haystack in this light.

As he approached the lake, he could see the two figures on the bank. They were calling onto the lake. He knew instantly it was sluggetts, their outlines were too distinctive to miss. Drunk, he thought. They always came over to the taverns in the Daccorian region, making a nuisance of themselves. They were well known for it. These two must have been off duty and taken advantage. Though they should have been inside the Slug Kingdom walls by now. Roper knew they were to be avoided, but he was curious about what they were doing by the lake. He walked nearer. They were too preoccupied with the lake to see him, until he was upon them. Roper could by now, see the fairy. She was being targeted by the two bullies. He knew he could not walk past and leave them to it.

"Now now, let the fairy go," he said carefully.

"That's no fairy! That be a ghost!" the tallest one cried.

"Ha, its not a ghost. I can assure you," said Roper.

"How do you know?" the other said.

"Because I have seen the Lady of the Lake and that is not her," he said.

"Doesn't mean, she's not a ghost," said the uglier one, holding his arrow straight at her, as if he were taking aim.

"Yeah, this lake is full of ghosts," added the other.

"Well, this little fairy should be allowed to go free," Roper added with some stern conviction.

"Well I disagree. She might be a ghost and I am not gonna take that chance,"

The other sluggett suddenly let go of his arrow and it flew into the air, missing Jee Hanna by inches.

"Now that's enough," Roper said.

"I don't think so. I want to be on the safe side. Try another, Stoby," he commanded.

"Yeah, was just little off that one. Close though," he replied as he loaded his bow for a second time.

"Hey! Leave her!" cried Roper reaching out to stop him.

"Why should we?" said the other sluggett, annoyed that this old man was in the way of them.

"What's she ever done to you?" said Roper, trying to distract the pair.

"Gave us a right fright! That's what," said Stoby.

"So you're gonna shoot at a defenceless fairy?" asked Roper, confused at their over reaction to the situation, but it was usual for a sluggett to behave badly.

"You gonna stop us?" cried the other, threateningly, as he aimed his bow now at Roper.

The next arrow sprang into the air, as the other sluggett was getting impatient. Jee Hanna froze, as she watched it fly towards her. Roper lunged at him, trying to grab the bow. The other sluggett went for him and tackled him to the ground. The arrow flew past closer than ever. Jee Hanna was trying to be brave but fear flooded into her. Another arrow narrowly missed. Tears dripped out from each eye, she blinked to hold them back, but they fell onto her cheeks.

With the sluggett watching his arrow fall into the water so close, Jee Hanna took her chance. She bend down and hid her whole body under the water, holding her breath as she plunged into it's icy murk. The cold was as dangerous as the sluggetts and she realised the moment she had done this, that it was a stupid thing to do! The cold water felt like an ice block on her skin. The cold seeped into her bones rotting her temperature to an icy core, far below what it should have been. The low temperature enough to kill a tiny fairy. She wondered if she would freeze in the pool and join her family that night. She was not ready to die. She swam forward, her legs pushed with all their might. She felt as if they would almost shatter with the cold.

The sluggetts had noticed,

"She's gone! Where's she gone?" one cried.

Roper was one the floor catching his breath from the knock down he had taken. The sluggett still on top of him, keeping him grounded.

"Has she disappeared? She was a ghost," said Stoby.

Jee Hanna raised her head carefully, trying to breathe upwards and tilt her mouth out of the water. She needed to breathe again, desperate not to be seen. She tried to find some ground to place her feet on. It was slippy on the rocks, which were covered in moss and weeds. She struggled to stay still. The slippery rocks, the cold and the fright were all against her tonight. Her foot found a place, but no sooner had she placed it, it skidded off causing her to fall, splashing in terror as she did.

"She's over there! Over there!" cried the sluggett. His arrow ready and aiming again.

Roper got to his feet, trying to stop the sluggett. The other jumped onto his back and started hitting him vigourously.

"Let me shoot, you silly old man!" cried the sluggett.

"You're going to hurt her!" cried Roper.

"Let him shoot! Why don't ya!" shouted the other. Pounding on Roper's head and ears with his short arms trying to reach further round.

Jee Hanna spluttered and struggled. She was slipping all over the place. Her footing had gone altogether and she was fighting with the water, to keep her head above it. It was relentless. She was scared. She felt so alone in the black water. She felt her end was coming, shooting towards her like a wave of death, her body shutting down with each kick. It was hard to breath and when she did, more water splashed into her throat and choked her like a water snake around her neck. The water gushing into her, with every twist, as her body chilled to a dangerous temperature with every splash she took. Each splash taking all her energy. It drained her little body of strength. The water grew stronger.

Roper was too busy to help. His attacker was crawling over his back, like a wriggling worm, but the blows were grinding him down. He was not as young as he used to be. He shook his body one way and the other, but it was no use, the sluggett clung on, whipping and pummelling him. He could not help the fairy from drowning. His efforts to shrug off his attacker were failing.

Suddenly, a squawk rang out in the dark night sky. It's pitch so high, it warned every creature of the night. The sluggetts stopped and looked up.

"A falconette! Quick! Run!" they cried.

Roper Stern had too looked up, to see what creature had made such a noise. He was relieved to have the sluggett jump down from his back. The bird flew around the sluggettes heads. Squawking and circling, till she was sure they were acting on her noisy descent. The falconette swooped over the sluggetts, pecking and clawing at them. She picked up one of them by his shoulders and flew several meters before dropping him, as he scrambled back onto his feet and ran again, with his head down. The bird was after the sluggetts. She left Roper Stern. He was already in the water, swimming towards the bubbles he could see, from where Jee Hanna had gone down. He dove forwards and searched using frog legs actions to push him under the water to look for her. He came up for air and dove again. He did it again, reaching out his strong arms each time, hoping to grab the spider fairy in his hands. The water was fierce now. Its chilling power had pulled Jee Hanna under. She was sinking fast. The water's surface was becoming further away and she was drifting down towards the bottom of the lake. Further and further down, swam Roper and he felt some wisped of hair, and a small round head in his fingers as he grappled to pull her out. His hands held her head so tightly. He did not let go, until they reached the surface. The spider fairy's head came above and she gasped for breath in his arms. He held her up and swam kicking his legs with vigour, spurred him on to the side of the lake- to safety.

The sluggetts ran as fast as their slug little legs and stubby tails would let them. One dropped his helmet and didn't go back for it. They ran till they were out of sight. They feared the big bird and did not want to risk being eaten. They could be seen wobbling from side to side, in panic and haste.

Jee Hanna lay on the lakeside. She took several minutes to catch her breath. She wretched several times as the excess water she had swallowed gushed out of her mouth. She was cold and shivering, but soon managed to sit up. The falconette had swooped down next to the bedraggled pair. Jee Hanna was so pleased to see her and she flung her hands out. Falentona was too large a bird to mess with for the meal meat sluggetts, who she would have gladly eaten.

"Falentona. Falentona!" Jee Hanna cried out.

"Thank you, falconette," said Roper, who was recovering himself.

All three looked at each other and smiled. They had survived an ordeal. The bird squawked happily to see her friend Jee Hanna. Jee Hanna reached out her arms to put them around Falentona's large feathery neck and rest her head against it. It felt so good, to feel the soft feathers, so wonderful after the waters chill. The warm bird with thick skin to warm the little fairy, like a hot pillow.

"You two know each other?" Roper asked.

"We live together. We are...family," said Jee Hanna. And for the final time that night, tears came to her again and she wept joyfully into the falconette's downy neck.

"Falentona," said the bird. "And who shall we give our greatest thanks to?" she said, her black eyes homing down on Roper like a new best friend.

"Roper Stern. I'm Roper Stern," he said and laughed.

"Well, Roper. Would you like a ride home on my back? It's quicker than walking and you look like you could do with a rest," she offered.

"Yes. Yes, I could do with the rest," he replied. His thoughts returned to Luca, who he had not helped so successfully.

The spider fairy and the old man climbed on board the large falconette's back. They sat so comfy, with ample room and held on tightly to her feathers. Up and away she went as her legs sprang her body upwards and tucked under her belly, as her flight began.

"It's not far. Just follow the path to the row of houses up ahead," said Roper, directing the bird.

"Yes, I see it," she said.

Jee Hanna was quiet. Exhausted from her experience, she sat and listened to her older companions chatter on.

"What brought you out on such a night?" Falconetta asked.

"I was looking for a boy. My good friend and neighbour- her boy was missing. It is not like him," he said.

"You didn't find him?" she asked.

"No," he said sadly. "Unless Luca has made it home by himself, but I will not know till I return. I hope so,"

Jee Hanna cut in, with glee she hoped she could help her rescuer.

"Luca?" she said.

"Yes, Luca. How did you know?" he asked, confused at her knowing the boy's name.

"We found him today. We brought him home," she answered.

"So that's where you and Dexy have been," interrupted Falentona.

"Yes. We saved a Luca. We took him home. He is safe," she said. "He was hurt but he is going to be ok."

Roper smiled and the relief washed over him like a hot shower. It was good news-the best! The boy was safe. Luca was safe. It was all he needed to know.

They flew down to the houses as they reached the spot.

"I will drop you down and you can wake up Dexy. I guess he won't be too pleased. Roper, I am glad we have met. I thank you for saving our little princess, Jee Hanna. I will get back and tell the others we shall see you at home tomorrow, a little later than planned," said the falconette. And with that she flew into the sky, like a dark angel.

Jee Hanna shivered, whilst Roper knocked on the door. The horses were neighing loudly and Dexy woke up as soon as he heard them. Ava had woken abruptly and rushed down to see what the noise was. She recognised Roper's voice and quickly opened the door. She greeted the two of them, with a confused but welcoming look.

"Come in. Goodness. You are both drenched. What happened?" she said.

Jee Hanna crept in. She knew Dexy would be livid. He rushed over, putting on his leather waistcoat.

"I'm sorry," she said. "I went to the lake," she apologised.

Dexy raised his eyes to the sky. He was not surprised. She had always been an independent child and he had not the heart to shout at her, as she dripped lake water on the stone floor, her wings crumpled and bashed to pieces.

"Let's get you warm," he replied, practical as ever.

Jee Hanna was amazed that he had not told her off. Maybe she would have to wait till they were on their own. Maybe he was being polite in front of Ava.

"Is Luca ok? I hear they found him," Roper asked Ava, as she passed around some warm towels.

"Luca is fast asleep. He will be ok," said Ava. "I am sorry you were out so late looking for him. Thank you so much Roper!" she said.

"Reckon it was a good job I was," he said and winked at the little spider fairy, who was shivering less and less. He had not found Luca, but without him who knows what would have happened to Jee Hanna this night.

"Yes, wasn't it. Dare I ask why are you so wet?" asked Dexy.

"I...I...I'm sorry," was all Jee Hanna could say. Her voice chattered with a shivery coldness. "Roper save me from the lake."

"Shall we save all the details for tomorrow?" Ava helped her out.

"Yeah," she replied nervously.

"Ran into some nasty sluggetts, didn't you?" said Roper kindly.

"Falentona saved us," said Jee Hanna. "She was looking for us."

"Yes, it was lucky for all of us, that she arrived when she did," said Roper.

"Well, I am glad everyone is home safely now," said Ava. She was rubbing Jee Hanna's hair dry gently and methodically.

"Well, it's been one of those days, I'd say," said Dexy, he was happy she was safe. He guessed where she had been already, he should have known it, if he hadn't been thinking about Luca he thought he wouldn't have let the little fairy out of his sight. But he told himself it was done and not to reprimand himself too much. He found parenting Jee Hanna harder than Jax, he felt he had to protect her more and he would never forgive himself if anything ever happened to her.

"Yes, it has. Now I must be getting back, or my wife will be sending out a search party for me! Goodnight all. I will be back tomorrow to see Luca and no doubt, Ettie will want to see him too," said Roper as he put down the towels and headed for the door to make his was home.

Jee Hanna wondered who Ettie was. Was she a friend of Luca's?

"Goodnight. Thank you," said Dexy.

"See you tomorrow, Roper and thank you so much for all your efforts today," said Ava.

"Well am glad the boy is safe. And you young lady, stay out of trouble," said Roper and left.

"Yes, did you hear? Stay out of trouble," said Dexy.

"Sounds like you had a nasty ordeal too," said Ava kindly, smiling at Jee Hanna, like a daughter.

"I...I saw my family...they were in the lake," she said. She wanted to tell them all.

"You should not have been at the lake," reminded Dexy.

"You saw your family?" said Ava.

"Yes, they were there, with the lady," she replied.

"Ah, so you saw the White Lady," said Ava. She knew of the lake.

"It was wonderful," Jee Hanna sighed. She could not even hear Dexy's reprimands as she remembered her moments at the lake. She would do it all again in an instant. It had all been worth it.

"Well, you took a chance and it paid off," Ava spoke from the heart.

"Yes," replied Jee Hanna. She understood.

"Now, it really is time we all went back to bed. Jee Hanna, your hair is nearly dry. I will get you some dry clothes and heat your bed up," said Ava, in a motherly tone.

"It is certainly time for bed. Tomorrow we should be on the road early, but I guess now that Falentona can tell the others that we are safe, there is less of a rush," yawned Dexy.

Jee Hanna was in agreement. She could not wait for sleep. She now had a dream she could replay in her mind again and again. Her family were closer to her than ever. She had fresh clear views of them, ready to fill her sleepy dreams, till morning. The happiness that filled her heart was so great. The peace the lake had brought to her thoughts could never be taken away. She told herself everything was always going to be this happy. She smiled as she remembered her beloved family. The family she had been longing to see again since she was a child. She closed her eyes and saw them again as they had been at the lake- flying, dancing and singing.

Little did she know, they were now part of a journey that had begun and nothing was going to stop, not wind, nor time...changes were already on their way.

Chapter 5. Returnings

The motion had already been set in place. The time carried these changes towards them, as time could not stand still.

The new day had cracked open and sunshine filled the house through the windows, enough to waken sleepy heads from the night before. They had all slept late. Ava was the first up. She checked on her son in his bed, who was still fast asleep. She smiled and touched his cheek and soft hair. She thought of his father and longed for him to be able to do the same. His face was cut and bruised but he was safe now.

Dexy heard her moving around the loft and pulled himself up, aware that he was not at home. He looked over to her and smiled. They nodded, each showing they were pleased that Luca was going to be ok. He looked over to Jee Hanna. She hadn't stirred. He would leave her for longer, until they were ready to go.

"Breakfast?" Ava whispered over to him.

"Please," he whispered back, nodding and yawning himself to help wake up.

Ava went down to the kitchen area and began. The kettle on the stove, some bread in the oven and some sausages into a pan. She had empty stomachs to fill. Dexy got dressed and joined her. They busied themselves with the breakfast making. The nettle tea bubbles as the boiling water poured into two cups.

"Tea?" she said.

She was nervous around him. He was a stranger, yet he knew all about her. She wanted to avoid any more talk of the past. She no longer thought of herself as royal, it had been too many years now for her to think like that. She hoped she had made herself clear to him last night. Dexy was not about to bring up the conversation from the night before. He had other plans. He wanted to get back and speak with the others. He could wait. It was better to wait.

"How is he?" said Dexy.

"He seems ok. I guess we will know more when he wakes. I can take a look at him then. The sleep will have done him good. And Jee Hanna," she added.

"Yes, she has had an adventure too," he smiled.

"I am glad they are safe. I don't think I will be letting Luca out of my sight for some time," she realised what she said.

"Yes. I don't blame you. I think I shall be the same with my little one. They both keep us on our toes, eh?" he laughed.

The polite conversation continued, as the bread warmed and the sausages sizzled. The smell wafted around the small house, promising a tasty savoury feast. Movements in the loft, presented a sleepy Jee Hanna. She stretched and her wings fluttered as she flew down to the kitchen.

"Morning young lady," said Dexy, in a dubious tone.

She looked sheepish. She knew she had caused unnecessary concern.

"Did you sleep well?" asked Ava.

"Oh yes, very well thank you," said the spider fairy, as she sat on the rug by the fire.

No mention of the night's events reassured her, though she knew full well that once out of the house where they were guests, she would be told off for what she had done. Dexy would not let her get away with it that easily. For now though, they were all on their best behaviour and ate a hearty morning breakfast with gusto and appetite. Ava was pleased to be able to feed her hungry guests.

"How is Luca?" asked Jee Hanna, with her mouth full of bread.

"He's fine. Asleep at the moment, but am sure the smell of food will wake him soon," said Ava.

Bustling noises outside the door told of more visitors. There was a knock and Ava saw her good friend, Roper Stern with his daughter Ettie outside, through the window. She waved and opened the door.

"Hello, how are you?" she hugged Roper and Ettie as they came in.

"Bit tired. How's Luca. Brought Ettie to see him, she couldn't wait," laughed Roper.

Jee Hanna looked at the small brown haired girl with Roper. She was curious to see the little girl. She felt a pang of jealousy as she wondered about her friendship with Luca. She felt pushed aside. She watched the small pretty girl walk into the house, comfortable, as if she had spent many hours there and was at home here.

"He's in the loft, still asleep. Go on up and see if he's waking. Need to get him up," Ava said to Ettie, who didn't need a second invitation, as she clambered up the ladder and into the loft, to see her dear friend.

"Thanks," she called.

Jee Hanna watched her again and smiled at Roper, her rescuer from the night before.

"How are you?" he asked.

"Fine," she replied, shyly.

"Thank you for bringing her home," said Dexy. "Who knows what might have happened if you hadn't been there.

Jee Hanna squirmed and looked guilty.

"Thank you for getting Luca home. It seems we are equally grateful," he smiled.

"Tea?" said Ava. "There are sausages going spare too," she added.

"Tea, thanks. Already eaten though," he replied.

Ava made more tea, whilst the group chatted and smiled in a polite way that is necessary for new acquaintances.

Ettie was up in the loft, excited to see Luca again. She sat herself next to his bed and whispered gently into his ear.

"Luca? It's Ettie," she called.

Luca was stirring. The noise and smells the cooked sausages had brought him round. He felt stiff pain as he opened his eyes but managed to pull himself up into a sitting position.

"Ouch," he cried.

"Does it hurt? You look terrible," Ettie comforted her friend. "What happened?"

"Some boys," he said.

"I missed you. I'm glad you're home. Can't believe what happened... You'll be back to your old self in no time," she said, sympathetically.

"I hope so, ow," Luca groaned as he moved again, forgetting he was not his old self yet and the aches and pains would be there for a while yet.

Ava brought up some tea for them both. She put the cups into their hands carefully.

"It's hot. How you feeling? Did you sleep well?" she said.

"Yeah, is it late?" he asked.

"A little later than normal... you can stay in bed as long as you like today," she said.

"No, I think I'll get up," he said, but on trying moaned some more. His bruises reminded him of yesterday's events. "Ouch."

"Poor thing," smiled Ettie.

Ava returned to her guests.

"We should be making a move. We'll get our stuff together and get out of your way," said Dexy.

"There's no rush," replied Ava, trying to be polite and make amends for her abruptness last night with Dexy.

"No, we'll get back on the road," Dexy answered, he knew he could not change things today and wanted to get back to the mountains and collect his thoughts.

Jee Hanna was ready too. She wanted to see Luca, but it was difficult with his old friend by his side. She felt a bit put out, but ready to get back to the mountains too.

When everything was collected, they fed the horses and made their way out. It was time that they left. They had stayed longer than expected.

"Bye Luca!" called Dexy.

"Thank you!" he called back.

"Thank you, I am so grateful," said Ava with great feeling.

Dexy thought that if this had been years ago he would be bowing down now to his queen, but she was a lonely villager now. He knew she had left her past where it was and ten years was a long time.

Ava looked closely at Dexy too, wondering what he was thinking, bearing in mind their conversation from last night. He waved at her and looked at her intensely, which made her think he hadn't forgotten anything. She knew she would be seeing him again. Then he winked, it was an impulsive moment, but regretted it instantly. He felt foolish in the circumstances. He hid his embarrassment well, making himself busy with the horses. They were ready to leave. Roper helped with their bags and loaded them onto the horses. They were finally ready to go.

They mounted the horses and waved as they trotted into the distance. They smiled in the sun as it shone proudly onto their backs, like glorified heroes of the day. They felt warm inside and out, as they had done a kind deed and made good acquaintances. Jee Hanna remembered Luca lying on the ground, like a fallen deer and how he recovered overnight into a bright young boy. A boy that she liked a lot! She enjoyed thinking of him, now they had left and daydreamed of them spending more time together. She hoped she would see him again one day.

Back on the road, Dexy and Jee Hanna could relax. It was the first time since they found the boy they felt at ease again. They rode in contented happy silence for a while, as the woods were around them. It was relaxing to soak in the trees and birds twitters and enjoy a relaxed harmony. After a while Dexy spoke again.

"That was a really silly thing you did last night," scolded Dexy.

"I know," said Jee Hanna. She was expecting these words.

"I would have taken you to the lake myself," he continued.

"Would you?" she said.

"Yes," he replied.

"I had to go," she said.

"In the middle of the night?" he asked.

"I know. I wasn't thinking," she said sheepishly.

"If anything had happened to you..." he broke off.

"I know," she said again.

"Don't ever..." he started.

"I won't," she finished.

They smiled at each other- an understanding of their conversation.

Their horses trotted peacefully through the Daccorian region. They knew they would be home within the hour. The sun continued to beat down shining onto their pathway. The breeze was warm and swept kindly past their ears and shoulders. It was an exciting prospect to be close now, after their journey had been interrupted and disturbed. They would soon see their mountain. They would soon see their craggy home. Its glorious high haven winning their hearts as if it had always been home. They anticipated their return and the reaction of the others to their stories.

Jee Hanna wanted to tell them all of her family on the lake and recount it back as much as possible to each of them, to relive her wonderful experience. She wanted to tell them about the boy, Luca, her special new friend. She wanted to talk about him and the lake.

Dexy had many thoughts looming; he was planning a meeting. He wanted to discuss important matters. He had discovered more information than he ever dreamed he would find in the last day- this had to be shared with his friends, the outsiders, in the mountains, and the freedom warriors. They needed to think about what could be done. Luca was an important part of any plan. His existence was important. His royal blood was important. His father would want him to act. He knew his old friend the King would approve of his plans for the boy, even if his mother wasn't willing. He would call an important meeting as soon as he was back home. The freedom warriors needed to make some plans... definite plans! Plans that would change, not only their lives, but the lives of many others...things would never be the same...they now had proof that the boy king existed, something they had never had before- it was always an hope or an 'if', but now he knew of Luca and of his true heir to the throne, they would stop at nothing to get him back his kingdom, their kingdom! Dexy would make sure of it. The meeting would make sure of it! There were many desperate to make sure of it!

Chapter 6. The Glass Queen

Narla was a 'glass-heart'.

These were people who would fall in love once. If their love was rejected their heart would turn to glass. It was an instant thing and irreversible. They would never love again, for their heart would shatter and they would die. They can only reverse this by winning true love, but this very rare since they had not gained the love in the first place. Most glass-hearts would grow bitter; you can see it in their cold uncurious, glazed eyes, which never shone. A glass heart is rare, but when you meet a glass heart, you know every time. They are cold and they cannot hide their glass heart from the world.

Narla was not bitter, for she could not allow herself that; however she was a 'glass-heart.' Today, she looked out of her stone tower, one of many, in the castle, as she did every day and gazed at the world below her from her bedroom, wrapping her silk dressing gown around her slim twig-elegant figure.

She owned all she could see: the lakes, the mountains, the woodlands and the marshes along the seacoast. Her power had grown since the Great War. She had gained more lands from The Slug King whom she had supported during the many battles and helped him to victory. He had given her many presents in the last ten years. He had the split lands beyond the mountains, as he knew he could not hold them entirely on his own, with only his army of sluggetts. Rather than risk their take over by his enemies, he gave them to his friends. They were lands, but that was all. He could afford to give them away. He respected and admired this icy lady. He hoped one day that he would turn her warm again, but he was deluded. He was not attractive, warm, but he did have a certain charm and he was highly intelligent for a sluggett. However, he was still a poor contender for her heart, even if it had turned to glass. She never minded his lavish gifts and thought him a fool, like a silly puppy dog in her presence. She would dine with him when she had to, or if she needed to ask favour, but she would keep their meals to a minimum. Keeping him at arms length, which made his heart beat faster each time he visited and the presents emulated his beating foolish heart. It was sad.

Unamused by the green mountainous views and blue sky, she sighed heavily and angrily as the view disappointed her as it did everyday. Her heart sank at a view. It made her feel empty. What was the point of them to her? She cared nothing for them... Grass was to be eaten by sheep, rather than ran through with bare feet on a warm day. The birds singing annoyed her. It seemed so tuneless to her. A sunset would fill her with sadness and remind her of others who would love in this world. She could not utter glad words for these things; she thought it nonsense and simple. She had had enough of love. It had treated her cruelly.

She turned her thoughts to what she would wear for dinner. Which silk dress and cloak would please her? She twiddled her long dark brown locks, which finished just past her shoulders wondering how she would wear it, glamorous curls or elegant straight. She went over to her large silver wardrobe; it's doors with mirrors and elaborate silver twining in the shape of twisted leaves. It was full with colourful garments, long gowns and cloaks. She rippled her hands along her velvety outfits and smiled, she felt some happiness from them. She took out the lightest pale pink satin dress with small white daisies, which fell around the neck into a v shape, down to the waist. She loved this dress. It matched her beauty. It would look good this evening. She laid it on her master bed, which was as big as a dining table, ready for later.

As she walked slowly around her room, holding her head high as if she were practising an entrance, with her slim pointy nose in the air. She noticed the door creep open, pushed by a podgy little foot, with mucky brown slip -on shoes, a disgrace on their own. In it's space stood a small otter man, who was so small and dumpy that his clothes draped over him in a ridiculous way, which made him look clown-like. Even his small sliver rimmed glasses slid down onto his large red nose and perched on the end precariously. His brown otter hair looked as if it had been gelled back into small peaks, in an effort to look smart, but his white hairy whiskers gave away his age and he was no spring chick, despite his efforts to look current.

"Yes?" Narla said slowly.

"I have your beauty cream from the Slug Pit King. Where would you like me to put it?" asked the small butler.

Narla had always used this age old cream for her youthful skin, it was made with two per cent of slug slime and the rest secret ingredients, but it worked and kept her young. She had it delivered once a month.

"Put it on my dressing table, as usual. Did Dagon not tell you where it should go?"

she nodded to her silver-mirrored dressing table, which sparkled in the sunlight, which shone in from the window.

"Are you new to butlering?'" she asked.

"Yes, me lady," replied the ludicrous old otter man, who trundled over to the dressing table in a flat-footed way.

This infuriated the queen, as she watched him in disbelief. His little legs looked so short they were mainly unseen under his little barrelled body. He reminded her of an acorn on legs and each scuff of his feet sent her a new irritation. His efforts to walk efficiently looked strange. His clothes swam around him like wrinkled washing. He fell short of the mark of what Narla was used to. He was not the sort of butler she needed, it would not do, she thought.

"Bevan Hislop- at your service," he added. Did he have a lisp too, she wondered?

"Not for long," she whispered under her breath, his service would be short, she thought as she managed a half-smile in his direction.

Bevan carried the large pot of slug cream to the dresser, as if he were holding a chalice in an offertory procession. He gave the pot more importance than it required. Narla looked on in utter disgust, as she ran her hands through her long hair in order for something to do, while she waited for him and tried not to show too much distain, (those who knew her, would see straight away he had not made a good first impression.) His integrity was comical. It would not do. How annoying; she agreed to herself.

Bevan Hislop had been fired from his last job, for his hiccups and clumsiness. Brother to Mrs. Weedy, the housekeeper who had given him the job while Dragot was away in the Saccorian region.

Narla turned away from the small dumpy creature and turned to the mirror to check her neck skin and look for blemishes. She was engrossed. She inspected like a beautiful peacock stretching its neck tall. She could not see, thankfully, that Bevan had snagged one of his brown slip on shoes on a nail, which held the wooden floor in place. He was stuck and shaking his leg managed to fall backwards. A quick thinking backward roll had him on his feet again, but the loose pot lid had spilt slug cream all over his head and chest area, and as he got to his feet, even worse, he saw that splashes of the cream had covered the Queen, who was dripping in slime too. The two of them stood in complete horror at what had occurred. Eventually the Queen roared,

"Get him out!" she screamed.

She ran at him, she lunged at his feet and grabbed his brown shoes like a raging banshee. The shoes in each hand were hurled out of the tower window with a great force. They looked like strange ugly birds, as they flew through the cloudless sky outside.

"Don't ever come in here again. Do you hear? Get out! Get...out!" her voice raged on.

Poor Bevan scrambling to his bare feet, took himself out of the room as fast as his legs would carry him, wheezing as he went. The queen's fury was not something he wanted to hang round for!

Chapter 7. The Bracelet

"If you take something that does not belong to you, then remember there will always be a price. It will come back and find you. It will demand its own price."

It was a busy market day, and Aviras was getting ready to go into the city It was his shopping day. He liked the choices of food that could be bought there. The sun was a glorious colour in the bright blue sky and Aviras was raring to go. He enjoyed market day. The market stalls were always bustling with people and the excitement of the day was clear from the huge grin on his face. Aviras loved it as much as anyone else.

He raced along the dusty road tracks until he was there. It took him half an hour at this brisk pace. He felt like a man as he walked tall in through the city walls. He smelt the food from the moment he entered. The noise was a constant flurry of voices and movement. He made his way through the stalls. Shoulder to shoulder with others, all after something from the market. He looked forward to bartering with stallholders, who were immersed in their trading and wondered if he could get the best prices for everything. It was a challenge he wanted. He wore his best, cotton jacket, which was a berry brown, with long sleeves and large pockets. His green work trousers, full of pockets would be useful too. He was muscular and tall for his age and his thick black hair swept down over his face and stopped at his angular jawline. He had a bag of roonies, that he could spend. It was money he had collected; from those he had bullied with his gang in the week, some of his own, and some from his mum. She never asked for the change, so the better the price he got, meant the more roonies he kept for himself. Aviras felt the world owed him. He loved money and he got it any way or where he could. Market day was his day.

The market, inside the city walls, which surrounded the area now known as the Slug Kingdom, happened every Thursday. The white town houses of these city streets were sophisticated and worlds apart from the thatched huts in the Daccorian region. These houses were splendid white, with red brick tiled roofs and plants outside the porch ways. Their white walls reflected the sun well and kept the houses cool from the heat. They were expensive and most of the people and creatures who lived in these areas were rich and could afford to pay large tax fees to the king. The sluggetts soldiers were always present in the area and acted like the Slug King's police force in the city. Though they caused more disputes than they ever solved. It was a vibrant place to be and the hub of the city could be felt, as the lively market got underway. The stalls lined the wide cobbled streets and all led to a market square, which was tiled in limestone and was the hub of the market action. To some it may have looked like bedlam, but it was well organised and the money flowed from buyer to seller at a fast pace. The sound of business and bargains filled his ears. The crowds and bustle was exciting. He loved market day, where he felt like a man of the world with money in his pocket and a purpose for the day.

Aviras knew where most of the stalls he needed were. He had to go to for the food, using the same places his mother liked each time, as she had shown him on many occasion, before she allowed him to go alone. Then, once his mother's shopping was done he had the freedom to go anywhere he liked. It was a freedom he cherished. This was the real world. It was where he loved to be- out of the village life where nothing ever happened. Here was alive here and he felt at home in the city. The crowds, the chickens, the stalls, the people, the bustle of creatures and all things together in the one place gave him a buzz. He needed to buy saffron; the best quality. His mother only liked the best and he always went to the same stall for it. It was further up the street, a slightly uphill walk, but Aviras didn't mind. He soaked in the sun and the ambience of the market day.

He reached the spice stall. It had colourful herbs and spices in every colour and bags of each stood proud. The smell was glorious and every blend of herb and spice gave a beautiful rich aroma. Each bag was brim full and had wooden scoops, to take as much or as little as you needed. The usual man was there. He was dark and had a long beard and turban hat. His skin was crumpled from too much sun. He was old, but slim and wore a long cream smock, with a turquoise scarf draped around his neck. It was discoloured from the sweat that ran from his face and onto his neck. His teeth were brown, apart from two gold ones, which shone like jewels in his mouth. It made him look unusual, but memorable. His hands were full of powdery spices that had stuck down his nails, they looked stained with orange marks.

"Can I help you?" he asked Aviras as he finished with one customer and saw the boy looking.

"Saffron, please. And chillies," said Aviras.

"Two scoops enough?" he asked as he shook the bag to see how full it was.

"Thanks. That's plenty," said Aviras, as the man filled the bag.

The man watched the boy as he took his leather pouch of money off his belt. The sun sparked on the bracelet Aviras was wearing from the day before. It caught the man's eye instantly.

"Nice piece of silver," said the man and pointed.

Aviras saw he was referring to the bracelet. He was a bit taken a back at first, but thought quickly.

"It was my...father's," said the boy.

"Your father's?' he said slowly. "I see. It's nice. Do you mind if I look?" said the man.

Aviras saw no harm in the man looking. He saw no reason to refuse.

"Er, no," he said, handing it to the man.

The man took it up close to his eye, inspecting it closely. He looked on the back and stroked the edges, as if he knew he would find an inscription. He smiled and handed it back to the boy.

"Anything else," he asked.

"Chillies, about a quart worth," said Aviras as he placed the bracelet back on his wrist.

"Good. Seven roonies," said the man.

Aviras handed them over. He did not barter. He thought it would not go down well, after showing the expensive bracelet. He wondered if he should put it away for the rest of his shopping excursion. It might not help him achieve the best prices, as it was an exquisite piece. As he walked away, with his bags, he took the bracelet off and placed it in his pocket. This did not go unnoticed by the stall keeper, who hadn't taken his eye off the boy for one second, since he had turned to walk away. He was studying the boy very carefully. The bracelet had given him a strange interest in the boy.

"Look after my stall will you, Tanni," he said abruptly to a woman next to him, selling fruit and vegetables.

"What? Where?" she hardly had time to object. "Hey where you going?" she called, but it was too late.

He was behind the boy and following his every move, her words, he hardly noticed.

Aviras wandered along the streets. He was spoilt for choice at the range of tables filled with goods. Food of every colour and origin, lay on every available space. The objects; pots, pans, glassware, tools and cloth was spread out for sale. They market sellers engrossed in their work, shouting and calling to attract the most buyers.

The man kept out of sight, but followed the boy, carefully not letting him out of his view through the streets, his stall in the distance now. Aviras stopped to look at some belts. He wanted a new one. He picked and tried a few around his waist for size and comfort. He did not notice the man watching his every move. Whilst he was busy, the man looked around. He saw some sluggetts nearby and went over to a couple who were laughing in the cool breeze, which helped the busy day. He spoke to them for a few moments and pointed to the boy. They walked with him, interested in what he had said. Aviras was oblivious. It was a shock to him when they surrounded him and spoke.

"Would you like to come with us," one of them asked.

Aviras swung round. He put the belt back on the table. He looked at them bemused.

"I think you need to come with us," they said.

"Is this the lad?' the other asked.

The stall keeper nodded.

"I am arresting you for taking goods without paying. Stealing is a crime in the Slug Kingdom," the sluggetts stated.

"Stealing?" Aviras said, alarmed by the accusation.

"This man informs me that you took spices from his stall without paying. That is a crime," said the sluggett soldier.

Stealing was taken seriously and the sluggetts meant business.

"I paid. I paid for them?" Aviras said with panic in his voice.

"I believe you did not pay. You need to come with us now," said the sluggetts.

The man sneered back at Aviras. He looked ugly, like an old dog. He knew the boy could do nothing. Aviras had never been challenged like this, but he spoke up for himself again.

"I paid. Seven roonies. I paid for the spices," he claimed again, with a lump forming in his throat.

"We can do this nicely or the hard way. Either way; you need to come with us," said the sluggetts.

Aviras was confused. He had no choice. He walked along, in front of the sluggetts and the keeper, as they prodded him forward. He knew they would take him to the castle to be dealt with. He hoped that the misunderstanding would be sorted out. But he worried. He could not understand why the man would lie. He had definitely paid. The man was lying. Why would he lie? There was nothing else he could do. His thoughts raced. He could feel a slow sweat built under his arms and on his back, as they headed up the castle. Sluggetts and man right behind. Not letting him get away. Aviras knew he could argue no more, as it would only do him more harm than good.

The Slug Palace loomed in front of them. One sluggett now in front and leading the way. It was white and splendid, a larger extension of the houses in the city centre. The stairs and gates were cleaned every day and the palace walls shone in the sunshine, showing a spectacular backdrop for the city.

Aviras could only speculate as to what was about to happen. He guessed that he would be brought in front of the Slug King. An overwhelming thought. He had heard stories of how thieves were taken to the slug pit, or worse, killed to made an example of. There was no court, just the decision of the Slug King here, a king with no desire for truth or justice. He was interested in making his power known. He loved nothing more than to hear a story and decide a man or creature's fate on the spot, with seconds of thought. Aviras wondered what the man would say, if he would continue to lie about him? He knew he had paid him, seven roonies, but what would that matter if he was not believed. It was his word against the man's.

The sluggetts looked pleased to be doing a worthy job and walked on their little legs and tails, with a pride and purpose. It was ugly. The man looked anxious to speak with the King. Aviras did not look at him for most of the walk, but when he did get the chance to look over. He tried to read the man. Why did he wish him harm? The confusion of the situation was worrying him the most. The fear it had installed in him outweighed his anger. His gut knew he was in danger.

The marble doors were large and wide. They opened up hinged in bronze. Each an expensive addition the Slug King had added to the palace. He loved anything lavish and his taste was for the exquisite. Each one they walked through was swiftly closed behind them by two sluggetts on door duty. The sound of them closing, gave Aviras a nervous pain in his stomach that worsened each time the door banged shut. It seemed final. It intimidated him and it was meant to. By the time a prisoner reached the Slug King, they were usually in a state. Some would plead and others would beg, or cry, or whimper, but it all fell on deaf ears, as the King was a cruel creature and nothing touched him. He saw strength in bringing enemies to their knees.

The last door shut. The huge open room, with windows looking out onto the city, was a grand sight. Long, lounging seats were placed at every window to see the view. The splendour of the objects in the room, the polished marble tiled floor and the velvet curtains, all oozed the elegance of a wealthy castle. The walls added a vibrant feel, dark red and vivid, with gold braided borders. Yet, Aviras hardly noticed the décor, his eyes were fixed solidly on the vision of the king in front of him. The sight was abhorrent. A detestable sight to any eyes, let alone one of a prisoner, about to find out his fate.

The Slug Pit King swigged from his golden goblet and threw the wine down his neck, before leaning forward, to see what his darling sluggetts had brought to him. He loved amusement like this.

"What have you brought me?" he asked with clear pleasure.

"Dear King, we have brought before your Royalist Highness, a thief!" said the sluggetts, with slimy charm oozing from every dribbling pore.

The King looked delighted again. His piggy eyes, which were too close together, glared at Aviras. He clenched in small chubby hands, which looked strange in size, next to his huge, fat belly that stuck out, hanging over the throne, where he did not fit. His legs chaffed together, each time he moved position, with tiny feet, wearing velvet slippers, hanging down, almost touching the ground. The sight was nauseating for Aviras, who felt his stomach wretch and turn.

"Well, well. I thought we got rid of all thieves a few years ago. The only ones alive are rotting in my Slug Pit. I wonder...do we need to show we are not weak in my kingdom again? Are the people getting careless and thinking they can do what they like?" said the king.

His mouth was a hole and looked mean and bottomless, like every sluggett, with gums that slouched and dripped with gooey slime.

The sluggetts watched with glee as their victim was questioned. They loved the spectacle, although they looked totally surprised, as the man, who had been keeping out of sight, spoke up.

"I brought the boy to you. He did not steal from me," said the man, stepping into the king's eye line.

They sluggetts nearly choked on their own dribble at his statement, not what they were expecting. They had been told he was a thief.

"So he is not a thief?" said the king, slowly, showing he was confused but intrigued enough to let the man continue.

"No. He has not stolen from me. He paid for his spices. But I wanted to show you something. If I may?" he said, pausing to seek approval from the king.

"Please, please do. Be my guest...I'm all ears! I can't wait to hear. Please continue," he commanded, as he wiggled his glass in the air as a sign to the servant to refill his wine goblet.

His legs swung freely as he did, like a small child being entertained.

"This boy is wearing a bracelet. I noticed it instantly. He took it off after visiting my stall, but he has it in his pocket," said the man, enjoying his own tale.

Aviras was in shock. He could not think fast enough to deal with all of the information. It was a far cry from the boy who had watched his gang lay into Luca, the day before. Both Aviras and the Slug King, were both listening in silent amazement.

"Is this true? Let's see! Let me see," said the king.

"I believe he was hiding the bracelet after I saw it," said the man.

"I hid it because I didn't want it to stop me bartering for goods...!" Aviras found his voice. The words sprawled out.

"Be quiet, you! Let me see the bracelet!" the king snapped impatiently and infuriated.

"It is nice, yes?" said the man, as if he was back on his stall, selling his spices.

"It is, it is," the king nodded and inspected the object carefully. "But why is this of any concern to me?"

The man interrupted him.

"The bracelet is from the old kingdom. It belonged to King Marcus. It was from the royal household," said the man.

"What?" cried Aviras, again he couldn't help himself.

"King Marcus! Don't ever mention that name in my kingdom! Don't say it! How dare you! Guards!" yelled the king, pointing to guards to get the man.

He howled.

"Wait! I know, because I used to work for him. I polished the silver and jewellery. It was my job," the man spoke quickly as his mouth began to dry and he saw the guards advancing towards him. "Please, I...it was the bracelet the King Mar...sorry, would wear. It was his bracelet. I know because the inscription says it," finished the man.

"You're telling me this belonged to...that person, who we shall not say? So how have you got it boy?" asked the king.

"It's not mine! I...I...found it!" he cried.

The man continued, interrupting.

"You told me it was your father's! It is said, rumours...and...it is said, that the king had a son. A baby was born to the queen after the Great War. If he survived, then that might explain the bracelet," he announced.

"What! I don't believe what I am hearing. This is outrageous!" cried the king.

"Please, I am only saying what I know," said the man.

"Well you seem to know a lot, don't you?" said the king in a disgusted way, swigging the new wine, like a necessary medicine.

"I found the bracelet, only yesterday. It's not my father's! It's not mine!" Aviras took his moment to speak up for himself, in a loud whine.

"Yes, well you would say that wouldn't you?" snapped the king. "Let me think. Let me think."

The sluggetts watched uneasy as the king pondered the new information.

"Yes, I have heard rumours of a son who survived, but I have never had any reason to believe them. Probably made up by the creatures and people, as a last hope. As you can see I have been in power for over ten years and I can't see it changing," he said.

"Please, I found it. It is not mine. I took it," said Aviras.

"You took it? So you are a thief, then," said the king.

"No…I…no," Aviras knew to admit to anything more would be dangerous.

"Tell me, how old are you boy?" said the king.

"Fourteen," said Aviras.

"So, this son that you speak of, would be just ten, am I right?" inquired the king, triumphantly.

"He would be, yes," said the market seller.

"Then, he is not the boy," said the king.

Aviras felt some relief.

"No, no he is not. But it is a piece that I have cleaned and I know of its value," said the man.

"You are right it is valuable. I agree. The question is, where is it from? Can you shed any light?" asked the king to the boy.

"I don't know! Really, I found it!" protested Aviras.

"You found it. You took it. You found it. Make your mind up, son," said the king menacingly.

The other servants in the room were also listening. Everyone had become enthralled with the mystery of the bracelet. There was more to be heard. All eyes were on the king and the boy.

"I don't know where it's from? Really, I..." he cried, tears were close to his eyes, but he knew he could not cry.

"I think you need your memory refreshing. I think a bit of time in the Slug Pit will help, don't you?" said the king.

"Please, no!" shouted Aviras. He had heard the stories of the pit.

"Listen here. I want to know where you got that bracelet. You tell me! And you tell me now!" he eyes rolled back in his head. He was getting impatient.

"I took it... from a boy," said Aviras.

"A boy?" said the king.

"I don't know him. I don't know who he was. I took it from him, yesterday," said Aviras trembling.

The eyebrows around the room rose. Everyone had gone pin quiet to hear the next words.

"Tell me. This boy, how old would you say he was?" said the king.

Everyone knew what he was thinking. Could this boy be the king's son? The heir to the throne?

"He was...er. Well, I don't know. Maybe eleven or twelve?"

"Could he have been ten years old, do you think?" said the king suspiciously.

"I don't know. I suppose. I'm not sure," stuttered Aviras.

"Take him to the Slug Pit! He will speak after a stint in there! I want to know more! You better start telling me all you know, when I return. You need to have a long think, while I'm away," he told Aviras. "Take him away!"

"No!" cried the boy, but the sluggetts needed no more instruction and grabbed each of his arms.

"I need to get ready for my dinner," the king changed the subject and went to get up and leave.

"Er...your Highness," coughed the man who had been listening closely.

"What? Yes, you may go," the king swept out his arm to send him away.

"But...you highness. I..er. I was hoping..." said the man.

"You were hoping...?" said the curious king.

"I was hoping for some, er, a...well. I was thinking maybe I would be...rewarded for my trouble?" he spat out.

"A reward? Ha! A reward? I might have known you'd want something out of this. Tell me, why did you bring the boy, if you worked for his father, you must have been...grateful to him, so why betray him?" said the Slug King. He was more intelligent than most sluggetts, whose brains were small and squashy.

"His father sacked me," said the man, hatefully.

"Why, would he sack, such a hard worker as yourself?" said the king wanting to get the full truth from the man.

"I was caught stealing. I took some silver bowls. I am not proud. It was a long time ago and I needed the roonies. I had debts," he said in a self-conscious, mournful tone.

"And your debts? Have they been paid?" said the slug.

"They have," replied the man, quietly.

"So why do you need a reward?" laughed the king.

"I just thought..." the man gave up, his attempts.

"Oh let's think. Oh why not? Yes. Get the man a bag of gold roonies, someone. Get him some money. Why not?" laughing to himself.

The Slug King liked to be unpredictable. He enjoyed his own turn around on the matter. It surprised everyone.

The man looked stunned. In his amazement, he bowed, still unsure if the king meant what he said, or if it was just another game. The sluggetts were unsure too and hesitated.

"Get him his reward!" he yelled impatiently, clicking his fingers at a dopey sluggett.

The sluggett jumped and rushed off and came back quickly with a decent sized bag of roonies. The man finally smiled as he took it. He turned to leave. He had no thought for the boy he had brought before the king. It was not his problem. He had his money. It had been worth his trouble after all.

"And now I need to get ready. Dressers? Come with me. I need something that is going to impress my fair lady queen. I have a beautiful bracelet to show her. This will do me no harm at all. No harm at all. The boy, I will deal with him when I return," he concluded.

He left the hall, with a flick of tail as his little legs jumped to the floor and a scurry of servants ready to dress him followed.

The Slug King looked like a funny little worm, but he was always working on plans in his mind. He was shrewd and cruel, though he looked like an over excited child, he was clever. A sluggett with a brain made him a formidable character, who could not be underestimated, however short and insignificant he might have looked. His mind craved power and respect. He would get both by any method. When he stood up tall his stomach stuck out, but this did not mean he was a fool. His foolish outline was misleading and many an enemy had fallen, making the mistake that he was a prat of no consequence. It was not a mistake you could afford to make.

Aviras was in trouble. He knew it. He cursed himself for taking the bracelet. Why had he not been more careful? It was too late to contemplate now, as he was led forwards along the corridors, down into the darker part of the castle where only prisoners were kept. Who was the boy he had beaten and stolen from? What was happening? Why was the bracelet so important? His shopping abruptly halted, he knew not why, and now, his life on hold in danger, even? He had time to reflect on all of it. The Slug Pit was dark and as they pushed him into a cell, and locked the bars firmly behind him, he kicked the wall in frustration and anger. This would soon be replaced with fear, everyone knew the Pit was no place for hope.

Gerrado was being dressed. The Slug King's main dresser made him look taller at every opportunity. He had heeled slippers and his extensive wardrobe of refined clothes, were something of a rainbow. His favourite item, a light gold coat, she had handmade for him. It was stylish and the length did him some favours, extending his calves with clever sewing. She placed it on his shoulders while he admired himself in a large mirror, in a back room saved for clothes and dressing. He was vain, his dresser knew him well, and knew what pleased him. He looked pleased with his reflection and pushed his shoulders back, sticking his chest out to see how good he could look. The other sluggetts looked on and made noises to show approval of his look, nodding their heads with great enthusiasm.

Daffni was a tailor of fantastic skill. She made dresses for Queen Narla too. They all liked her elegant work, it made them look so well dressed. She was calm and confident with the clothes she provided. It was a triumph. Everyone could see the king was happy with his attire. She was an attractive sluggett herself.

"Can I ride in this? I'm taking the horse," he said.

"I would put your weather coat over it, as it will not be warm enough in the wind," she replied.

"Yes, I will do that," he said.

"Thank you. I think I am ready," he confirmed.

"Yes, you look knock out," she answered, always full of praise and compliments for her master.

"Gold slippers ready?" he asked.

"In your bag, you can put them on when you arrive. Need help with your riding boots?"

"No, I'll manage. Get me my coat and then you can go," he said.

Outside, the Slug King left, jumping up, putting his foot into the saddle and hurling himself over and onto his horses back. He kicked his heels into the beast and it shot off, galloping through the fields and down towards the queen's castle. It would take a couple of hours to ride there. The king was healthy and ready to work up an appetite for a meal with his beautiful friend, Narla.

Chapter 8. The Visitor

Bevan Hislop was making himself busy, as he set the table for the Queen. He was eager to please and went about his work cheerfully. He whistled and hummed. He did not like silence. He was a happy worker and enjoyed getting things done. The castle dining room needed to be buffed and polished to the highest standard and the table prepared for dinner. It's oak table and chairs were very grand and well carved and set the dining scene well. The side cupboards held lots of glass bowls and glasses, which could be set out for any number of guests. There was ample on display. The candlesticks shone, two on some sideboards and giving more elegance to a glistening room of decadence and order. This dining room wanted for nothing. It was a true vision of dining glory. It was decorated with dark blue walls, with gold leaves painted, which gave it a royal glow.

Narla was expecting her visitor and she wanted everything to be ready on time. She was not totally excited at the thought of her visitor, but she knew it was in her best interest to keep him sweet and she enjoyed his company. Gerrado was a good friend to have and she was happy to have him over for food. He was hoping there was more to it, but there never would be. She was not interested in any type of partnership, though she kept him keen. The table had to be set with glasses and cutlery, the big vases needed polishing and filling with fresh flowers, the marble floor was to be polished; the job list that Mrs. Tweedy the house keeper had been given was endless. Bevan her nephew was here to help, as she was getting old and the usual butler was away on business for the queen.

Bevan had been allowed to stay on at the palace, since his first encounter with the queen, which had not gone well. Her face cream spilling everywhere had not impressed her. He was clumsy and it was not something that could be changed, but his intentions were good. She only allowed him to stay on because of their short staffing problem, so she agreed to let him help out, hoping he would have the sense to keep out of her sight and in the background. She liked her servants to be seen and not heard, apart from her trusted Dragot, who was away. She relied on his advice on all matters, but with him away, she had to make do. Bevan was small but he worked like a donkey, if a clumsy one. He was fast and firm with a duster and his precise table setting was admirable. His aunt had always known he would do well in the household, as long as he could keep his clumsy episodes to a minimum. His diligence was in no doubt. His swift cleaning and polishing were all going well and no accidents had occurred so far today, which made him skip around the furniture with a gleeful spring.

The queen looked in on him half way through. She gasped in utter disgust at the view of him, but could not criticise the quality of his work. And so with table set and room cleaned, the sun shone through the windows and set an idyllic scene ready for her noble guest. As she left the dining room, Bevan smiled to himself and thought about his new achievements. He was going to like his new position. It was going to be fun. Great fun! He felt at home in the castle. Its rooms were fine and waiting to be cleaned. He could make himself indispensable here. It was the perfect job for him.

Gerrado, the Slug King arrived hours later, on time if not a little sweaty and out of breath. The ride was bound to leave him this way. The queen greeted him well with a small kiss on the cheek, a little shocked at his damp appearance from the vigorous horse ride. She showed him through to the castle, which he had allowed her keep for many years. They walked together, through the hallway. His short legs struggled to keep up with her elegant strides. He was relieved when Mrs. Tweedy appeared to assist him.

"Let me take your coat, Sir. And riding boots?" said Mrs. Tweedy, who had been waiting for the visitor all day and now her stomach was a bag of nerves, especially with her nephew waiting on.

She waddled off with his coat and boots which he took off and replaced his gold slippers on his tiny feet. They were not the most attractive, but did suit him well. She wandered up a grand staircase that led up from the entrance. Bevan led him into the dining room, which he had been preparing all day.

Queen Narla was beautiful. She was tall and thin; her curves were modest but in the right places. Her skin and hair shone like silk. It was clear she knew it and the Slug King became like a bumbling wreck in her presence. His keenness to impress was embarrassing at times, but he was no different to most who met her. Gerrado enjoyed a challenge and it was good for him to be with someone who was not afraid of him. Queen Narla did have a fearless streak. She did not care what happened to her and it left her with an untouchable charm. Her history had left her on her own and no one could understand why such a woman would choose this life when she would have the choice of anyone she wanted. It was a mystery, but it kept this suitor as keen as a beagle looking for chops.

"You look well Gerrado," she said, as they sat at the set table.

She took the head place and he sat at the side of her.

"Thank you. The riding keeps me fit," he replied, pleased at the compliment.

"You look beautiful, my dear," he said as he touched her hand.

She withdrew it straight away. Too much encouragement at this early point might be a mistake, she thought. She looked at his large stomach, as if wondering how he could think himself fit, with such a large girth.

"White wine? I have some new bottles of Sauvignon which are very nice," she asked.

"Perfect," he replied as they settled into their seats.

"I have brought some more cream. I hear there was an accident with the other pot," he said.

On hearing this Bevan shrunk behind the door, not wanting the queen to see him at this precise moment. He did not want to exasperate her. She looked annoyed at the reminder of the lost pot of cream.

"Yes, there was. Thank you, we shall take more care with the new pot," she replied haughtily and glancing over at Bevan anyway.

"Oh it is no bother, you know I can bring some anytime. Not that you need it," he said, wasting no time to fill her with compliments.

"Oh you are too kind. I am getting old. We all need a little extra help when trying to stay young," she laughed.

Gerrado melted in her presence; he was like a different person. His harsh exterior disappeared and his need to show a soft and caring side would take over.

His enemies would be amazed at his change. She was a beautiful queen and many had fallen under her spell. Though she only had one man in her heart and no one else would come close her. She knew it. She didn't mind Gerrado visiting and paying her compliments and she enjoyed his company. He was an interesting king. He was wealthy and powerful, so his visits did no harm at all. They got on well.

Bevan carried the first course onto the table. He placed their dishes in front of them and carefully ladled the soup into each bowl. The first course of salmon and prawn soup was received well. Bevan was thrilled not to spill any under pressure. The queen eyed him carefully. Her eyes burning into him as he brought some bread. It didn't matter to him, as he enjoyed serving. He was a happy servant. He stood back to the side whilst they ate, until the soup slurping stopped and then he would clear away, ready for the next course. It was an easy job, if his nerves could hold out. He listened carefully to their conversations, but was careful not to show any interest on his face, and so looked on as if he were daydreaming. Most servants could not help but listen to conversations, it was a given. The king and queen made small talk for the first course, and the soup went down well whilst talking about the latest weather and funny stories, and then the conversation became more about recent goings on…and of course Gerrado had lots to tell. He was desperate to know what the queen would make of the 'bracelet and boy' story. He was keen to show her the bracelet. Bevan continued to bring in hot dishes of vegetables and potatoes, to match the roast duck that was being served in a rich orange gravy sauce. The gravy he spilled a little onto the saucer, but the two were in deep conversation and so did not notice.

"A funny thing happened this morning," Gerrado began.

"Oh yes, what?" said the queen, enjoying his stories as usual. They usually told of some poor soul being taken to the Slug Pit for some reason or other.

"A boy was brought to me. He was ordinary, as far as I could tell. I was told he had been thieving in the city. One of the market holders had caught him. Anyway, turns out he wasn't a thief, but the market holder had seen a bracelet on this boy and thought it should be brought to my attention," Gerrado continued, as he got the bracelet out of his coat pocket and place it on the table for the queen to inspect.

"Hum, is lovely, yes," she said as she picked it up to admire it.

"This man from the market tells me that it belonged to King Marcus. What do you think about that?" said Gerrado.

"It could be. Who could be sure?" she said.

"Well the man reckoned it was his as he used to clean all the jewels for the king. He says it was the one he wore," said Gerrado.

"You think he's right?" she asked.

"I don't know. But why would he lie?" said Gerrado.

"For money?" she said.

"Yes, maybe. We don't know. The inscription, do you know what it says?" he asked.

"No, I have no idea. I could find out. I could get some people to look at it," she added.

Bevan was very interested in all their talk. He stood back next to the door, with his hands by his sides. His mind racing. He had known the old king well. He had worked for him many years ago, with his aunt. They had been part of the royal household. He remembered King Marcus fondly. It looked like his bracelet. If he could get closer, he would be able to read the inscription. He knew that it would read, "A great king."

"What about the boy. Where did he get it from?" she asked.

"Ah, well he was very cagey. Couldn't get a word of truth from him. Says he found it. Or took it. He says it wasn't his. I have put him in the pit until he is prepared to talk," he said.

"I guess the pit will make him see sense," she added.

"It's not that I want to put my pit to use like this, you know, but when I am told lies, I just don't have much choice. A king has to have the truth. He must punish liars," he went on.

"Yes, it's true. It is hard to be in power. It is necessary to gain control with any method. If you show any weakness, it is never a good thing," she said.

"Marcus was weak. That's why he lost the war. He let others lead him. He took advice. He was a weak man. It showed. My power has been so strong over the last ten years. I have no problems. The people in the Daccorian region work hard for me. They pay their taxes. It is necessary to keep the kingdom healthy. The sluggett army is strong and undefeatable. The Loban Masters have enough with their land, but they hand its riches over. They lost the war. I let them live in their ancient burial grounds, but they lost. I won. I won and have to keep everything in its place otherwise it was all for nothing. It is for the good of the kingdom. But a king must lead, otherwise chaos ensues," he finished.

The queen nodded. She had liked King Marcus, but she knew that the Slug King was ruthless and she understood how he worked. He ran a strong kingdom, even if many in it were repressed and downtrodden. But she understood that with power came responsibility. She knew he held power higher than responsibility. He was a cruel king and that's one of the reasons he had stayed in power so long.

"So the boy. I wonder how he got this bracelet and if it was from King Marcus?" she returned to the point.

"It could be the bracelet, but the boy is a mystery. I will get answers from him on my return, no doubt about that," he said, scoffing down his dinner with great appetite. "Delicious! Regards to the cook!" he added.

"Let me know what you find out," she added.

It certainly was an intriguing story. She had never heard the Slug King talk much about King Marcus. He was always keen to speak of the future and never dwelled on the past.

Bevan's lips were becoming moist with the news. He was listening carefully. Who was the boy, he wondered to himself?

"I will. I will. When I find out where this boy got the bracelet from I shall track down its original owner. Have you heard talk that the king had a son?" he asked.

"Yes, I have heard rumours. But he was never found was he? The queen escaped, they say, but she was never found either," she said.

"And with King Marcus dead, they would be on their own," he added.

"Do you believe the queen survived and had a son?" she said.

"I never thought about it till now," he said.

"And now?" she asked.

"Now? I shall have to give it some thought. I mean I can't have this, this...story filtering down into my kingdom. Who knows where it could lead? I mean, if the creatures and people thought there was a new king, of Marcus blood, alive...well, you know what creatures and people are like. It might give them some sort of hope. Or some might use it as an opportunity to hurt me. It will have to be handled with care, that much I know," he said as he swigged more wine and become more relaxed.

"So there could be a boy?" she asked.

"If there is, he is as good as dead, when I get my hands on him and I will. I will. The other boy will talk. If the boy is alive, I will find him. I will find him and eliminate him, without a doubt," he concluded.

Bevan moved to clear away the empty plates. He picked them up and took them out into the kitchen, His ears ringing from the information he was gathering. An heir to the throne of King Marcus was great news, indeed. He wondered where this boy could be. He knew, whoever he was, his life was already in grave danger.

'Oh my poem, I nearly forgot," said Gerrado, who had taken to writing poetry for the queen. "Shall I read it?"

"Please do," choked the queen, clinging onto her wine goblet for help with the next moments that would follow. She had never got used to his poetry reading, but the king seemed to find a necessary part of their meetings. "What's it called?" she asked trying to seem interested.

"You. It's just called you," he replied.

She held the glass so hard it was lucky she didn't break it.

"You," he paused and the continued to read his well-prepared poem.

"You are as sweet as a red red rose,

From the top of your head and down to your toes!

The way you shake my hand is as lovely as a rose

and I like your pointy nose.

My lady true, so kind and strong,

With each other we belong,

It is true you are the woman of my dreams,

A lady of many extremes, I wonder do you like ice cream.

I would give to you the stars, the moon, my all,

You are part of me, and as our friendship grows,

I hope it will never, never, never, never end!"

The queen's smile remained fixed through the whole reading. Mrs. Tweedy saved her, as she came in to clear for the last course.

"Was everything alright for you mam?" she asked.

Coughing on wine, "Yes, it was lovely... perfect," she added, looking at Gerrado. He looked delighted.

Mrs Tweedy smiled and took the plates away. She was helped by Bevan who was buzzing and bumbling around, not wanting to miss any more of their conversation that night. It could prove important to him. He was always on the look-out for information. He liked to be seen as a fool. It served his purpose well.

Chapter 9. The Freedom Warriors.

Jee Hanna and Dexy made the final climb along the mountain edge, it was good to be home at last. The horses had been left in fields at the bottom of the mountain, to graze and rest. Then the final walk up the mountainside had been easy today, with happy steps they took, glad to be finally home. They stopped outside the cave entrance, placing down their bags. It was hard to tell it was an entrance at all, but it was cleverly disguised with some branches and leaves so the opening was masked.

"Hello!" Jee Hanna called out, she couldn't wait to see everyone again. They seemed to have been gone so long.

Inside, the crew were cooking a hearty dinner of pumpkin soup and soda buns. They were waiting for their friends to arrive at any moment.

"Was that Jee Hanna?" said Falentona.

"Sure was," said Gobber jumping up to greet them, making his way through the cave to the front entrance. His pimples bulging with excitement and green eyes brightening at the thought of seeing his friends again, especially if they had food in tow. "They're here!"

Jax followed behind him, eager to see his brother and Jee Hanna again. He had missed them the most. Keto looked up and smiled at the sound of Jee Hanna's voice. Samlit picked up his guitar and began to strum and jolly tune to mark the occasion. Falconette kept her eye on the food, keeping it warm.

There was a short thin corridor that he walked down before reaching the area at the front of the mountain. Jax was keen to see his older brother again, he overtook Gobber who ran at a slower pace. He could hear their footsteps approaching. He smiled to hear his friends once again. It had been far too long they had been gone.

"Hello!" Gobber called, not minding that he had been pushed into second place. He understood Jax's impatience.

"Hello!" echoed back Jee Hanna and Dexy at the same moment.

They walked through the final bend and all met once again to joyful hellos and happy hugs. It had been a tense few days and they were pleased to see each other again. Falentona had told them bits of the story, but they knew they would hear it all from Jee Hanna as she repeated her adventure. They knew nothing of what Dexy had learned. Even Jee Hanna was oblivious to the news he had. Dexy wanted to call a meeting as soon as possible, but he kept it to himself for now. It was vital, but for the moment he was pleased to be back bringing them the rations they had gone for in the first place. His hand-picked family fussed around them both for the next few hours. Greetings and laughing was passed back and forth by all. Falentona took her eyes off the soup for a big long look at her little Jee Hanna who she had saved the night before from harm. Keto smiled and nodded at them, chewing an old herb leaf. He didn't move much, but his wrinkled lined in happiness showed his smiling face was pleased. They were a gleeful group and the soup was happily dished out to the hungry creatures.

"Pumpkin soup?" she asked, knowing the answer.

"Yes please," cried Jee Hanna.

"I'm starving!" shouted Gobber.

Everyone laughed. Things were back to normal in the Silver Mountains. Samlit sang a tune they all knew well.

"Hee Ya! Hay Ya! Heeyawah! Haywa!" he taped and banged his feet in tune causing as much noise as possible. A sure sign of his happiness to see his friends back at home. "Glad you're here again! Glad you're home with us! We have missed you so!" he sang with all his might.

"I see you have made some new friends," said Falentona.

"Yes, we have," replied Jee Hanna.

"We have made some new friends, yes," added Dexy, with more importance in his voice than they understood at the time.

"Luca. He was hurt. We saved him," said Jee Hanna, hugging her Samlit and Keto.

"Was he ok?" asked Gobber, scratching his bottom.

"He will be after a few day's rest," said Dexy.

"We got him home to his mum," said Jee Hanna looking pleased with herself, enjoying all the attention and fuss.

"And I hear you had a lucky escape," said Keto.

"I...well, yes. Thank you Falentona. You came at just the right time," she said, jumping to hug the falcon lady.

"It was lucky," she said, stirring the hot soup and putting her other arm around the little spider fairy.

"Thank you so much," kissed Jee Hanna.

"Gave me a right heart attack," said Dexy, sitting himself down at last and shaking his head.

Everyone laughed, knowing the worry she would have caused him.

"I saw my family," she said quietly.

"Yes, yes we heard. I guess it was something you needed to do, darling," said Falentona, full of understanding and motherly love for the spider fairy.

Jee Hanna smiled, glad of her approval that was so important to her. She knew she had so much to be thankful for. She was glad to share her news with her best friends, her new family.

"I need to call a meeting," said Dexy, changing the subject.

The others looked at him and slowed down their eating to look curiously at him. They knew this meant there was news.

"A meeting?" said Gobber.

"Yes a freedom warriors meeting," he said.

"So you have news?" said Keto. "I thought as much... I dreamt you had news. I was thinking you had more to tell," he said, often reading the future in dreams.

"I do have news, but I want to wait till the others arrive. Falentona, can you take these messages to them, after lunch?" he asked.

"I will," she said.

"So we have to wait till the meeting? Can you give us any clues, Dexy?" asked Jax.

"I can tell you when the others arrive. Till then, you can wait. I want them here by midnight. The day will go quickly. You won't have to wait long," he replied.

Everyone ate the soup. They pondered the news that Dexy had hinted at. They knew it must be of some consequence and they guessed it was news of the uprising that was being planned by several fractions of the Daccorian area who wanted the kingdom back that they were robbed of ten years ago. They knew they would have to wait for Dexy and the news. There would be no more talk of it until the meeting later.

Jee Hanna wondered what it could be too, she did not understand. She had not realised that 'Luca' (her new friend) was 'the news!' She just thought he was a boy like any other... She did not know he was the key to freedom and the lost heir to the throne. A new king! And indeed Luca knew nothing of these plans and legacies and of how his life could be changing quickly into something he not recognize. His life had been as a boy, not a Prince waiting to be crowned and made into a King!

Chapter 10. The Loban Masters

A Loban Master is free in honour of self.
Fight for these and you will find; your courage, your strength and
your truth.

Everything in the Loban Master quarters was grand and ancient. The room was tall and long, made of large square stone clad walls, with windows lining the top of the room, that would hold fifty Loban Masters, if needed. The large oval table was full of food fit for a King. It had seats for twelve placed around it, one at the head, which was more elaborate in size and wooden carvings. They were grand and comfortable with armrests and silver cushioned seats of silk.

A pig's head rested in the middle and various vegetables looked colourful around it on a silver tray. The thick oak table was magnificently laid, with fine cutlery, three-bar silver candlesticks and sparkling wine glasses. It was a feast. The food looked too good to eat. It was bright and shiny, covered in glazes and herbs. The meat smelt strong. It laced the air with savoury tones and would defy anyone's mouth not to water in anticipation.

The Loban Masters always ate well. They needed to keep their large frames strong. Their meaty figures and features were something to behold. Their backs were shelled and hard, like lobsters. Their hands were pincers, for they had two large claws, which snapped together. They clothed themselves in fur and sheepskins, a clue to their hunting skills. The Loban Masters had existed for hundreds of years. They were from times of old. Their ancient dwellings displayed history all around. Their faces told of their fore fathers.

Sedgefield Maross was the leader. He was every bit a Loban Master, his face just as a great Master should be, solid and square, though he was not a king. His face would redden quickly, due to his love of wine and fine foods, a sign of his age and experience. His hair was parted down the middle, grey and plaited on each side, in two bunches, the back in wavy locks of wiry white. He rose to his feet to make a toast, as he always did when they ate.

"To the Loban Masters! May we rise again and have back what is rightfully ours. Down with the Slug Kingdom and all who support it. Victory we shall have!" he raised his glass to the ceiling and everyone followed with,

"Victory we shall have!"

Sedgefield had not stopped fuming since his lands had been taken from him in the Great War. His anger still raged at the thought of what had happened. He had found it hard to come to terms with the occupation of a sluggett army, who guarded the ancient burial grounds of their fathers. The previous king had respected their ownership and they had lived happily along side each other, but the Slug Pit King was another matter, a law unto himself. A tyrant! A vagabond! A slime! He had the morals of a gnat. He had the brain of a flea, and yet he was in charge now and had been for ten years. It was an insult! Maross had spent every day of those ten years making plans and plotting to win back his Ancient ground. He had a small fierce army, of two hundred, but they were tiny compared to the nearly a thousand sluggetts. He had waited and waited and would not strike till he was ready, for fear of another failure would be more than he could take and he did not want to be humiliated again.

Some of the Loban Masters were allowed to carry on with their archaeological digs, but it was all under the watchful eye of the sluggetts, who guarded every inch of the ancient grounds; their watchful eyes making it impossible for any great artefacts to be kept, since they were given straight to the Slug Pit King. His castle was dripping with finds from this area.

The Ancient burial grounds contained a wealth of time worn objects, crumbling walls of buildings lost years ago. Vintage finds included jewellery, clothing, utensils, tools made from a range of clay, stone, bronze, silver, gold. The best finds encrusted with diamonds and opals, emeralds and rubies. The old ships and boat boughs also of great worth, but all handed over to the Slug King. He kept it all. The Loban Masters were not in a position to argue, however they did have some rare secret finds which the sluggetts had not found and so could not be confiscated. They kept these safe in a locked cellar where they would not be found, but compared to what they should have had; it was an insulting fraction. Yet, they treasured these beloved locked away items all the more for their scarcity. The one thing everyone was looking to find was a book, which had been hinted at in old letters and carvings, it told of stories and power, of the Ancient Loban forefathers. No one had found this book yet. It was still far underground, or destroyed, they assumed. Whatever the treasures were, the Loban Masters all agreed on one thing, and that was that they belonged to them and no one else. It was only right that one day they would get back their land and historically grand tokens of the past.

"Eat up!" cried Maross. "Who knows when we shall need our strength again?"

He bit into a pig's trotter and chewed it with vigour.

"Strength and honour!" he continued.

Another toast, as he raised his glass with a tip into the air again.

The chorus followed faithfully. They knew Maross was a fan of the toast, even if they were a bit clichéd. He chewed knowingly and nodded at the Loban Master to his left.

Here was Tarron Tippencloak, his second in command. His friend for many years... They had grown up together and fought in the Great War side by side. He was a jolly soul the smile across his face rarely left him, even in his sleep he would grin. He liked a joke and a drink. Though he often spat out bad wine with no manners or worry. The stone floors of the Loban Master Quarters were often covered in small wine pools of his spit. He always had time for drinking and was always last to leave any social gathering, that was his nature. His skills on a battlefield were second to none. His muscular arms could swing a sword around his head and take three sluggetts out in one swing. He looked like a bull, partly due to the fact that he had a gold nose ring, which hung solidly, just out of the way above his mouth, and also from the way his head rested on his wide neck and chunky shoulders. His hair was plaited in the same way as Maross, in two bunches, but his hair was a dark almost black colour, which made him look sleeker and younger and the whites of his eyes stood out, both in battle and when he laughed.

"Did you see that sluggett today; fall into a hole by the new dig? So clumsy! Made me laugh though," said Tarron.

"They are clumsy by nature those sluggetts. There isn't one of them yet that I have seen with their helmet on straight," added Maross.

"How many are we harbouring now?" asked Tarron.

"The occupation is a small few, I guess no more than a hundred. They won't spare more of their army on us old warriors; too worried about an uprising from the Daccorian Region! That is always being whispered about. It won't be far off, the uprising will come and that is what they are most afraid of! We don't seem to worry them too much... for now; little do they know we too are building ourselves back again. Loban Masters will not be kept down anymore," he started ranting as he always did at meal times...

"We will have our day, that is for sure and I can't wait to get my hands on some pasty slimy sluggetts, they really are the pits!" he realised what he had said. "Ha! The pits! Ha, ha, ha!"

Laughter could be heard, filling the large eating room, filled with the Loban Masters, as it was most nights. The laughs were never far away from this crew. They loved Sedgefield's rants about the sluggett occupation they were always entertaining!

The Slug King had given them a rather grand monastery and quarters, right on the edge of the ancient grounds, as he thought it would keep them sweet. They had never been happy to be demoted and humiliated, and they would not stop till they owned what was rightfully theirs again. It had been so long people might forget. But ten years is a milli-second to a Loban Master, whose existence and ancestors had been around for thousands.

Falentona flew over the Ancient burial grounds. She glided around, looking for the best place to land. She could see some of the historian Loban Masters busy at work in the digging grounds. She admired their intricate work. She watched them scrape and chisel into the ground with care and attention. Finally she flew to one of the round turrets. It was an old monastery which they used for bedrooms and living quarters. They were self-sufficient with vegetable and herb gardens that kept them in fine food. They were like monks for daily chores and life, but they also knew how to fight. (They had fought hard in the Great War. On the side of King Marcus who they lived with peacefully and side by side. But now under the Slug King, occupation was to be endured. They were allowed to stay in their burial grounds and were expected to be grateful for that. They would have given anything to have overthrown the Slug King and avoid this situation.) Falentona landed and placed the note down. It was picked up by one of the workers. He was a typical large Loban Master and thanked her.

"For Sedgefield?" he asked.

She nodded and flew away, as quickly as she had landed, like an athletic giant of the sky. The note from the Freedom warriors, informed him of the meeting. He read and folded it up again, looking pleased and thoughtful as he replied to Falentona.

"I will attend."

Chapter 11. Reflections

Don't blame the mirror for your refection. You can only see what you are ready to be.

Luca sat up talking to his best friend. They had lots to catch up on. He was feeling much better after a sausage sandwich breakfast and seeing his good friend Ettie. Ettie always made him feel better. She was a girl of thirteen, but small for her age. Her red shiny hair was cute and freckles dotted on her face evenly.
"Are you ok? What happened?" she asked, eager to hear the whole story.
"I can't remember too much. It all happened so quickly. I knew the moment I saw those boys I was in trouble, but there was nowhere to run, so I had to take it," he began the sorry tale.
"Were you scared?" she asked.
"Too quick to be scared, guess I was. One minute I was walking along minding my own business, next minute I was on the ground being kicked to pieces," he looked pained to remember it.
"I'm glad you got home. It was lucky, those people came," she said
"Dad said the spider fairy nearly drowned in the White Lake. He said it was lucky he was out looking for you," said Ettie.

"Why did she go to the lake?" he asked.

"She went to see her family. The spider fairies are nearly all extinct, you know. I guess she must feel lonely sometimes," she said.

"So she saw them?" he asked.

"Yeah, I think so. Dad said she did," said Ettie.

"It's not fair, is it? I go all the time to the Lake to see my father and he never comes. She goes once and sees her family. Why is that?" Luca said crossly.

"I don't know. It's just the way things are. You might see him one day," she tried to reassure him again.

"Maybe my father doesn't come because I'm a disappointment. Maybe that's it," said Luca.

"Now why would you think that? Don't be so ridiculous," she said. "Sometimes answers are not always there for us when we want them. The lake might never show your father, are you going to spend the rest of your life waiting for him and making yourself miserable?" she said using tough words to help.

She knew Luca was visiting the lake more than he should and he was making himself unhappy. She wanted to help, but she didn't know why his father never appeared, or what to say to Luca when he asked her about it. It did seem so unfair that the fairy had been able to see her family at once, after one visit, but what could she say to Luca. It was tricky.

"I know. I am lucky. I must put the lake to the back of my mind and concentrate on getting better again," he smiled.

His arms and chest ached terribly still and he knew a few days in bed would do him some good, but he wanted to get up and do the things he always did. It would be too boring to rest. He was home and that was good, even though his aching limbs were sore and tired. He could still hear Aviras' voice in his head, 'Give me the bracelet! Give it to me!'

"You look like you've been through the mangle. Not your best look, a black eye and cut lip, but you'll be as good as new in no time. See, nurse Ettie is here," she put her hands out acting the part, wanting to make him laugh.

"I know. Ettie, though, the worst part is that I wore my father's bracelet. You know the one mum gave me," he continued, moving his covers away as he felt warm and clammy and placing his feet outside the covers for an airing.

"I didn't think you wore it. I thought..." she said.

"I know, I'm not meant to. I just wanted to wear it. It makes me feel lucky," he smiled, unsure.

"Oh dear, not so lucky, dilly," she laughed, but knew it was a shame for him. "Your poor thing."

"I know. I know. I'm so stupid. It was so stupid of me. I should have known," his eyes went tearful as his face showed his anger.

"Well you weren't to know you were gonna be jumped on. It's not your fault that those boys took it,"

"I should have listened," he said.

"Well we all do things we wish we could change and when do you ever listen? You never know you might get it back," she tried to cheer him up and squeezed his hand as she slurped her mug of warm tea. "Those boys, we can find them and get it back."

"I don't know. I wish we could," he said eventually.

"We could try. It's not impossible," she comforted him. "Does your mum know it's gone?"

"Don't know," he said rubbing his head as the pains came back like dull waves.

"Well then. Let's see if we can get it back. We can try," she was happy to hatch a new plan with him and offer some hope.

Ava was downstairs talking with Roper. They were talking too. He could see her face was full of worry. He assumed it was for her son and his injuries.

"Ava, you know he's going to be fine. Those cuts and bruises may look bad, but he will heal quickly," he said, with his eyes narrowing with emphasis on the word heal.

"I know. You are right and the main thing is he is home. I just can't believe this has happened," she said, squeezing her arms around herself. "Everything's such a mess," she added looking over Roper's head and out of the window.

"Come on now. He's home! He's tucked up in bad and he'll be fine. We need to find out which boys did it and speak to their parents," he added.

"I'm not sure that's a good idea. I want to keep it quiet," she said.

Roper stayed silent for a while. He was shocked at her answer. He would have thought she would want to find the gang and sort things out. Why would she not want to find the boys? They needed to be spoken to at least. If he got his hands on them, he would make sure they never did it again. Her reaction was certainly strange and unexpected.

"Now don't you want to find those thugs and give them a piece of your mind? They must be from the village. I am sure a few questions would bring them to light," he said, getting up from the chair and putting his mug on the side, wiping his mouth from the wholesome breakfast he'd polished off.

"Roper, I think it should be left alone. Luca is my main concern," she said again, shocking him further.

"Yes, if he is your main concern, why not find those maggots and make them pay? They can't get away with it," he said.

"They already have. What good would it do now? It won't do Luca any good now," she said, rubbing her face anxiously.

"Surely it's about what's right and wrong?" he was getting frustrated with her replies, but trying not to show it.

He was amazed, he assumed she would agree wholly with him, like any parent would.

"It's hard to explain. I just don't think it's a priority at the moment," she said trying to sound convincing.

"Well, hum, I guess," Roper did not want to say too much for fear that they would fall out and he could see she needed his support at this time, so he kept quiet. She must have been tired from a restless night maybe she would change her mind in a few days. For now he knew it was best to leave the subject.

"We should be going," he made his excuses politely. "Ettie! You ready? If there's anything you need, you just shout. You hear?" he was always kindness itself.

"Coming! Bye Luca. See you later maybe? Shall I come round this afternoon if I can?" she asked.

"Yeah, that be good," he replied.

Ettie jumped up and climbed down the stair ladder, into the kitchen. She rushed to the door and her father followed, waving to signal a farewell. Ava went to the door to close it behind them. She was deep in thought. Her mind a whirlwind of what repercussions might be happening. She climbed up the ladder and went to check on Luca. She smiled,

"Need anything?" she asked.

"No," smiled Luca.

She stroked his hair and his eyes became sleepy again, as he dozed off into a comfortable healing sleep. Ava watched him lie there, wondering how safe they would stay and wishing she had never let him out of her sight. She took a moment to speak to her husband Marcus, in her mind. What should she do? What choices did she have? No answers came rushing. It was hard being on her own. She looked into the face of her son and felt a heart ache like none she had ever felt before. She wondered if her heart might snap. She wondered if she would ever feel safe for him again. She knew they were both in danger. Their discovery had made it so!

Chapter 12. The Meeting

The freedom warriors waited and planned for their time to come again...

when it came they would know.

The freedom warriors sat round the fire in a circle. It was the best way to conduct a meeting of this sort where everyone could see each other and everyone could speak. All of them were involved and even Jee Hanna was allowed to stay. She needed to know things that were happening as much as anyone else. They were waiting for Sedgefield Moss. He was due any minute. He had been before and knew the way. They were expecting him.

Tea was made. It kept them awake at the late hour. The night was upon them, but they were wide awake at the prospect of the meeting ahead of them. Dexy and Gobber had some glasses of beer too, they knew Sedgefield would not want tea and they enjoyed as drink. Jax had been allowed some too and he was pleased to be included in the beer drinks.

They heard a ruffling and Dexy went up to the entrance. It was not Sedgefield, but a welcome and expected visitor all the same.

"Bevan. Glad you could make it at short notice," said Dexy.

"Wouldn't miss it for the world. It's been too long," he said, shaking Dexy's hand and wandering in walking along the corridor and into the hub of the cave where everyone sat waiting.

They greeted Bevan with ample hellos and offers of food and drink. He took the tea and sat next to Keto, where a space was evident. They smiled, they were the older members of the group and knew their wise offerings were always greatly listened to and appreciated. The cave was deceptively large and they sat around, ledges had been carved into walls for seats, some had cushions, which added extra comfort. It was a cosy home, but practical more than anything else.

"Long time since I was here. The place looks good. Have you expanded? Looks bigger," he said, glancing around at them all with a knowing smile.

"No I don't think it's bigger since you were last here. We have some new rooms at the back. Jee Hanna has her own bedroom now, don't you?" said Falentona.

"Yes," she said with pride.

"Well aren't you growing up?" he chuckled. "A young lady before me, hey?"

Jee Hanna smiled with more swelling pride. She had always like Bevan and he always made a fuss of her on his visits. He was a small funny looking creature, his silky otter tufts were always gleaming and his little spectacles on the end of his nose balanced precariously.

"She is growing fast, as is Jax," said Falentona, smiling with pride at her family sat around.

"You look well, Bevan," said Gobber.

"I have a new job. I'm at the castle with Queen Narla," he said.

"I didn't know," said Keto.

"No, it's a new job. My aunt helped me get it," he explained.

"You enjoying?" said Keto.

"Yes, I do enjoy it. And it means I can be a good source of information for you too," he said.

"Ah, that is a good thing," said Falentona.

"In fact I am glad we have a meeting. I have lots of news," he said, enjoying the nettle tea and finishing his first cup already.

"I think Dexy has news too," said Gobber. "Yes we definitely needed a meeting."

"Long overdue," said Bevan.

"Speaking of overdue. Where is Sedgefield?" said Gobber. "He's always late that fellow."

"He has got the furthest to come," reminded Keto.

"I'm here!" said a deep voice appearing from nowhere. "Sorry I'm late. Pass me a beer and let's start," he laughed and sat down, squashing Jax and Samlit into a slightly uncomfortable corner. For such a heavy man, it was hard to think they had not heard him coming.

Sedgefield was the largest of all of them. His wiry ringlets and plaits hung down his face and made him look like a warrior, as he liked to seem fierce. He had looked this way since he was twenty but he was now in his fifties, some grey hairs showed it. His large shoulders and back, squashed into his place and his thighs were as big as boulders. He was something to behold, with his fur skin rug over his shoulders and bronze clasps to make his look official and important. His hands were huge and looked like he could squash a small creature in one go.

"Thanks. Hello to all of you. You all know each other, as we have met many times over the years. I have called an urgent meeting because I have some news, which needs careful discussion," Dexy said in a serious voice.

The group listened in silence. They were keen to know what news Dexy had. The last meeting was over six months ago and they had had little to discuss, it had been a quiet and practical formality, but now this meeting was different.

"Yesterday Jee Hanna and I saved a boy who had been beaten and left in a ditch. We took the boy, Luca home to his mother. On the way home, I started to notice that he seemed familiar to me. At first it puzzled me, but then it became like a nagging itch and I could not understand what it was about this boy that was drawing me to him. When he was able to speak, he told me that the thugs who attacked him, had taken a bracelet, which belonged to him. This bracelet was the key to the puzzle," Dexy stopped for breath and looked to see the faces around him.

Each freedom warrior looked at him with great curiosity, hanging on each of Dexy's words as if they were laced with golden threads. No one spoke, as they were keen to hear more from Dexy. He had always been their leader, and they were proud of this.

Jee Hanna listened, she was the most surprised, as she knew nothing of Dexy's thoughts about Luca. Why she was stunned at what she was hearing. He hadn't mentioned anything to her about Luca. She felt a bit silly, but listened anyway, putting her own feelings aside. The others waited for Dexy to explain further the significance of the boy.

"It was soon after that, when I realised who this boy Luca was. The bracelet from his father, a father we knew and loved, King Marcus. His father who had died. I looked at the boy and I knew who he was. His face, the image of King Marcus. Here in front of me was the son of the king. I believe that his mother did escape and had a child, as the stories say. I believe that Luca is that child. He was the child who we could only hope existed," Dexy paused to see the others reaction.

"Can you be sure? It's a lot to have us believe all based on a bracelet and a boy who reminds you of the old king?" Sedgefield started first with the questions.

"Did you ask him? I mean did you question him?" said Falentona.

"Was it him?" said Gobber.

They all had questions. Each wanted to ask more, but knew they should listen to Dexy for longer to gain more idea of what had happened.

"It was him! The more I looked, the more I knew it was him! He was too ill to start asking questions. I couldn't ask him, as he didn't seem to know his father was a king and so it was difficult. The more I looked at him, the more I knew. His mannerisms, even his voice was familiar. I am in no doubt," said Dexy.

"Well, if you're in no doubt, then that's good enough for me," said Gobber with pride.

"There's always doubt," warned Falentona, adding caution.

"Is Luca a king?" asked Jee Hanna.

"Maybe you were seeing what you wanted to see," said Falentona, again adding caution.

"If he is the heir to the throne, then we have more reason than ever to rise up against that slug of a king," Sedgefield wasted no time to denounce the Slug King, who he hated so fervently.

"We need to protect the boy, that is what we must do," said Dexy.

"We can do that. I'm sure," said Gobber.

"I haven't finished… " Dexy interrupted them all. When I took Luca home, I spoke to his mother. She calls herself Ava now but I knew it was Queen Amber. She vaguely remembered me. She has changed her name and everything she has done since the Great War has been to cover up their royal past. She lives a simple life and keeps her secret well, so well that she hasn't even told Luca of his royal blood. She wants to keep him out of any uprising. She does not want me to help her at all and she sees me knowing about them as a big threat," cautioned Dexy.

"That's understandable," said Falentona.

"She has a responsibility to the kingdom!" cried Sedgefield, outraged at what he was hearing.

"It's very tricky, that's for sure," said Jax in amazement.

Jee Hanna had gone quiet. She was in such shock that Luca the boy she had saved was so much more than she had realised. She was numb with all the news. Bevan who had been quiet so far moved himself forward and coughed a few times, in order to make way for him to speak.

"I have more news, along the same lines. As you know, I am working for Queen Narla. She had her friend, the Slug King over for dinner last night. He told her about a boy who had been brought to him, wearing the old king's bracelet."

Sedgefield interrupted, "What? They have the boy?"

"Let me finish. This boy had found the bracelet, or taken it, something, and it had been spotted in the city by a market seller, who took the boy to the king," said Bevan.

"So the boy with the bracelet…?" said Gobber, trying to work it out.

"He was the boy who attacked Luca...?" said Keto, understanding what had happened.

"Serves him right!" Gobber cried, always hating injustice.

"It seems that way," answered Bevan, slurping on an empty cup of tea.

"So the Slug King has the bracelet?" Dexy asked.

"And the boy who took it," said Keto, sharp as a razor as always.

"The boy was taken to the Slug Pit. Gerrado is going to question him tomorrow. I am sure he will find out exactly where he got that bracelet from. He is keen to eliminate any threat to his throne," said Bevan.

"So Luca is in danger," said Falentona.

"It seems that way," answered Keto.

"I knew this would happen. I said they would come looking for him. I told Ava, Queen Amber that everything would change," said Dexy.

"So we need a plan," said Falentona.

"I thought she would agree to letting him come here to live with us. We could keep him safe and she could still see him, but she would not agree to it," he added.

"Well I'm not surprised. What mother would hand her son over to a bunch of strangers?" Falentona said, shaking her head.

"We need to get the boy," said Sedgefield.

"We need to stay calm," said Keto.

"Keto's right. We can't just take the boy. I offered him shelter in the mountains with us but if she won't not allow it," said Dexy.

"Surely this changes things the fact that the Slug King will shortly be looking for her boy, without doubt," said Gobber.

"Well, I can understand it. She has kept them safe for over ten years. She doesn't want things to change," said Falentona.

"But everything has changed," Dexy said, swigging his beer down.

"Indeed it has," said Gobber.

"The boy should be told where he is from. Who he really is! Everyone should know their roots," said Keto.

"It will be a shock,' said Falentona.

"But he does need to know! Apart from anything else he is in real danger," said Gobber.

"The Slug King will come looking for him, that's for sure," said Bevan.

"So what can we do?" said Jax.

"Well you need to speak to his mother again, Dexy," said Falentona.

"He's already spoken to her and she won't listen," said Sedgefield who was the least impatient of them all.

"No, he needs to tell her everything. She will see this time she has no choice. The Slug King will be searching for them, it is too dangerous for them to stay put," said Falentona.

"I was going to go back anyway. I want to take some medicine for Luca to help heal his bruises. Keto, you have some that I can take?" asked Dexy. "She will need to know of these developments too as they put Luca in even more danger," he added.

"Yes, of course," he said.

"I guess that will be a good reason to see her," said Bevan.

"Can I go with you?" asked Jee Hanna, but got no answer.

"She needs telling, not asking," Sedgefield was not the most caring of the group and saw no use in treading lightly.

"Well you need to go soon, as there may not be much time," said Bevan.

"Time is running out," added Samlit, who had been very quiet, but was always deep in thought when not singing.

"What if she refuses to listen? Like last time?" said Sedgefield, wanting to cover all bases.

"What, refuse to see sense with Dexy explaining. She's a woman, she will fall under his spell, surely," laughed Gobber. The others didn't find his joke funny.

"Hum, I'm not so sure. A woman who is set on keeping her son's identity secret at all costs," said Dexy.

"Well it's no secret anymore is it?" said Gobber.

"No, it's one big problem," said Dexy. "And we need to fix it."

"Well I think that's a start. If you go tomorrow and speak to her," said Falentona.

"We need to do more than that," said Sedgefield.

"I still don't think she will let him come to the mountains with us. She might decide to run away. On their own," said Keto.

"Yes, we need to know what she's gonna do," said Bevan.

"But we can't possibly know what she will do," Gobber cried.

"She will do what she thinks is best for Luca,' said Falentona.

"What do you think that will be?" said Jax.

"To run," answered Dexy.

"I hope not," said Bevan.

"You're gonna have to be persuasive, Dexy," said Falentona.

"I can be persuasive," said Sedgefield. "Maybe I should talk to her."

They all knew what Sedgefield meant by this. His type of persuasion was not as gentle as others. It was not what any of them wanted.

"No we don't want heavy handed threats! That will do us no good and you're not to go anywhere near them," said Dexy, crossly.

"Go in too lightly and we risk losing them," disagreed Sedgefield. "No one wants that!"

"If Dexy speaks to her, we can meet again and decide what the next move is from that," said Bevan. "If she agrees to let us take care of the boy for now to keep him safe, then we haven't any problem,"

"If she doesn't agree, then we need another plan," said Gobber, helpfully.

"Well let's hope that time doesn't run out while she is deciding, because if the Slug King gets his hands on him before we do, then the boy is as good as dead," said Sedgefield. "Mark my words. Make sure she understands that," he continued shaking his head, still not happy.

Jee Hanna gasped at hearing this.

"Well what do you suggest? I can't kidnap him," said Dexy. "We have to work together."

"He's right. We need to see what she says, then decide," said Gobber.

"All agreed?" asked Dexy.

A chorus of nods and agreement went round.

"Agreed."

"More tea? Beer?" Falentona could see they needed refreshing.

"Please," said Bevan holding out his cup.

"Beer," said Gobber and Jax.

"Large one," said Sedgefield.

The group sighed and drank together, each one thinking about what would be the best way to proceed. Jee Hanna could not believe she has saved the boy who had seemed so nice to her. Could he really be a king?

Chapter 13. Medicine and a Map

Step ahead with your mind and your feet will follow thoughts.

Dexy set out once again. He was as early as the birds which sang morning songs from the trees down below the mountainside, as he climbed down, with his rucksack firmly on his shoulder. It had medicine for Luca- a good reason for him to return to them without arousing too much alarm. He knew he could not risk waiting any longer to speak to Ava. It may cost them too much. His mind was still thinking of the boy he had rescued and how it had been a long time since he had been reminded of his old friend; the boy's father.

The day was dull with clouds that were damp and full of rain ready to pour by lunchtime. The still air was wet and cold and it woke him up quicker than any wash in a steam would have done. He knew the quickest route down the mountainside. His strides were so vigorous that he had to watch he did not break into a run with the momentum from the steep edges; the rocks could be deceptive and lethal and the grass was slippery too on this dampest of mornings. His urgency was clear but he knew a fall would be disastrous today. He was well prepared and his thoughts were focussed on the appointment ahead with Queen Amber, or Ava Lockharth, whichever was right?

At last at the bottom of the mountain he found his horse grazing on the damp fresh sprigs of grass, which covered the area like a green tufted carpet. He mounted his horse and set off at a gallop through the fields and then on into the wood. He rode for a couple of hours at this pace and then trotted for the last hour through the village lanes. He was an experienced horseman and knew these so parts well. He could not believe that the son of King Marcus had been living so close to him for all these years. It was unbelievable; the son they had dared not dream existed till now.

Approaching, he climbed down from his horse and walked towards the house. He tidied himself up as best he could, running his hands through his hair and checking all his buttons were done and brown riding boots clean of mud. He was a tall handsome man, eyes that shone like green pools and eyelashes which gave him an almost pretty look, yet his square chin and jaw line was as manly as a lion and his stubbly rough chin made him gruff and bristled too. His hair was wet from the rain and curled on his forehead in ringlets that stuck flat. He recognised the cottage. It was thatched, not too large, but enough for a family of two to live comfortably in; the type which was typical in this village. The wooded door was closed and he wished he could see inside before knocking, but he knew his nerve would have to keep strong for it would be an important visit and he wanted it to go well. He knocked and made sure it could be heard but it was not too loud either, so as not to alarm. Inside movement could be heard and he waved as he saw Ava peeped through the window to check on the visitor. She looked concerned.

"Hello?" she said carefully.

"Brought some medicine for Luca. Hope that's ok?" he asked, nervously.

He was more nervous than he realised.

"That's fine," she let him in.

"How is he?" he asked.

"He's sleeping," she smiled. "He's ok. He's young and strong."

"That's good. This cream will help his bruises and the medicine is good for healing and strength. So I'm told. They do work. I know they do, I've used them many times," he explained, as he handed them to her from his rucksack.

"Thank you," she replied and looked at them with interest as she put them on the side.

"Would you like a drink?" she offered.

"No. Thanks," he said.

"Is it a fleeting visit?" she asked, but had a feeling it was not.

"Err. Well, I would like to speak to you," he said, getting more of his confidence back.

He was too aware that he was speaking to a queen and it was strange, in these surroundings.

"I though you might. Come to change my mind?" she said sitting down in one of the chairs by the hearth.

"Well, I have things I need to tell you, my lady," he said giving her old title and sitting in the chair opposite.

"You don't need to speak to me like that. I am not a queen any more," she whispered.

"You will always be," he added honourably.

"What is it you need to tell me?" she asked, sitting up straight and moving into a position she could hold with comfort looking straight at him.

His eyes were piercing and full of integrity that she could not help but want to trust him.

"The bracelet that one of the gang stole from Luca; I think it has turned up in the hands of the Slug King and I am guessing it is only a matter of time before he realises who's it was and will want to know where it has come from. I think there is a strong possibility that he will come looking for Luca," Dexy tried to explain.

"Well that's convenient isn't it? Is that what you think will make me hand my son over to you to take him to the mountains to hide for the rest of his life until you want to go to war?" she said, the warmth in her voice faded.

"It is an option. I think to protect him," he said trying to show her they meant no harm.

"How many times do I have to say? I will not hand him over," she said.

"I know, but he is in danger. I want to protect him, like I did his father," he said, knowing to mention his father at this point was a mistake.

"Don't mention his father. His father is not here anymore. We are a different family now," she added. "Nothing is like it was then when his father was alive.

"I mean you no harm, my lady, I just want to help," he said.

"You can help by leaving us alone. I am grateful to you for helping Luca, but it does not mean we owe you," she said.

"Maybe not me, but what about the kingdom? What do you owe it? The creatures and people who went to war to save it? Everyone lost. Families were destroyed and things changed for many people, not just you and your son," he was getting cross that she could be so adamant when it was so clear things were changing.

"I am here to warn you. The Slug King will come looking. He will not leave an heir alive, even if he thinks it might not be true, he will still come. He has the boy who took the bracelet locked in his Slug Pit and how long do you think it will be before this boy talks and tells him how he got it. You don't have much time," Dexy warned her.

The queen paused for a long time. She was thinking. She was thinking about the choices she had. She could let Luca go with Dexy, a man she hardly knew, but yet she trusted him. They could all go to the mountains to live as outsiders, but to live like that forever, and what would she tell Luca? Or she could wait and take the chance that no one would find them. Or she could move on with Luca, hide again in another village, as they had done ten years ago. She would have to start all over again and make a new life for them many miles from here. They were no great choices.

"I need some time to think," she said. "Can I have a couple of days?"

"You can, but it could be dangerous. If the Slug King comes looking," he added.

"A couple of days, surely that will be ok?" she said.

Dexy shrugged.

"Who knows? We think he will come soon," he said.

"We?" she asked.

"The freedom warriors," Dexy added.

"You have told others about this?" she looked horrified.

"I have a duty to my friends," he said.

"But no duty to the queen?" she asked.

"I thought you were no longer a queen?" he concluded, looking slightly amused that she had become her old self and shown signs of a queen again.

"You had no right to tell others," she said. "The more people and creatures that know about this, the more danger we are in. It will become common knowledge and I will have no choice but to leave and where will we run?" she asked.

"I had every right." He said. "These creatures and people fought for you in the great war. They would fight again for their kingdom to be taken back from a cruel and selfish king. I had every right to tell them. They suffered and I had some hope of a life away from that. What I know and what I learned, I have every right to tell whom I chose and to make plans as I chose. As you say I am no longer governed by anyone. I am an outsider," he spoke well.

"I am left with little choice, but I want some time to think," she said.

"Or time to run?" he checked her reaction.

It was a thought that had crossed both their minds.

Would she run and hide again?

"Where would I go? I would if I knew where," she added.

"Listen. I thought we might not agree, but if he does come, you may need our help. I have a map for you; it shows the route to our Silver Mountain. It will bring you to us, if you need to us. Please take it," said Dexy as he handed it over, hoping she would take it.

"Thank you," she took it. "What choice did she have?"

Dexy sighed; it was a least one small victory. She had taken the map; she could reach them if she changed her mind. She was not going to hand Luca over for his own safety, so short of kidnapping him, there was no more he could do.

"Are we friends again?" he asked sympathetically.

"We are friends. We always will be. I just need to figure out what I'm gonna do for myself," she said.

"Well, you know where we are," he replied, getting up to leave.

"I do now," she laughed as she waved the map at him.

Dexy felt strange impulse. He leaned over to kiss her as he left. It was awkward. She went to kiss him back, but then moved away. They looked at each other. It was a moment they both felt. It was not something they had seen coming. Was he a reminder of her past, her husband? She longed for any connection to those days.

Dexy left, looking back once as he took his horse and rode off towards the Loban Master burial grounds. The afternoon had been a strange one. He wanted to speak with Sedgefield and keep him up to date with things.

Chapter 14. Aviras and the Slug King

***Dark souls are still close to the light; their shadows will lead them,
just as your light leads you.***

In a dark prison cell, Aviras was getting used to the dark light in the Slug Pit. It was damp and cold, with empty moaning sounds filling the unpleasant air. There were sluggett soldiers placed all around the walls, which were filled with glowing torches that stuck out, but the darkness was still always there, like a wolf at the door. The darkness filled each space, a beast of its own, with black shadows on the walls in shapes that twisted and spread like monsters crawling. Even when eyes grew accustomed to the darkness, it was hard to see in the black gaping spaces, which blocked out any inch light and ultimately hope. A large cavern that stretched wide and long and deep making a circular prison for its captures.

Each sluggett guard had a small arch to stand in around the walls, which were jagged and rough and left mud paths circling around the pit and the prisoner cabins. They stood in rows, the arches every twenty footsteps apart, a candle lit in each arch, giving each snivelling sluggett, a craggy silhouette of their own in the shadows. The prisoners were kept in mud caves that were closed by metal bar doors, locked with padlocks. There were from two to four prisoners in each cave.

All had been there varying lengths of time. Each prison cell looked out onto the pit reminding the prisoners that escape was futile and pointless, as the giant slug pit in the ground sloshed around below. It slurped and gurgled below them like a giant cesspool. It was often bubbling. Mud and slime mixed well and its depth was unknown, with thick gulps of clotted sewage pushing up towards the top constantly. Many had been thrown or fallen to their death there, some survived and managed to crawl out an experience never wanted to be repeated; a warning to all who went against the sluggetts and their king. It was a sad grave pit as well as a threat. The sluggetts also looked down and out onto it, the central attraction in a devil's playground. It was foreboding as it was clear that anyone stepping out of line would be thrown down and any lion's den would be the same.

Aviras's knees had gone to jelly the first time he laid eyes on its murky bog. Most would experience some sort of stomach flip or turn or wobbly legs, at their first sight of the pit. He could smell its rank pungent, overpowering, powerful, slimy smell, as he was led around past the other cells and placed in a small cave cell on his own, by two hardened sluggetts. The darkness masked the reality of its bare caved walls of slime and mud, oozing down from the ceiling to the floor. Aviras was given his own cell. It was small with a bowl and bucket that was all it contained. The doors quickly locked behind him and the keys kept safely on sluggetts warden belts.

The sluggetts returned to their posts in their own archways, as they always did and never moved again until their duty was done. It was a strange place where no hope outside existed. It was a place where if you thought too much about where you where then you would probably go mad. It was not a place for children, though there were some here. The creatures that had been banished were from all walks of life. Many had committed no crime. Some had just been in the wrong place at the wrong time. Some were small time petty crooks, few deserved to be there. Most had been unlucky. Some might have said that Aviras did deserve to be there, after what he had done to Luca and others. He was scared. His thoughts were only on how and when he would be released. It never left his mind. His relief came then next day when the Slug King came back to speak with him. One long and lonely night in the darkness had been endless had been quite enough for his mean fragile soul to bear.

Gerrado the slug king was on his way to the pit. He was keen to start his search for the boy and keen to speak with Aviras. He hoped his night in the pit would make him keen to talk and tell him all he needed to know about the bracelet and the boy who threatened his throne. He brought his young son, Worrom with him, as the young slug had wanted desperately to see the sorry prisoner and begged to be taken to see him, not wanting to be left out. They walked with certainty and purpose, it was a quick and intimidating pace, 'business' could never wait long with Gerrado; he liked to work quickly. Sluggetts surrounded them both to give them an air of importance, which they didn't need as they walked with such pomp. These sluggetts carried spears horizontally and marched in time to the pace of their king. The son loved his entrance to the slug pit as he saw the prisoners scramble to their feet and move to see them enter. They marched round the pit until they reached Aviras.

"Get up boy!" the king demanded as he entered the unlocked cell.

Aviras jumped up quicker than a fox at a chicken. He was keen to be released. The moaning by other prisoners in the pit had driven his mad.

"Sir?" he said.

"I want you to tell me as quickly as you can who you got the bracelet from and where I find them," said the king slowly.

"I took it from a boy. I don't know his name but he is from the village by the White Lake in the Daccorian region. I have seen him there. I think he lives there," he said.

"Could you show me?" he asked.

"Yes. I am sure," he said although he was not at all sure, but he was prepared to say anything to get out of the Slug Pit.

"You will stay with me until we find this boy. I will swap your life for his, so if you find him you will be free. If not, you will stay here forever. Is that clear?" he asked, knowing it would be crystal clear for the boy.

"Yes sir," replied the boy.

"Even if he isn't the son of old dead King Marcus, I want him found. It is better to be safe and sure on this matter. The only heir to my throne will be my son, Worrom. He shall rule when I am gone and nothing is going to stop that," said the king.

The sweat poured from Aviras. He knew he had a good chance of finding the boy. He was already working out which area he would show them first and where he was most likely to be.

"Can you tell my artist what he looks like too? I want some posters made of the boy's face. You will have to come up into the palace to do this. I will fetch you in an hour. Once the posters are drawn up, we can head into the village and start looking for the boy. If you think of anything else tell one of my guards and they will sort it,"

"Thank you, sir."

A polite boy stood in front of the king. He was a far cry from the boy with his gang of friends. He was paying a good price for his bullying and stealing, he had already vowed never to take what didn't belong to him again and cursed his own arrogance at wearing the bracelet in the market, but it was all too late, his nasty deeds were done and his punishment was not over yet. He seemed so scared of the Slug King, or maybe it was the pit that installed a great deal of fear into everyone. Or maybe he knew how the mind of a bully worked and maybe he saw himself in the Slug King and knew he would be treated mercilessly if he didn't come up with 'the goods...'

Luca was 'the goods'. Little did he know, as he concentrated on getting well again, sleeping peacefully; that in few hours time, half a kingdom would be searching for him.

Chapter 15. Sedgefield's Secret

Trust your own truth and timing.
'Findings' are always well-timed to the exact moment.

The next day, early morning again Dexy made his way through the village, past the lake and onto the open fields which lead out to the Saccorian region, the clouds loomed over each hill chilling the air and threatening a down pour. He was keen to see Sedgefield and keep him informed of the current situation and continued with his coat wrapped tightly round his body keeping out the cold. He travelled east. It was only another twenty miles before the ancient burial grounds were in firmly sight.

His horse a keen runner, moved swiftly along the path, which ran along the cornfields, the day became grizzly and the rain began to pour down as the temperature had suggested earlier. It pelted down slowly at first and then increasing, the constant drops hitting his face and hands with a fresh and clean splash. The clouds built into more grey looming bundles and the miserable sky was broken into a constant drizzling rain, but Dexy didn't slow, he galloped through the lashing water. His mind full; skin wet and hands clinging to his reins, riding on. He was hoping that Ava would reconsider her options and come to them for help. It was the only way he could see of protecting the boy, but she had to be in favour otherwise his efforts would be in vain. He galloped for miles, deep in thought, till the fields were long behind him and he could see the Ancient burial monastery walls ahead. The rain stopped and the sun began to blast through again, baking his damp clothes to crispy covers.

On arriving, he could see the sluggett guards placed around the outside ancient grounds. The small walls showed a large garden maze of excavation work, which showed where old rooms had once been were being uncovered daily. It was a busy excavation sight. Loban master's dug in the hard rocks and softer clay with small trawls and pointed pickets. They were scattered around each half metre deep, square or rectangular trough, which was being dug out and chipped into, like ants on a cherry pie, not stopping for a moment. It was slow work and they carried on in all weathers. Buckets, old cloths and tools lay everywhere. The days were long and tiring as the slow painstaking work continued. The thrill of finding more treasures of their ancestors spurred them on. Each worked under the watchful eye of the sluggetts, who stood sullenly with helmets and full armour clad bodies. They were instructed to note any significant finds. The Loban Masters had got used to this, but loathed every minute under the sluggetts watchful eyes. He knew they would not bother him, as visitors were allowed. It was only the historical objects they were interested in and their duty was to watch for objects of old that were pulled out of the ground, anything worthy of taking back to the Slug King.

Dexy spotted Sedgefield over in a small trench, busy at work, scraping tiny bits of soil from an area surrounded by pegs and string and labels showing progress. He waved. Sedgefield stopped digging and put down his tools. Waiting for him to make his way over, not wanting to stand on the excavation grounds, Dexy watched his old friend clamber over, shaking his dusty hands on his stomach and then on a scraggy cloth he picked up off the ground.

"Dexy! Good to see you. News?" asked Sedgefield moving along a squared area of wall where others were working and onto the path, keeping an eye on the sluggetts as he spoke.

"Some," he said carefully.

"Shall we go inside?" Sedgefield knew they would not want to risk being overheard, though the dopey sluggetts were disinterested in the two and looked bored, but dutiful.

Once inside the old mansion house, which had large solid grey walls, simple but grand by scale, the two knew they could talk freely. Their muddy boots marking the creamy white tiles in a long hallway that lead into a big hall.

"Drink after your journey? Beer?" he said.

"That would be great thanks," said Dexy who was getting parched after declining a drink earlier that morning and his water bottle now empty.

Sedgefield sorted the drinks and they sat in a conservatory room, which had glass panelling so they could look out onto the excavation sight and watch the work being done.

"So you've see them- the boy and his mother?" he said.

"I've just come from there. She won't let me take him," started Dexy.

"She needs to be told. He's not safe," he added.

"I think she is slowly realising that he is not safe. If she has bit of time to think about it, she will see we are right," Dexy said. "It's been a shock for her after ten years of secrecy."

"I realise that, but does she have time? It seems the Slug King will waste no time in looking for the boy and he will waste no time in deciding what to do with him. We haven't got time. It could cost us all dearly. Can't she see that?" he was annoyed by the news.

"I know. I just want us to do things pRoperly. She is the queen," he said, finishing the water.

"She was the queen. It seems she has forgotten how to act like one," he said, passing the glass of elderflower water over before he had an answer.

"Thanks. She's a mother too. She's trying to do the best for Luca," Dexy sympathised.

"But it's not the best. She is putting him in danger. I think we should just go back and take him. No choice. No discussion. She can thank us later," Sedgefield saw things plainly. "I could do it, if you want. I can see you would find it difficult," he offered.

"I just can't agree to that. It goes against the grain," said Dexy.

"You always were an honourable bugger. Maybe that's why Marcus trusted you," he laughed.

"Yes, he trusted me and I let him down. I didn't protect him. She knows I let him down. She can't forgive me and I think it's the reason why she's not gonna trust me with her son's life now," he said sadly.

"Well she can't hide on her own and the Slug King will be on his tail. You're all she's got!" he said.

Dexy had stopped listening for a moment. He was thinking about his distant memories of that day when Marcus had fallen in battle. His mind would drift back to that day often. He was tormented by that day...

They had been surrounded by sluggetts and stood little of a chance. Dexy held them off while he got Marcus into the safe hands of Sedgefield. The King was weak after a few blows had got him, but he was well enough to go with Sedgefield who carried him as far as he could. That was the last Dexy ever saw of Marcus. Dexy thought the king had been taken to safety. He didn't know that would be the last time he would see the king alive. Sedgefield came to him with the news that the king was very ill and couldn't be moved. The fever he had never left him, it surged through his body and all the medicine they gave him failed. He had infection and it raged through him till he took his last breath. Finally the king had given up the fight and died. It was the final blow, the war had been lost and power was in the sluggetts hands, the king dead and hope for the future gone. That was ten years ago...

Dexy snapped back into the present, gulping his water to revive him and his haunted thoughts. He wished he too had left the battleground with the king and helped him through his last days, he believed he would survive the battle and had never forgiven himself that he didn't. He looked at Sedgefield again, ready to talk, "I think we have a bit of time," he said.

"Well I hope your right about that," replied Sedgefield. "You must be hungry. Fancy some lunch, before the others get their hands on it? It will be being served about now in the dining hall," Sedgefield was always hungry himself and liked the chance to talk and eat at the same time.

"Please," said Dexy, grateful for refreshments.

The two walked into a large dining hall, with a table filled with plates of various buffet food.

"Help yourself," commanded Sedgefield as he handed a large white dining plate to Dexy.

Dexy was keen to eat and knew it would do him good for the rest of the day. His stomach had been feeling empty since he'd left Ava's house. The food looked beautiful. It's colours made his mouth water as he threw some breaded chicken and small sausages onto his plate. There was a range of salads and vegetables, all grown by the Loban Masters themselves in their extensive garden's which were very well cared for. The array of meats and potatoes was plenty for the hungry traveller. Sedgefield tucked in too, his appetite was as healthy as any man.

Tarragon approached from the excavation area. He looked agitated.

"Problem?" said Sedgefield.

"Yep…one of our Masters, Jermous found some old small coins and put them into his pocket with for 'safe keeping', but a sluggett saw him and thinks he wasn't going to declare his findings and wants to arrest him," sighed Tarragon.

"Great jucticus!" cursed Sedgefield. "I will come and speak to them," he said. "Happens all the time," he nodded to Dexy. "Help yourself to more food, back in a bit."

Dexy was enjoying relaxing and eating well made home cooked food, in such nutritious abundance. It was a luxury to have something that had not been over a campfire. He wondered how the Loban Masters kept so calm while the sluggetts watched their every move day in, day out. It must have been blood boiling to have this occupation in front of them. They had lost their freedom in the Great War- it had taken many lives and changes many others. Dexy chewed and savoured his gastronomic delights, until he could eat no more.

Sedgefield could be seen at the excavation area, deep in talks with a couple of sluggetts and the Loban Master who was in trouble. He was protesting his innocence but it was not washing with the sluggetts. It looked like things were going to take a while to sorting out. Dexy decided he needed a quick wash. He had been there before and knew the bathroom area. He walked through the dining area and down a short hallway to the bathroom. As he got closer, a Loban Master passed him and smiled, seeing he wanted the bathroom,

"That one's out of order. You'll have to use the one on the lower floor. Just head down to the staircase and follow along and it's the third door on you right," he said helpfully.

"Thanks," said Dexy.

He knew his way around the main areas but had not been on the lower floors before, the sleeping area for most of the Loban Masters. The stone staircase was narrow, as it curved round to the lower ground. This level was darker and colder than that of the ground floor. Dexy walked along looking for the bathroom. He counted to the third door along and opened it, a big wooden door with some bars at the top of the window. It didn't feel like a bathroom. It wasn't. He had opened a large bedroom. He could see a man sat on the bed with his back to him. There was a lit fire and cushions and chairs he could see. Unseen Dexy crept out.

He went to the next door and this smaller one felt more like it and as he opened it, he saw he was right this time- a bathroom. Dexy was happy to wash. His underarms and face refreshed after a splash of water and soap, after his ride in the rain. He splashed clean water on his hair too for extra refreshment. As he was washing, he heard a strange sound. It was a voice moaning and wailing, like an animal. Clean and brighter, Dexy walked out listening to the noise. It was coming from the room from before. Glancing in again through the door to see what was happening. The grey haired man, who sat on the bed facing the fire, was rocking backwards and forwards, moaning. Dexy stared. Suddenly the man turned round. He wailed at Dexy. He face looked like an old man, groaning and grunting like an animal in pain. Dexy stood in horror, transfixed with the sight of the mad old man. He watched him continued to make the awful sounds, which made his ears ache. Dexy looked at the man. It was hard to see what he looked like. He crept further in,

"Are you ok?" he asked, moving closer still to see if the strange moaning man was alright.

The man turned and looked at Dexy. He looked confused to be spoken to. He stopped moaning and watched Dexy with eyes like a frightened rabbit. As he stopped his face changed into a more human one. Dexy stood staring. Dexy could not believe his eyes. He stared at the man. He looked at him with amazement growing. He stepped closer and stared and stared. Eventually he spat out the words, which were struggling to come from him mouth,

"Marcus...Marcus?" he said, in utter astonishment.

Dexy could not believe what he was seeing. The man a grey old crazy, but Dexy could see it was Marcus. His stubble and unbrushed hair made it difficult at first, but something was unmistakable, underneath the hair and moans, this man was the old king. The man looked back at Dexy with wide blank eyes. Dexy's words had made no obvious impact on him. He seemed vacant and child-like, though he looked old and gnarled. His face looked as if he recognised Dexy for one split second, then he started to laugh, and Dexy went to hug him, but the man flinched back, horrified and the laugh turned into a howling maddening laugh which seemed to get right inside the head as the laugh of a mad crazy man. Dexy stopped with fright himself, and recoiled as his old friend changed back into the old man he hardly recognised. He heard someone come in the room behind him. He spun round to see. His horror was growing. It was Sedgefield.

"So you found him then?" he said.

"Is it?" asked Dexy slowly, not taking his eyes from the sight of the old grey man in front of him.

"I'm afraid it is. Though he is not as you remember him. And I doubt he will remember you," he replied sadly, as he moved them out of the room and shut the door behind them.

"It's Marcus?" asked Dexy again in disbelief.

"It is…though he has no idea who he is," said Sedgefield.

Dexy stood in stunned silence for a moment and then began to speak…

"You didn't think to tell me the king was alive!" cried Dexy in continuing horror.

"If word got out that the king was like this, it would have done us great damage," said Sedgefield.

"You kept this from me for all these years? You made me think…You said…" Dexy broke off, his words were failing him, his mind rushing with questions. He had struggled so much with the King's death, blaming himself for it and now to find him alive was almost too much.

"Think about it, Dexy. We had no choice. We voted to keep it secret and I think we made the best decision,"

"No, you had a choice! You kept this from me! You kept it from us all! You had no right!" said Dexy in anger, raging with inside fury.

"You are wrong! We had to do what we could and we knew a king who is alive but mad and demented is no good to our cause... you must see that. We did the only thing we could- we cared for him as best we could. It's not been easy you know. He is not an easy patient," he continued.

"Patient! Patient!" Dexy screamed. "He is the king!"

"He was the king! Now he is just an old tired man who has problems. No memory of being a king. We do what we can to help," said Sedgefield firmly.

"Did you not think I would want to know! It's been years! I thought he was dead! I thought it was my fault!" cried Dexy.

"Well he would have been better dead," Sedgefield was not backing down.

"No! No he deserved better than to be locked away down here," said Dexy.

"Oh and you think he would have been safe anywhere else? In the mountains with you perhaps? He'd have cost you all your lives by now with his howling, or worse, jumped off the mountain edge when he doesn't know where he is. You can attack me all you like, but with all respect, you have no idea and you have no right to criticise me. I did what needed to be done!" Sedgefield bawled back.

"What about the news of his son? Was that not cause enough to tell me? Say something? He has a family!" cried Dexy.

"There was nothing to say. The man is gone. A family changes nothing. He is no use to them. He is a burden- one that I have been willing to bear. That is not your king in there. We feed him and keep him, but his mind is gone. He is not the Marcus you once knew. You have to understand," said Sedgefield as they walked up to the hall on the second floor, Dexy being steered away from the room.

"He is still a man. One that I knew very well. I could have helped him! I want to help him!" said Dexy sadly.

"You think he would know who you are? He is hard work. Like a child some days and an animal on others. He doesn't know who he is. He's gone. He's a mad man, no use to himself or others. We have taken very good care of him. You didn't need the burden of it," said Sedgefield.

"It is my duty to serve the king," cried Dexy.

"Then you should thank me for what I have done for all these years."

"Thank you?" asked Dexy.

"We have carried this burden alone," he said.

"I should have been told," he snapped.

"Will you tell the others?" asked Sedgefield.

"Of course I will," answered Dexy.

"And Queen Amber?" he asked.

Dexy paused. He did not know what to say, for the thought of the queen and her son knowing of this man, their husband and father. They would have to be told, surely? This was something that would have to be thought about.

"You see. It's not that simple," replied Sedgefield.

Dexy glared at him.

"I will be back. Don't think I have finished with you," he growled.

"Oh I know you will be back. I have too much that you want. You'll be back," Sedgefield added.

Dexy walked out furious and confused at the same time. The horse ride home would give him time to think. He needed to think. He wanted to be pleased that his old friend the King was alive, but in that state was it really a cause for celebration. He jumped on his horse and galloped, each stride eased his pounding head, each hoof print marking a the road like a stamp of honour that Dexy's heart felt now towards his King. The King was alive...wasn't that all that mattered? Marcus was alive!

Dexy sat back at home in the Silver Mountains, amongst friends.

"So King Marcus is alive?" said Jax in disbelief.

"I don't believe it!" cried Gobber.

"Oh believe it, believe it!" shouted Dexy shaking his head and chewing some bread with anger.

"I am surprised that Sedgefield kept it from you," said Falentona shaking her head.

"I'm not, that Loban Master is a law to himself!" muttered Dexy.

"The cheek, after all we've done for him!" cried Gobber.

"He is untrustworthy!" cried Jax.

"He had his own agenda," added Keto.

"They should have told us! I cant believe it, I really can't," ranted Falentona.

All of them were aghast with the news that King Marcus was alive, even if his mind was not as it once had been, It was still a great shock and they still felt betrayed by Sedgefield and the Loban Masters to have not been told. It was incredible to think they had kept him there all these years while they all assumed him dead. It was going to take some time to sink in.

"What you gonna do?" said Falentona eventually after moments of silence ended.

"I don't know. I need to think. Any ideas?" said Dexy.

"Well yes thinking is a good move, don't want to rush anything. We must see the actions of Sedgefield as a compassionate decision, am sure he acted out of the best intentions," said Keto, wise and calm as ever.

"He should have told Dexy!" cried Gobber again.

"Can't believe he didn't, is unbelievable!" said Jax.

"Talking about why he did it will get us nowhere now. The fact is that he is alive and what do we do now?" said Dexy.

"What sort of state was he in when you saw him? I mean was he able to talk?" asked Falentona.

"He certainly didn't know who I was. He was rocking and seemed confused. He isn't himself," said Dexy.

"Not capable of leading his kingdom back to the throne," said Gobber disappointedly.

"It is still his throne whatever state he is in," said Dexy. "We still want our kingdom back and the fact that he is alive can only help our cause."

"Not if he is as bad as you say. It might not help the cause," said Keto.

"How?" said Gobber frustrated.

"People want strong leaders and this might show weakness and make a laughing stock for those prepared to follow a king like this," said Keto.

"What about the queen? Surely she is the best leader we have in terms of strength; the boy is too young," said Falentona.

"I think she is right. The queen would be a good leader, and he could be kept secret, or at least out of the way," agreed Gobber.

"The queen who wants nothing to do with our war and our uprising?" said Keto. "But everything has changed. She might not have a choice. If she wants to remain in hiding she has a big task on her hands, especially with Gerrado looking for the boy. What she wants might not be an option any more. She might lead if she knows her husband is alive. She will have to do something. She cannot hide in the village anymore. Soon the Slug King will be looking for her and her son and then she will need people to fight for her again. She has no choice to want peace," said Dexy.

These discussions continued long into the night in the Silver Mountains. The outsiders discussing each angle every option available and each point of view that could be valuable. It was necessary to be prepared and to plan and to decide unanimously what their next move should be. The next move was to be as important for them as they would ever imagine. This move would be the first into the next war. A war, which they knew was on the way and looming over them all.

Chapter 16. The Search

They looked and found only what they could not see.

It took Gerrado all day to organise his search. Gerrado, the Slug King was getting ready for the search into the village by the White Lake, as the Aviras had informed him. His determination to find the boy, possible heir to his throne, showed on his face and in each of his abrupt and purposeful movements. He had to make sure he was ruled out as contender for the throne.

He had powered up a team of forty or so sluggetts; some carried flyers and all had details of the boy, as given to him by Aviras that morning, who had also had to relay the face of to an artist and so each sluggett had a portrait copy of Luca to carry with them, though it looked like many other boys too. There was a swiftness about them and their determination to complete the task ahead showed. Their dedication to their king shown through clenched and busy faces, as animated as sluggett could be.

Gerrado fixed his gloves firmly on each hand and looked at each helper, ensuring they were ready and serious of the business that was before them. He was pacing more than usual and becoming ratty with the sluggetts, as usual.

"Father, can I come with you?" asked Worrom, as he watched his father saddle up his horse.

"No son. I want you here at the castle where I can keep my eye on you," he replied.

The small sluggett boy looked disappointed and stamped his foot, but it made no impression on his father who always meant what he said and stuck to it. Gerrado was actually a very good father and loved and protected his son dearly. Sluggetts had hearts, even if it was only for their own kind. Worrom though only young, was used to getting his own way, but his father meant what he said and he could not have his small son around to worry about during the task in hand on this bountiful morning. He looked gently at him and smiled as he realised who he was doing this for, his son would follow in his footsteps one day...

The horses were ready and they marched forward from the castle walls, and into the city. They rode with purpose and pace. The horses' hooves made a heavy noise, which echoed through the city as they went. They wanted a victory and each sluggett knew they would be rewarded handsomely for the boy and that their search was to continue long into the day and night, until the boy was found, and so it showed in their rations and appropriate clothing for all weathers. They carried weapons in case of resistance; it was unlikely from the villagers of the White Lake who were poor and defenceless and indeed paid high taxes each month without complaint.

They travelled south, taking the roads that led down from the city and into the countryside. It was an hour or so before they reached the lake. Villagers along the way stared and wondered what was at hand. They dreaded the sluggetts and this hefty presence was never a welcome sight. They knew they were looking for

someone, it had happened before when prisoners were wanted, usually for unpaid taxes. They stopped in their tracks and bowed to the king as he rode by. They shivered at the thought of him in their village again, it was always a chilling sight.
"Have you seen this boy?" asked some of the leading sluggetts, slowing the horses down and waving their posters at the villagers, who were nearby.

Heads shook. No one wanted to help the sluggetts. After passing the lake, the army of sluggetts slowed with their King, as he spoke to them.
"I will offer a reward. I want you to go to each house in this village up ahead and knock on every door. Two thousand roonies for anyone who has information," he commanded and road on further into the nearby village.

The sluggetts understood. The money would get someone to talk. They began their search of the village, knocking at each house and the news quickly spread of the search for the boy.

Ettie was walking home. She had been to collect some water from the lake. She was greeted by the sight of the sluggetts ahead of her and shuddered. Was it tax day? No that was not till the end of the month. So why were they here? They must have been on the look-out for a prisoner or a traitor. Two sluggetts approached her on foot. They carried their flyers and shouted to her,
"Do you know this boy?" they asked.
Ettie turned and looked at the picture. Her heart missed a beat when she saw the resemblance to her dearest friend Luca. She hoped they were not after him. Her bucket of water slopped as she shivered at the thought. She had frozen for a second and could not reply.
"Did you hear what we said?" cried the impatient sluggett. "Do you know this

boy?"

"No. No I don't," she managed to reply.

"Are you sure?" asked the other, not convinced by her answer.

Ettie could feel her face burn with terror. Again she replied.

"No, I don't know him."

The sluggetts snarled and walked off down the path to more houses further ahead. There were swarms of them everywhere and every house was to be visited, that was not in doubt.

Thinking fast, Ettie knew she had to move swiftly... She wanted to warn Luca, but she couldn't risk being seen going straight to his house, for fear that they would see and follow. She walked off the path and down a side field. Her pace increased and her water surged over the side of the bucket as her thoughts turned to Luca and her heart beat faster in her little body, her legs almost buckling underneath her to get home. Her desire to get to him before the sluggetts presence became overwhelming in the village. She reached the back of the house and tapped rapidly the back window to see if Ava and Luca were in.

Ava could see the little girl. She came to the window and looked at her with a puzzled stare and went to the back door.

"What's wrong with the front door?" she asked her laughing. Then she saw the look of fear on Ettie's face and quickly added, "Come in, what's wrong?"

Ettie ran in through the back leaving her water bucket, which was now almost empty outside, its contents no longer important.

"It's the sluggetts! They're looking for a boy! They are looking for a boy. I think they want Luca! They boy there looking for!" she could not get her words out fast enough.

"Slow down. Why do you think they want Luca? What's happened?" said Ava trying to make some sense of the little girl.

"They're on their way!" she cried, tears were starting to well and the little girl's was now chocking with each sorry word. "There's no time!"

Ava could see that this was bad news and that Luca was in danger.

"Tell me again," she said to be sure, shaking Ettie a little to get some sense and clarity.

"I was walking back from the lake and they were everywhere... the Slug King. He is looking for a boy. They have a picture. I think they want Luca. They are coming!" she cried, tears flooding down her cheeks.

"How much time do we have?" she asked, seeing the limits of the situation.

"Not long, they were at the lake only ten minutes ago. They will be here in no time," said Ettie.

Ava was already getting ready.

"Luca!" she called. He was upstairs asleep. She ran up the ladder to shake him. "Luca! Get up!"

Ava shook her son awake. His eyes rolling back into their sockets to avoid the light, until her persistent shaking of him meant he could not avoid opening them any longer.

"Luca! Wake up! Wake up! There is no time to explain, but I want you to go with Ettie. Go to her house," she instructed him as she picked up some clothes and items from around the bedroom, throwing them into a cloth sack, her eyes glaring round like a hunting gawk looking for necessary items that her son might need for whatever lay ahead.

"Mum? What's going on?" he asked.

"Get your sandals on and your coat. There is no time. You have to go; go with Ettie. You must go now," she cried,

"What's happening?" said Luca.

"Ettie will explain. I want you to go with her and wait at her house till it is safe. You must stay there, with Roper till I can send a message to you. Do not let anyone see you. Do you understand?" she continued to pick up bits of clothes and put them into bag for him as she spoke, rushing round as fast as she could.

"The sluggetts are looking for a boy. He looks like you," said Ettie as Luca climbed down the stairs looking dazed and confused at his mother's strange behaviour.

"We can't take any chances. Just go with Ettie. The map! Where's the map?" she seemed distracted as she raced around the house looking for the paper that Dexy had given her earlier that week.

Then, as they picked up bits from around the house that might be needed, they heard jangling armour walking up to the door. They could see out of the window that's two sluggetts were on their way. Time was running out.

Ava found the map and folded it, giving it to Luca as she hugged him with all her strength.

"Take this map. You will need it. It will get you to the Silver Mountains, Dexy is there."

"I don't understand," said Luca who was wide awake now from his sleep that had been so abruptly interrupted by a frantic mother.

"There's no time to explain. Please Luca, just do as I say!" she hugged him again.

"Go out the back! Go to Dexy in the mountains!"

She had so little time to give him instructions of help...

Outside there was movement and the sluggetts could be heard walking towards the house.

"Quick there's no time," she said rushing to the window to see how many were walking up the path as she heard the crunching of their boots on the gravely path.

Two sluggetts approached.

"Luca, hide! Quick!" she called out to him watching the window.

Ettie and Luca looked around to see any place for a hide out. Luca could not think straight and his head was starting to hurt from all the panic, still sore from his beating. Ettie called to him,

"In here."

The basket of washing which stood tucked in the corner was small but made a good enough den for Luca to curl in. Ettie emptied the clothes as fast as she could and bundled her dear friend into the bottom, the sprayed the clothes on top of him. While Ava stalled the sluggetts as they banged on the door.

"One minute!" she called, taking her time and making sure Luca was well out of sight in the laundry basket, as Ettie placed the last piece of clothes on top of it.

Ava eventually opened the door, trying to look calm and composed, thought it was difficult under the circumstances, but she knew she could not afford to show fear now and put her son in more danger.

"What is it?" she asked innocently, as the sluggetts leaned on the doorframe and pointed at the picture that had a resounding resemblance to her only son.

"This boy, do you know him?" they asked, prodding the poster fiercely.

"No," she said as nonchalantly as she could, keeping the door minimally open.

"Are you sure?" one sluggett asked.

"I don't think I know him," she replied again as calmly as she could for a mother protecting her son from whatever might be due.

"Thank you. Good day!" they said, seemingly satisfied with the situation.

Ava sighed and closed the door behind them. She fell back on the door and closed her eyes as if this would all go away.

"Do you think it is him they want?" asked Ettie.

"Oh, I am sure of it," Ava replied, surprising Ettie for she had not expected such a resounding yes.

"You have to get Luca away from here, to the mountains. Do you understand?"

"Yes," said Ettie but she didn't really understand anything at all. She knew nothing of what was going on and could not understand why the sluggetts would all be looking for Luca.

"Go to your house and tell Roper to get Luca to safety. Give your father the map. He can take him," she said.

Their conversation was intense and Luca still hadn't moved from the basket. The muffled sounds were confusing for him under all the clothes and he knew it was better to stay hidden until he was signalled to appear. For now the voices were too hazy to make out safety or danger.

A sudden knock again, startled the two inside the house. They had not noticed more sluggetts approaching. There were more of them this time. A hefty crowd of four sluggetts; armed and forceful stood outside. The second knock at the door proved this, as the thud could be heard clearly by Luca in his hiding basket.

"Open up! Open up there!" shouted the sluggett, these were more aggressive in tone.

Ava went pale as she opened the door for a second time that day under immense pressure. Ettie froze as her heart pounded, she wanted to be brave but she felt her legs go to jelly and her throat turn as dry as a feather .

"You have a son?" he didn't wait to be polite.

The questioning was more intense and to the point. The sluggetts burst in past Ava and into the kitchen area. Ava could hardly speak.

"Yeess?" she said carefully.

"Where is your son?" the sluggett demanded.

"My son is not here."

"Where is he?"

"He is away at his uncle's… on holiday," said Ava. She could not think what to say in such a short moment and she knew they expected an answer.

"Is this your son?" the sluggett held up the poster again as Ava watched the picture haunt her as she focused on the face.

"No, no. It looks a little like him, but it is not him," she said.

"We'll we hear it is a lot like him. Where is his uncle's house?"

"What is this all about? Why do you want the boy?" she asked.

"The king wants to speak with the boy," said the sluggett.

"The King does want to speak with this boy," a voice from the doorway chilled the room as Ava saw the Slug King, Gerrado step into her house and removed his gloves putting them on the side, indicating he would be here for the time being. Ettie watched without breathing as she seemed to have forgotten how to for the moment. He looked mean and powerful, even though his stature was small and his eyes old.

"You see, I would very much like to speak to your son," said Gerrado, looming into Ava's face as he made his point clear and his words lingered on for seconds after he spoke them, like a ringing through the house. His eyes delving deep into hers, looking for answers to his questions more than any words could say.

"My son is away," repeated Ava, holding his gaze back and calmly, like a war of pupil's had begun and blinking was forbidden.

"Convenient. Away where?" he asked, wanting to smile at her courage but cross at her lies if they were...for he had had five different villagers send them to this house, the house where Luca Lockharth lived, the boy whose picture he held in his hand and the boy who was now so conveniently 'away'.

"He...he is staying with his uncle for a week," she managed to get her answer out.

"Staying with his uncle," the king spoke slowly and coldly as if he did not believe a word of it. "You won't mind if my guards search the place will you?" he added.

"I..." Ava could not answer, the words failed her and her heart missed it's beat.

"Don't worry, it is just a precaution; I am sure you are telling us the truth, so you have nothing to worry about. You see I need to find this boy, he has been brought to my attention in the last few days and I would like to speak with him. Sit down and relax, my guards won't take long and we will be on our way, oh and of course I shall want to speak to your boy when he returns," he watched every inch of her face as he spoke and sat on the chair by the fire as he made himself at home in her house.

The Slug King moved with an air of importance that he had built into a great act over the years. He felt supreme and in a small and simple house like this with wooden furniture and a loft bedroom. He moved slowly at times, but flicked his riding cloak up as he sat on the chair quickly, the mixture of fast and slow movements when he wanted signalling his control over everything. He was proud and intelligent and not to be lied to; he knew when villagers had something to hide, he had seen it too many times before and he knew that face, that look and that despair, he had provoked it often on many a face.

The sluggett soldiers set about moving furniture and looking around the house. Two took the upper floor, which contained the beds and wardrobes. They shifted bedding and anything out of their way, which seemed it might provide a hiding spot for any small boy. The search continues for another ten minutes or so, but they could find nothing. Ava and Luca led a simple life and there was not much to search. The two sluggetts searching the bottom floor were also fruitless. Ava felt herself praying to her husband, that they would not find Luca, whom she believed to be an angel watching over them from morning through to night and beyond. She could hardly look, when one of them rested his dirty foot on the washing basket, where she knew inside, only inches away from his boot was her only beloved son. The basket his only protection between him and the sluggett guard. Ava and Ettie tried not to look at him as their glances may have given Luca away. They suspected nothing and moved around the house efficiently under the careful watch of the king, whose silence now was as bad as his every sentence when he spoke.

"Nothing, Sire," the sluggetts were sure.

Gerrado rose. He patted his gloves on his thighs, as he thought.

"Well it seems you have been lucky. Your son is away for the week. I would like to see him when he returns," he said.

Ava's thoughts were racing thinking of the time she had bought Luca to get him to some sort of safety in the mountains. Her heart was shaking with fear now, as she remembered that it was the very same enemy who had killed her dear beloved husband ten years ago. She was prepared to lay down her life to save her son. She knew the minute she seen the guards on her pathway, earlier, that she would die for her son if she had to. (One day she might have to.)

Gerrado had not finished his announcements,

"...till then you shall come with me. I would like you to stay at the palace...we have accommodation...ahem. I don't want you out of my sight, Ava. It is Ava? You see, if your son is the boy I want, and I suspect very much that he is, then it is in my interests to keep my eye on you too, because you will lead him to me. If your son wants to see you again, he shall have to come and get you himself. Guards!"

The guards rushed to her side and took hold of each arm tightly so that Ava was in their charge. They held her firmly and held each arm; she had no intention of struggling, as she wanted to get the guards away from the house and her son as fast as possible. She would not be going far without them.

Ettie gasped in horror. She could not believe what was happening. Ava was trapped. She knew that getting them away from the house would give Luca a chance to escape.

"You two stay here and guard the house. I don't want it left for a second. If we have missed the boy, he will have to come out at some point," commanded Gerrado.

He gave on last glance to Ettie.

"I suggest if you have a home to go to, little girl; that you go," he added.

Ettie froze again. She hated it when he looked at her; his yellow eyes were bulgy and cold with no compassion. She watched him leave with her beloved Ava held tightly by the two sluggetts. The jostled her slightly to push her out of the door as she looked back to Ettie with a longing glance that spoke a thousand words. She knew it was up to her, to get Luca to safety. With Ava gone, she knew it was up to her. She did not know how she would do this, but she knew it was time to help her friend and she was prepared to do anything for him. Anything she could to get him to safety. To the Silver Mountains? To the man Ava had spoken of, Dexy? Who could he be? Ettie's thoughts raced on. She hoped Luca would stay put for now in the washing basket, even with the king gone, there were still two burly sluggetts to be aware of and he would have to stay there for as long as it took until Ettie could think of a way out for him, or a better plan...

Ettie would never know how many people were relying on her at that moment. Not only a boy and his mother, but a kingdom. She did not know it, but these next moments were to be the most important she had ever had.

Chapter 17. Capture and Escape

Freedom can only ever exist in the mind.

Ava now led away held tightly by each arm, a guard on each side; she wasn't abandoning her son she had little choice but to leave with the guards. She glanced over at Ettie with a long gaze. Her beautiful eyes welling with tear drops that she blinked back as quickly as they had arrived in the corners of her eyes. A terrible unsettling in her stomach, carried up into her throat like a ball that she couldn't swallow. Her heart started to ache with sadness and fear.

Detesting the Slug King, and seeing him again after all these years struck terror in her heart. She didn't show it. She remembered his cruelty then and didn't underestimate it now. The thought of leaving her son was only bearable because she knew it kept him away from Gerrado. Her dignity was strong as she walked through village where she lived for the last ten years as a simple villager and was led away to the city. She felt like a queen again for the first time in many years as left her home and her son behind.

The villagers knew something was wrong. Some watched with pity, others with suspicion as the troop of prisoner and guards with Gerrado made a significant sight for all to see. They rode back to the castle (her old home where she had not been since the Great War) with guards either side of her she switched off from the curious villagers and wondered if her dear home had changed as it had been, once grand and happy with her family living there. She knew her memories would flood back like charging bulls into her mind if she let them...it had been years since she had dared to think of her old life, a queen with a husband and kingdom, so different to what she had grown to know in recent years, alone and struggling. The past she had left, and now her future was unknown, she concentrated on the present again and watched Gerrado ride back with his trophy and take glee in all the fear it caused.

The castle came into view it looked nothing like her old home now, with sluggetts stationed at every corner. It looked like a cage with sluggetts stationed around each wall and the once green gardens, now bare and ruined by marched on mud and lumps of dirt. She looked ahead and with every step hoped this led the army away from her son- the boy they really wanted. She was pleased they were heading away from him and hoped in her soul that he had a chance to escape...

***

Back at the house Ettie had understood what Ava was doing in leading them away. It was up to her now to keep Luca safe, though the reason for him being in such danger was still a puzzle. She still could not think why the guards would want him, after all Luca was just a boy. What could they want with her little friend she thought to herself?

The two guards who had been left behind to search the room looked at her mindlessly, as if their souls had been sold. They thought only of orders to be carried out without question or reason, they followed their orders. Ettie found it hard to look at them. They made her sick. They were ugly creatures and dribbled as they spoke. She couldn't leave Luca now he would not escape without her help as he hid in the washing basket undetected. A ball of terrified boy who told himself to keep still though he was suffocating under the piles of clothes.
"I came for the washing," she said quickly, trying not to make her words sound like a complete lie. She was never that good at lying.
"We do the washing sometimes," she added in an unconvincing tone, though they took little notice of the girl and were not interested in her which was good for the children.
 Ettie froze, clenching every tooth in her mouth as she waiting for their response.
"Well I guess you should take it then," replied the sluggett irritated by her menial presence.
"How long do we wait here," said the other as if she didn't exist?
"We'll wait a while longer then head back," said the other enjoying his chance to

sit on the wooden chairs in the kitchen by the fire, stretching his short arms over his head and kicking his legs out to relax.

Ettie moved over to the basket and prepared to lift with all her might, knowing her arms would need strength to lift Luca and make it look effortless. The guards watched her making her start to sweat nervously. She dared not say another word in case she aroused their suspicions. Luca was still, holding every muscle tightly inside the basket so as not to move. He could only hear their muffled voices through the washing pile. He knew his movement would cost him and so he crouched and stuck in a ball as small as he could though it hurt.

Ettie took the sides of the basket and felt for the weight. She braced herself for the lift, trying to keep a calm blank look on her face for the unsuspecting guards, both quite relaxed and making themselves at home on the kitchen chairs.

"Looks heavy," called the nearer sluggett to her leaning forward.

He had a softer face and seemed genuinely concerned for the girl carrying a large basket on her own.

Ettie tried not to look alarmed.

"A little," she replied.

"Here let me give you a hand with that," his words hit her like a punch to the stomach, as he stood up to help.

It was out of character for a sluggett to show any compassion, she felt his kindness striking like a sickening force, but tried to look unperturbed and puffed out her body showing she really was strong enough to manage the basket alone.

"No, honestly is fine," she pulled the basket away, out of his hands as he reached forward to grip the rim of the basket.

"It's fine," she added again, this time her voice had more urgency in it and she seemed alarmed.

"Sit down, Axon. The girl doesn't need any help," said the other sluggett whose face was like a crumpled old dishcloth, old and worn.

"It looks heavy that's all. She's a small thing to carry such a large basket," he whipped back at his fellow guard.

"Am used to it," Ettie added.

"We're not all lazy lumps like him you know," continued the sluggett. "Let me take it," he persisted.

Ettie jerked the basket away with such force she nearly dropped it and she alarmed both herself and the friendly sluggett.

"You would think you had something to hide in there," he laughed but as he did so and he heard his own words floating in the air, he realised that what he was saying...it was actually closer to the truth than he had imagined and his words hung over their heads until they sunk into their thick skulls.

"...Dirty laundry, no one likes that in public," Ettie managed as her throat seized up from dryness.

"Are you hiding something?" he asked slowly his tone becoming less helpful and more suspicious.

For all she tried, Ettie couldn't speak again. She tried to save the falling basket by her knees but the awkward angle was impossible to hold as it scraped down her leg and onto the floor. Luca was thrown from one side to the other and now laid in an awkward ball on his elbow, trying to keep hidden as the lid fell off and a few items of clothes tumbled onto the floor. Both sluggetts stopped and stared at the lop-sided basket in front of them. It had been a great hiding place, but not anymore.

Ettie saw the sluggetts' faces change with the realisation. Luca could not sustain balancing on the edge of the basket with his feet squashed and twisted. The top of his head was showed and one foot dangled out, his knee pushed down onto the ground with relief from the pain of his small curled shape. The sluggetts looked in horror at the boy unfolding in front of them seeing that he had been there all along. Luca like an apparition, small and tiny at first but the young boy got to his feet and ran past them kicking the basket out of his way and as fast as he could towards the back door.

He knew Ettie was behind him he could feel her at his back heel. The sluggetts clambered after them as they sprang into action, their adrenalin pumped giving them the surge to chase after the children.

"Luca, run!" she yelled in horror as she watched her friend emerge onto the kitchen floor in a heap.

Luca scrambled to his feet and ran for the back door as the sluggetts grabbed his sleeve, failing by inches. The sluggetts lunged at them swiping into the air hoping to catch either of them, luckily getting in the way of each other more than nearer the children. One managed to grab Luca' shoulder and yanked him back into the room out from the doorway, Ettie rushed and found some nearby salt on the side in a jar and threw it at them. (Salt was a sluggetts worst fear. It made them wince and it burnt their skin to slimy mush.) They recoiled in pain, but their armour protected them from too much injury and still they pounced at Luca again to gain a firm grip.

"Let me go!" Luca yelled as he kicked at the sluggetts legs and feet.

"No chance son," said Axon.

Luca wriggled and punched at their hollow faces, which loosened the sluggetts grip. Luca chocked, as his tunic was tight around his neck from the hold. He pulled himself free from their sweaty clutches. Each lunged at him again trying to grab at his shoulders, but missing as he ducked their grasps and ran for the back door.

Ettie continued to throw more salt as it slowed them down and made them cry in pain. She pelting it at them with all her might and headed in the same direction as Luca, her heart booming through her chest over towards the door. (They stood more chance of escaping from the back door.) The sluggetts furiously batted away the salt, which flew tirelessly in their direction like an annoying batch of flies. The children's young legs ran out of the back door and they didn't look back.

Ettie followed Luca. The adrenalin pumped into her legs as she ran down the back lane and over the hill out of sight. Luca headed for the woods for cover. It was a better idea than the house and she followed him with leaping through the grass as fast as she could move.

The sluggetts were slower than the children, as running in armour was difficult and the children were quick. They struggled to see the children as the ducked and dived over fences of each house. The woods were close and would give them a safe shelter until nightfall. There they could think and hatch a plan to save Luca's mum.

Luca and Ettie ran and ran until they were completely immersed in the heart of woods. The sluggetts were lazy followers, hungry for a soldier's wage rather than bound by duty. (A sluggett was not a natural soldier in terms of fitness with such stumpy legs, their jelly-like bellies hung low and wobbled with any movement made.) Speed could not be maintained for long, even if they were the King's soldiers! The sluggetts fell behind and in the distance now, lost sight of both children. They looked at the woods with confusion and stopped to catch their breath, too old to chase such young ones.

They began to curse.

"The blasted salt!" cried Axon wiping his face, looking for water in the troughs of villager's backfields to sooth their stinging faces.

"We don't get paid enough for this!" said the other whose eyes were red and streaming.

"Well we tried," said the defeatist sluggett.

"I nearly had him till you got in me way!" cried the other.

"Oh that's right blame me, nothing to do with the fact that you're old and due for retirement," the other snapped back.

"Yeah well what's your excuse, you've got ten years on me, how come you didn't catch them?" said Axon.

"Me eyes, me eyes! I can't see two sodding meters in front of me face after that little brat threw salt at me! Dunno how I'm meant to chase them when I cant even see!" he finished exasperated.

"Blasted girl!" the other added sitting down to take off his helmet on the grass for further rest.

"We wont catch 'em now they're well gone into the woods,"

"Guess we could tell Gerrado the house was empty, might save our bacon," he suggested.

"You know, you're right if he thinks we let them get away, we both won't see retirement," said the other.

"So is that the deal? We keep stum about the boy being at the house?"

"Can't hurt us that way, the other way we'll both end up in the pit,"

"Ok, shake on it," he said as he held out his arm.

"Deal!" they both shook the others grey measly hands.

So it was settled, as far as the two sluggetts were concerned they had never been in the house at all. They sloped back to the kingdom, sure that they had done their best. The sluggett way was a sloppy one and these two were no different!

In the safety of the trees, Luca and Ettie dived onto the ground and lay on their backs catching their breath back, they were far into the woods. It was a long time before they sat up, exhausted and careful not to make a noise that might have given them away, still unsure of who might be around. They were worn out from their darting run to the safety of the trees. They warmed a little at the thought that they had escaped the guards, but both felt the cold shock of the chase, which left them with a shivery fear each knowing this was not over. Each could hear their own heart pounding in their chest like a galloping horse on a beach. Their bodies felt shaken and tiny scratches began to show on their arms and legs from the scrambling that had got them over the fences and into the woods, both battered and bruised but safe for now. Ettie could not stop shaking she sat on a small patch of dark wet soil with twigs and leaves all over. She would have sat anywhere, as she needed to rest and take stock. Her breathing was tight but became normal again after a few minutes of stillness.

They were well hidden under a canvas of branches and greenery, draped across the floor like a net curtain letting the sun through its holes. Ettie stood up to shake the tiny twigs out of her hair as she had laid flat on the ground. The soil smelt wet and comforting, like an earth mother to them, a blanket on the ground that was soft and protective.

"Do you think we lost them?" said Luca.

"I think so," she shook with trembling shock no more words came out.

"I think they gave up," whispered Luca, seeing she was struggling to speak and trying to hide his real fright.

"What do you think they want?" she asked when she could speak again.

"They want me!" answered Luca in amazement.

"Why? What would they want you for?" asked Ettie.

"I have no idea," wondered a clueless Luca.

"Since when have you been an enemy to the king?" she asked.

"That is what I'd like to know," said Luca raising his eyebrow towards his hairline and shrugging.

"I think you're mum knew...she knew something," said Ettie cautiously.

"She would have told me," he said.

"Are you sure? I think she tried to tell you before we left,"

"We don't have secrets," he snapped.

"You do. I know most of them but you do...we all have secrets," she said like a girl older than her age.

Luca looked out beyond the woods and into the mountains thoughtful and pensive choosing not to answer his wise friend.

"What now?" she asked to change the subject.

"We keep moving into the woods," he replied. It was all he could think of at the time.

"Your mum gave you a map, do you think we should try and follow it?" asked Ettie.

"She said to find Dexy in the mountains," Luca replied as he felt in his pocket for the folder paper his mother had passed to him, his body started to ache again, as the adrenaline started to ease off and his pain rushed back into his bruised limbs still recovering from his beating.

"The mountains are beyond the woods we could make it," she added hopefully.

"We can't risk going back anyway," said Luca agreeing.

"If we head to the village it'll be crawling with sluggetts like it was today," she said.

"Yeah, you're right. I think we need to head to the mountains we'll be harder to track there," he added.

"You ok?" asked Ettie, who always got straight to the point.

"I don't know, I can't tell. It's not real," replied Luca.

"It's real alright!" said Ettie, flicking more soil from her ruined skirt.

"I know but I keep thinking it's a bad dream," said Luca.

"Well it ain't a dream this is all happening!" added Ettie.

"You hurt?" he replied glad that she was by his side and looked at his muddy friend.

"Nah, am ok I guess," she smiled reassuringly at her friend.

"Thanks for saving me," he said.

"It's ok," she laughed.

"You were brave," he added.

"I guess I had no choice," she said pleased.

"No you had a choice and you were brave," he replied.

"Well any time, I know you would do the same for me," she laughed.

"... guess I would," he laughed back the laughing relaxing them a little.

"You'd better... let's hope you never have the chance," she whispered and smiled at him again as their friendship melted into their hearts as it always did in times of happiness or trouble.

They talked no longer after that as they both needed time to contemplate what might be ahead of them in the next few hours or days ahead. So much had changed in a short space of time. It was hard for both of them to take in. Both were silent each in their own deep thoughts as they walked along.

Ettie knew she had put herself in danger helping Luca escape; that she would be on a wanted list as an enemy of the Slug Kingdom. If she risked returning home she would be putting her family, in danger. They would have to get to the mountains. This was the only place to be safe for now. Luca wondered to himself in these quiet minutes where his mother had been taken to and if he would see her again soon. He knew he needed to find this Dexy. He was the key to all of this; he would have answers.

The world he lived in had changed in seconds...

Those moments had made going back to his old life impossible. The Slug King was not an enemy he wanted. Was he the boy the king was looking for? But why?

He was a wretched fearful poisonous enemy, and now he was his enemy and Luca needed to know what he had done?

So the boy became a man, not slowly over years but in a split second of time. His mother was gone and he had to fend for himself. He felt different than he had ever felt before. His world had changed and he didn't know why.

Chapter 18. The Slug Pit

"Keep your eyes fixed on the horizon and the stars~
Never look down, it will only make your journey harder than it
needs to be.
Keep your eyes on the stars."

Ava Lockharth had been lead down to the depths of the castle grounds and into the underbelly of its lower cells, a new part of the castle that now existed. It was a horrible cold pit known to the villagers and townsfolk as The Slug Pit. The place where no one returned from and no creature would ever wish to be.

She tried to see Aviras' dusky figure through the darkness, but her eyes were not accustomed to the dark blackness still. Gerrado had found it amusing to put them together in a small dark cave of a cell. One of many, each full with up to three prisoners. She had no idea who Aviras was, to her he was just another prisoner probably wrongly accused and thrown into the pit out of shear unluckiness...

She smiled at him as she entered the cell and didn't see the keys being turned in the lock by a heavy fat sluggett guard, Tando one of Gerrado's finest. Her dark glowing eyes looked softly at Aviras like a new mother to a deer. He reminded her of her own small son, shocked to see young boys in a hell hole like this place. His tall broadness had been lost in the few days here at the pit and he was now a smaller boy himself sitting in the spidery corner on his own. He looked like he had been crying all night as teary muddy stains were on his face. She peered at him willing him to look as kindly at her as she was at him. Aviras looked wildly like a startled pig- his fear had got the better of him over night so he was jumpy and broken.

Ava reached out her hand to him, touching his arm, "Don't be afraid," she whispered to him kindly.

It was the first time he had felt hope since he had arrived.

Gerrado overheard. He laughed.

"Don't be afraid?" he chuckled to himself. "You wait, you wait till you hear what that young man's been up to! Then well see if you're quite so happy to comfort him! Pah!" he growled relishing in the thought that soon she would lean that it was all Aviras' fault. "Don't be afraid," he muttered to himself in utter disgust as he turned and left the Slug Pit cells.

Ava took no notice of Gerrado and bent down to speak to the boy. She knew he was frightened and her motherly instinct was to comfort the sorry sight of a human in front of her. The sight of him made her twice as glad that her son Luca was free. She wished Luca on to the Silver Mountains (with all her heart) and hoped Dexy would take care of him as he had promised her earlier. Dexy had warned her that this would happen, she should have listened to him. Her stubbornness had nearly cost her son his life. She shivered at the thought of Luca in the hands of Gerrado and prayed he would find his way to the mountains.

"I have a son," she began. "He's just like you, brave and handsome and kind."

Aviras stared at her. He didn't know who she was but he was glad of some company, she was warm and kind something that was lacking in the Slug Pit.

"I'm not kind," he replied.

"I bet you do kind things all the time," she encouraged him gently.

"That's just it, I deserve to be here. I hurt people. I...I steal...I take things that don't belong to me..." he stopped for tears would not let him continue.

"Well you seem nice to me... a friendly face in a mass of sluggetts. Hey you and me, we've gotta be there for each other," she said making everything seem simple again.

She was right they would have to support each other if they were to survive the Slug Pit it was the only way.

In the next few days she would find out what it would be like to be a prisoner of the Slug King. She knew Gerrado would stop at nothing to hurt her son, if he knew she was the old queen, whom he had driven out of the kingdom, ten years earlier. She hoped she had changed so much that she would not be recognisable, Gerrado would not see Queen Amber, but Ava Lockharth the person she had been for the last ten years- a lowly villager.

Gerrado in truth didn't care who she was, he planned to use her as bait to lure her son and other so called traitors right to his path and then kill them. He knew they would come looking for her. Gerrado was no fool. He knew how to win battles. He knew how to overthrow kingdoms. He knew every inch of winning and it had befriended him like a lucky clover over the years. He made sure he won at all costs, going the extra mile that others would see as a step too far, and for Gerrado losing was not an option, not today not ever and there was no cost that he would not pay. A small boy and his mother right or wrong, Queen or King were a small price for him to pay for his kingdom! He had hoped for the boy today at the end of his search, but was pleased he at least had the mother and believed it only a matter of time before he would catch up with the boy. Then he could throw them in the pit and never have to think of them again! Gone!

Back in the woods, Luca and Ettie had been walking for two hours, finding drinking water in small streams which trickled down the groves in the wooded area.

"What about your dad?" remembered Luca thinking of Ettie. "He'll be worrying."
Ettie kept walking,
"I know but we can't go back and there is nothing I can do. Maybe when we get to Dexy we can get a message back," she said hopefully. "We need to move before nightfall and get to the mountains."
"I agree we should make use of the daylight," he nodded but wondered how he would keep moving with his bones and bruises still aching.
"Let's see where we heading then," she wanted to keep positive and seeing her friend was in pain she focussed on the map in front of them.

The map was crumpled but clear enough and once through the woods the mountains were beyond...

They sat to study the map as they had been every twenty minutes, to check their way and only continued onwards when they felt ready to move through the woods. This wood they had played in many times now seemed confusing and grim and they had never gone this far in. The trees loomed over them like huge lonely ghosts warning them to go no further on a haunted abandoned path...

Old and sprinkled with full of great green leaves that kept out the sunlight. It smelt of dampness and the cold soaked through their clothes and settled on their skin sending sharp tingles to the core. They had no coats and they were freezing with every step. They trundled on side by side at a brisk pace which had kept them warm at first but now the coldness was inescapable, using what energy they had left to move forwards onto the mountains. Their battered legs were bruises and tired but as they moved deeper into the forest, they felt safer with each step away from the village. Finally, they reached the steep path at the bottom of the mountain. It was hard to see at first but it was marked with some stones, which were shown on the map. It had to be the place they were looking for. It was here that they had been striving to reach for the last few hours. The formidable mountain in front of them was unmistakable.

"This has got to be it," said Luca checking on the map.

"Looks steep and big enough," replied Ettie in agreement.

"Can't even see the top, do you think we can climb it?" asked Luca.

"Only one way to find out," she laughed never losing her sense of humour.

It was an overwhelming mountain where its misty top reached the sky, the clouds hung darkly threatening rain. The trickiest thing was it's steep narrow footpath with blank rock face on one side and grey gravely pathways underfoot. The height made it a grand old master that reached up through the sun's ripples, reflecting rays against its chalky, light, grey face. Its slippery moss was lethal and to slip was dangerous with such a long drop and slim path. Some had fallen and their lives were taken in a second in one slippery missed step. It was easy to see why most turned back and didn't attempt the climb. The craggy edges of this mountain could throw them off like pebbles to the bottom, but Ettie and Luca had no choice.

"Take it slowly, it's not worth rushing and we have no rope if we fall," warned Luca to Ettie.

"I wasn't planning on rushing this one," Ettie replied knowing her leather shoes were the worst kind for climbing offering little support for her ankles and feet.

It was daunting; they took it step by step and tried not to think of the dangers. Wet moss under their feet was like walking on slippery eels, their skin was like soft butter as it ripped on the stones with each slip. They concentrated and only spoke to check the other was ok. Ettie found she could cling onto odd branches that randomly stuck out of the mountainside and she held onto each one she found as long as she could.

Halfway up the path widened and was ample for the needs of their small feet. The mountain's deceptive cracks opened into large splits, with its old mean face it was a relentless walk. The path was drier and the stones less sharp, yet it was higher and a fall would hurt. A sheer drop to the right meant they could not risk complacency. Still two miles short of the dwelling cave that homed the 'outsiders' it was well hidden and as high as was possible to live in the altitude. The children could do nothing more than keep going. They knew the climb might kill them, but staying in the woods was not an option. Reaching Dexy and following the map was their only choice. Each step brought them nearer to safety, but each step was equal in danger, but all they knew was, they had to keep moving.

Chapter 19. A Hopeless Visit

Remember, hopelessness is always only one step away from hope.

Dexy was back on his travels to see Sedgefield. He wanted to arrange regular visits to Marcus. Away for the afternoon from the Silver Mountains. He had no idea what had happened that afternoon. He rode his horse through the outside of the village knowing a route through the fields and rivers, thinking of Ava, how he could tell her that her husband was alive, but not of sound mind, as she would remember him. How do you tell someone that? How he could resolve the unresolvable? He knew too that Gerrado would come looking for Luca, but even Dexy would have been surprised at the little time he had wasted in doing so. He had no idea that Luca was as of now on the run and would never again be safe in his old village by the lake with his mother.

With all of this on his mind he headed to the ancient burial grounds for a second time in two days to meet with Sedgefield. He wanted to see Marcus again and what he could do to help his long lost friend. Although he was still cross with Sedgefield, he knew that if Marcus had been well enough he would have surely told him of his existence, so with this in mind he expected the worst. He had told only Falentona where he was headed and why.

He arrived to a quiet burial ground. The walls were deserted, as it was evening when the Loban Masters took their last meal of the day and so most were in the large dining room. He knew he would find Sedgefield among them.

"Dexy," said Sedgefield getting up from the large dining table and wiping the food from his mouth with a serviette. "I didn't think I would see you again so soon...after last time. I'm glad you have come. Please sit with me, eat."

"Thank you, it's not food I came for," replied Dexy.

"Oh of that I am sure, but why talk on an empty stomach you must have been riding a while," he added smiling, not much worried Sedgefield where fallouts were concerned he was a Loban Master who did what he liked and fell out with many and often.

"I was hoping I could see Marcus," Dexy kept his voice low, though the other Loban Masters kept on eating and knew of the King anyway, it was they who had cared for him all these years.

"I thought it would have something to do with Marcus," he smiled, licking his greasy fingers enjoying his chicken wings and waving over a servant Loban to fill his and another empty cup with wine.

Dexy was not interested in the food in front of him. "I know you did what you had to do with the him but..."

Sedgefield interrupted, "I did what was necessary, yes," he agreed. "I have no problem that you see him, now you know he is alive I see no point in keeping him away from you. And you will see the same as I see- a man who is not of healthy mind, a danger to himself and others. You have hope in your heart for Marcus I can tell, but Dexy, do not hope too much... for Marcus has gone, if you're expecting to see your old friend...your old King, then you will be disappointed," Sedgefield was clear and firm with his words and stopped eating to say this which was rare.

"I don't know what I expect to see but I have to see him for myself. I want to speak to him, I need to..." Dexy broke off, he didn't finish as he didn't know what he needed to do, to see. He would have to take what he saw, whatever state Marcus had been in these ten years, he would have to accept it.

"I shall take you to him. He will be eating too," said Segdefield getting up and leaving the grand room, chewing what was left of his mouthful as he walked.

The noise of the dining hall grew fainter as they walked down towards the room where Marcus was living. Sedgefield told the Loban guards who manned the door to stand down and take a break. They entered. Dexy stayed behind him.

"Do you want to be alone? I can stay?" offered Sedgefield.

"No, I will be fine, leave us," said Dexy.

"Come see me when you are done we need to discuss the uprising and my Loban Masters are ready, it will be a chance for us to make plans. I take it we are friends again?" he asked.

"We are friends, we both have the same enemy!" Dexy smiled at him, he liked Segdefield and trusted him friendship. Their loathing of Gerrado made them permanent allies.

Sedgefield left closing the door behind him and Dexy turned to look at his dear friend a man who he hardly recognised. The large room had ample space it had a bed and table, a wardrobe and a fireplace, and a skylight window that let in some light. There was a work bench which had wooden bits around on the top and floor, it seemed this kept Marcus busy and bowls and small wooden statues of various sizes could be seen around that had been made. The fire burned brightly keeping the large room warm. Marcus didn't look up to see who had arrived. He continued to eat and stared blankly at his food placing each fork full carefully in his mouth like a machine. He was curled over his table and his bowl was held firmly as he took his food scooping it onto some bread like a piece of cutlery. He did not acknowledge Dexy at all.

"Marcus," Dexy spoke quietly as he moved towards him but got no response neither a look, movement or noise.

"Marcus," he said again moving closer so he could see his old friend. He had grown so old in the ten years apart that it was hard to remember how he had once been.

Dexy could not believe that his friend looked so old and worn. It had been ten years but his face showed twenty. He was much thinner and his eyes with lost sparkle, still blue but not as before, like two silver drops of rain that never smiled or remembered happiness. His skin was smooth but dull from lack of sunlight. He had a scar on the side of his face accompanied by a dint in his forehead, an old wound from the war. A strike from a sword had damaged his front lobes and sent him to the ground. His hair was long and grey though they cut it, it was wiry and dishevelled. He looked like a different man. He was a different man thought Dexy, but he could not forget his old friend as he stood opposite him stooping to see him and not frighten him.

"King Marcus, do you remember me? It is Dexy?" he whispered, but unsure if this man could hear at all from the way he looked so distant and undisturbed by his presence.

"It's Dexy. I was by your side when you fell...I'm sorry," he said again but it did nothing as Marcus continued to eat and stare at his bowl. "Do you remember me? I worked for you at the castle."

Marcus continued to eat and made no attempt to look at Dexy.

"I have news for you. I have found your wife, Ava...the Queen...Queen Amber...you have a son..." continued Dexy moving nearer again and speaking up.

"I'm Dexy, your servant, do you remember? Sire, you...you have a son... Luca," he said finally.

It was hard to take this man responding as blankly and carrying on as if there was no one there with him. Dexy found it unnerving but was determined to make a connection, to see something in the old king.

"You have a son, a son! He is brave and just like you," he told him moving closer slowly.

Dexy could see he was getting nowhere. The man was taking no notice of him and his words were of no interest either. The food was his focus and he ate slowly chewing the bread and making no other movement and looking ahead blankly.

"Do you like it here with the Loban Masters? They take good care of you?" Dexy tried again.

Unsure if he had seen it or imagined it he thought Marcus gave a little nod, it was so slight that it might have been a trick of his eye.

"You like it here?" he said again.

The nod returned it was definitely a nod. Dexy was pleased. He was getting somewhere so he continued...

"Do you make bowls? Who are the statues?" Dexy asked him walking over to the workbench in the corner and picking up some figures to admire the craftsmanship.

Marcus stopped eating as Dexy handled his work. Suddenly he made a loud pained cry it rang through the room like a horrid piece of noise shattering the calm. His was distressed. He pointed with vigour at his pots and rocked backwards and forwards the squawking cries became louder. Dexy backed off and places the pieces down, he moved back nearer to the bed putting his hands out to show he was not touching the wooden carvings.

"Don't worry I won't touch your work!" he tried to calm him. "I was only looking," but it did not stop the rocking and the noise.

Marcus continued to moan and hit his head with his hands as if he was very unhappy. Dexy's efforts to comfort him were in vain, so eventually he moved back away from Marcus to the bed, it seemed to be the only way he could show him that he was not going to hurt him.

Back on the wide bed, Dexy watched his friend behave so oddly that he could not do anymore but sit and stare in shock. He sat and watched. He didn't move or speak until stillness came back to Marcus and he seemed stable again.

Marcus rose out of his chair and went over to his workbench where he sat down to carve. His ignored Dexy again. He worked on his bowl, carving with skill and determination and defiance. He worked in silence and forgot his visitor.

Dexy wondered whether to leave, he sat on the bed watching his friend carve the figures and silently work. The minutes passed and the two of them ignored the other, Dexy stayed as he watched him whittling the wood in a trance. The communication was over. He continued working curled over his work, each piece carefully carved.

"You like to carve?" Dexy collected himself and tried to question him again.

"My bowls and figures, I work on my bowls and figures," said Marcus quietly without stopping from his carving.

Dexy walked over towards the man who had animal like behaviour and tried to speak to him again.

"Do you remember me Marcus?" he asked but nothing came as a reply.

"Do you remember me Marcus? He said again listening for an answer that didn't come.

"Marcus, do you remember me?" Dexy would not stop. He went closer again bent low, opposite him now he continued to speak the carving didn't put him off.

"You must try to remember me? Marcus you must try," he shouted again moving nearer and nearer to him but crouching low so as not to frighten him. Now up close and kneeling close to his friend, he asked again, "Do you remember me? Do you remember me? Try, try to remember me," he whispered through gritted teeth, willing him to remember.

"Marcus, I am Dexy, it's Dexy. Do you remember me?" as he put his arm on the man's hand to stop his constant carving.

Marcus stopped his work. He did not move. He was still for a whole minute as Dexy held his arm with the metal carving tool still in hand. The silence melted into the room and Dexy wondered what would happen but he held onto his arm squeezing it tighter in hope. Marcus stopped his work. He looked into Dexy's eyes. He growled a low tone as he pulled his arm away. He flung his arm out from Dexy's grip and pushed him off! The anger rising through his body. He let out a roar like an animal and his hand flew through the air taking the carving tool down and into Dexy's throat, stopping short of his jugular. Dexy fell back, knocked to the floor. Marcus crouched threateningly sill over Dexy like a raging bull frozen in time, his hand any closer would cut Dexy's throat! Dexy lay still and if he moved the blade would slice his skin open.

"I don't remember you!" Marcus replied, shaking with terror, coldly holding the sharp carving tool stiff in place to Dexy's neck ready to slice him dead in a second.

Dexy felt the cold ground underneath him and stayed there knowing if he flinched the man would strike him down.

This was what Sedgefield had warned him about. His worst fears came crashing through his mind it was not what he had wanted to see from his old dear friend. The Marcus he knew was gone. This was the man who was left an unpredictable creature who had no sense or comprehension of the reality around him.

Minutes passed till Marcus moved his hand away from him and put his tool back down on the bench. He went over to his bed and lay down with his back to Dexy, ignoring his visitor as if nothing had happened. Dexy knew that his friend had suffered terribly his injuries from the war had left him damaged and broken. This was how he lived out his days, tucked away in a room for his own safety. Dexy slowly got up and brushed the wooden chippings he had fallen in to the floor. The fire had burned closely to his face and the heat from it made his cheeks hot as well as the shock. He stood staring at his friend unable to know what to do next.

The door opened behind him. He turned to see Sedgefield had returned.

"Any joy?" he asked walking in seeing Marcus quiet on the bed.

Dexy couldn't even master a reply, but Sedgefield could see he was frustrated by the encounter, he knew without asking how things had gone.

"Well you need to come with me now. There is news from the village. It's news you will want to hear," said Sedgefield gravely.

They left Marcus to himself. Dexy was glad to leave the room he was beginning to feel sick in there with him.

"Come on there is talk," said Sedgefield.

They went back into the dining room there was a buzz in there- everyone was chatting. Loban Masters a blaze with food wine and news.

"Tarrogan is just back from the castle, he went taking the sluggetts back to the castle for the night. They are all talking about a boy and the search for him that Gerrado had laid on in the Daccorian village. They say he is looking for the 'lost king' and they say Gerrado has captured his mother. He is holding her in the Slug Pit, but the boy apparently has escaped," he told them rapidly as the words churned from his lips like a galloping waterfall.

Dexy forgot about Marcus and stood astounded by what he had heard.

"So I was right Luca was in danger," he added.

"So the boy is lucky to escape. Gerrado would have killed him on the spot, had he found him," said Sedgefield with certainty.

"Lucky for now but the boy must be found and we can keep him safe," said Dexy.

"You must find the boy before Gerrado!" he cried.

"I must go back to the mountains at once!" said Dexy.

"Your horse has been prepared and is waiting for you in the courtyard," said Sedgefield. "Remember we are together one this one. I want to help the boy and his father as much as you do. It suits all our interests. I have cared for his father all this time. It would have been easier to kill him, you know. Many said I should."

Dexy smiled, "But you and I are alike. We do what we think is right,"

"That we do," smiled Sedgefield. "That we do."

Dexy wasted no time and rode back to the mountains faster than he had ever ridden before. Luca had to be found before Gerrado got his hands on him! He was the real king and Dexy was the King's protector. He never forgot this. He owed Marcus that!

He owed them all...

Chapter 20 The Mountain Attack

"Look for fear and it will find you. Look for hope will it will find you."

The main and only entrance to the 'outsiders dwellings had secret lines of salt sprinkled at the doorway in case a sluggett soldier ever came looking. (Not that they would, as their lazy nature would not usually get them this far, even if it was an order from the Slug Pit King himself.) The sluggetts were often told to comb these woodland areas, which ran by the River Toga looking for 'outsiders' but they never went higher than they had to. They guessed the mountains would provide no home for any enemy because of its harsh conditions, but they were wrong...

The mountains of silver and grey shadows with hints of green foliage had always provided the 'outsiders' with enough to live on, though they would never swap it for their own homes from before the Great War- the homes and families they had lost. Each outsider had been forced into the mountains after the war...none of them ever believing that they would be there forever though some days it seemed like it. They had made a promise that they would one day win back the lands that had been lost in the Great War. They would give the Ancient burial grounds in the Loban area back to its rightful Loban Masters. They would find a noble and just king to take the place of Marcus. They hoped they could set free the downtrodden villagers and creatures who lived in the Daccorian region.

They were the Freedom Warriors! Whispers in the trees talked of them. Echoes in the mountains hinted at their plans and eagles could hear their busy chatter as they flew over their caves. They were preparing. The uprising grew closer with each day and some days it seemed so close you could touch it and other days it was far away and only a distant dream.

Each storage room packed with weapons and equipment; anything they would need. Salt stores by the bag full to fight against an army of sluggetts were kept well stocked. The Freedom Warriors, only spoken of in myth or legend, by the wolves and birds. They were alive, whether you believed it or not, they were alive and it was here that they lived out their days!

Ettie had scraped her legs so many times that she had lost count. She cursed the wretched mountain, every few minutes her toes stumped on a new bramble or stone on the narrow path. Luca was finding it no easier as his old wounds from days earlier were giving him jip. The two of them yelped and cried at different cruel slices of the mountains edge as it dug through their skin, but they carried on and never let this stop them. They were both desperate to find Dexy. They knew a hidden cave entrance would be somewhere so they had to keep climbing, no matter how ingrained the mud and dirt ground into their skin with each step. The map had instructions, but they were both unsure and the mountain's harsh steep face gave them enough to think about. Ettie was tired her little body was sore but she could not moan as it was her friend who was depending on her. She thought of her mother and father and hoped they were not worrying too much. She knew the news of Ava would reach them soon. She wanted them to know she was safe. They would know she must be with Luca. He stopped suddenly looking at the map again.

"The map says to go past where the moss and grass changes to rocks half way up, so I think we must be half way," he declared.

"I hope so," answered Ettie.

"The paths gets narrower be careful," warned Luca knowing they had to keep diligent as a slip would be fatal. The edge of the mountain gave a constant reminder of the danger.

"I know and it's getting darker now," she said. The light had been changing for the last hour and the next hour would leave them in darkness. They had some time but hoped their climb would not last into the night.

Up ahead the children could see the edge of the mountain stuck out into the path it blocked the way. The mound stuck out far over the path and presented a big problem. The children stopped to look at a cliff face. The mountain edge was curved and awkward to cross on foot without climbing around it, but how could they risk a climb with nothing to stop them falling off the edge of the cliff face?

"We can't get past," cried Luca.

"It's impossible! How can we get around it, might as well be a boulder in the middle of the path it's sticking out too far!" she exclaimed.

"Unless we climb round?" said Luca thinking carefully.

"But what if we fall. It's a clear drop. It would kill us," warned Ettie.

"I can't see any other way. If we don't climb around it then we're stuck!" he finished.

Ettie stood staring at the curved cliff face that stuck out so much and made crossing so difficult. There was no way round it on foot, but climbing with no rope would be dangerous, if not impossible.

"What shall we do? We have to carry on," she asked.

"We could get hold onto some vines that are coming out of the cliff to tie around ourselves at least then we are fixed to the cliff," he answered.

"I guess it's the only way," she added looking at the vines that trailed of the mountain like green ropes of strength.

"If we fall we can cling on to that and swing ourselves around the bump,"

"You make it sound easy," she said scratching her head. "I guess we have to try?" She tried to stay positive for Luca but was scared at the thought of clinging to a vine of a cliff face.

"It's all we can do. The vine should hold us. The wall is sticking out so much... it is the only way we can hope to get past," he said gritting his teeth in despair and kicking the ground.

"Come on, let's try," she said with a surge of bravery and began to tie a long leafy vine around her middle.

"Does it feel strong enough?" asked Luca as he did the same and tugged at his vine to see its strength.

"It seems to be," she said tugging at hers too.

"If it's long enough we can hold onto it as we climb round. I'll go first," he offered.

"Be careful," she cried as he started to place his foot on the edge, testing the vines strength by pulling it tight.

The sheer drop below was like a death trap. The wind was quiet today, but the air around still felt cold on their backs. Luca went slowly and climbed around the rock bit by bit, feeling his way with his feet and holding on with his hands. It took him a few minutes but he managed to get round. On the other side Ettie could no longer see him, but she knew as he called to her that he was safe on the other side of it.

"Shall I start?" she called to him.

"Yep! I'm good," he reassured her.

Ettie began using the same manoeuvres she had watched Luca make moments earlier. Her hands were smaller and she found it hard to get a grip on the cliff at first. It was cold and hard and didn't have much to hold onto. Slowly she lifted her foot off the ground from its safe path and started to peel around the cliff. She looked like a spider on a stone. Her body hung off into the evening's breath. She felt the breeze on her back it was cold enough to make her shiver. Her legs shaking. They were wobbly with fear. She stopped and took a moment to look up at the sky.

Luca called to her, "Don't stop! Keep going!"

"I can't!" she called back. She could feel her energy draining from her arms as they began to shake too.

"You can do it! Just don't stop!" he cried again, trying to help.

"Please Luca! I'm stuck," she yelled back with panic in her voice.

Tears fell down her cheeks. She knew she was in danger and the panic swept over her like a rushing wave. She shook and cried, her body too scared to move.

Luca reached out his hand to try and grab her. He was able to just about touch her but it was not enough to grab her or let her hold onto him.

"You only have three more steps Ettie," he tried to help again.

"I can't move! I can't do it!" she cried, sobbing beyond control.

The next minute felt like a slow hour, but she felt her body fold and pull back from the edge, she let go with one hand and caught hold of a branch, but it swung her off to the left and her feet lost footing and swung into the air below her. She only had one hand on the rock. It wasn't enough to hold her.

"Ettie!" screamed Luca seeing her little legs dangling down.

"I'm falling!" she cried and with that she let go and her body threw back falling down, the ground below waited patiently. Her body fell like a leaf from a tree swirling and twisting in the air.

Luca saw her she looked like she was flying at first but then with each drop in height she fell at a gathering pace as the ground was hurtling towards her. He screamed and tried to throw the vine he had around his waist out to her, but it was no good she was falling and she had no way of grabbing anything. Luca was helpless

"Noooo!" cried Luca.

"Help me!" called Ettie but it was too late, her little body was bulleting down and she was falling to what could only be her death...

Chapter 21. Mountain Dwellings and Discoveries

Dexy headed back to the mountains. He needed to find Luca before Gerrado.

It was a route he knew well and he was back by the woodlands in no time at all. He left his horse in one of the villagers' fields as it had always grazed there by arrangement, then he ran through the woods as fast as he could to the mountains edge. He went up the mountain with ease, he had his own route and avoided the difficult areas with ease. (The children had read the map well but not well enough to help their journey, it would be impossible to know the mountainside as well as Dexy did.)

Looking up at the mountain he spotted the figure falling down from the edge, he could see it was a girl. Her hair sticking up past her face with gravity and arms and legs flaying- horrific sight. The child was bending in all shapes as the wind pushed her further to the ground. Her legs splayed and arms grasped out, but nothing was there to help her. She battled in the air. Her cry was thin as the air took it away- the noise, a haunting sound though the woodlands. Dexy gasped and felt sick. He leapt up the mountain running to reach the children, knowing he was too late.

Falentona too had seen the falling girl. She had been circling for a few minutes and spotted the children heading up to the mountainside moments earlier. She had sharp eagle eyes and could spot a mouse from hundreds of meters up, so these two were easy to see. The seconds after the fall, she homed in on the girl. Her body was her target. She swooped lower; her magnificent wings stretched out like an Archangel. She glided down through the air with ease and accuracy and dipped under the little girl's body, whisking her up onto her back. Ettie clung on to the fleecy feathers with all her might. She felt the bird save her falling body with a clear glide underneath her back. Her strength returning in time to let her hang on to the huge bird of prey who had come to her rescue just in time. Ettie had been waiting for a terrible bump that would come on reaching the ground, but all that came were soft downy feather, saved by a large kind bird who was cosier than a blanket on a cold night. She was like a large warm carpet and Ettie dipped into the safety of her feathers, like nothing she had felt before. She had seconds to spare.

Dexy still watching, tears filled his eyes, thanking his eagle friend in his heart for her quick thinking and her ability to always be there when needed. Luca too was watching, with every hair on his body sticking up in fright, they changed to relief and he put his head in his hands and fell to his knees. He sobbed in thankfulness that his dearest friend was safe.

Falentona landed on the mountain edge next to him and smiled.
"Climb on too," she commanded. "You look like you could do with a ride."
"We want to get to Dexy in the mountains," Luca replied.
"I know little one that is where I will take you. Do not be afraid now Dexy will be pleased to see you both," she nodded.

Luca grabbed onto Ettie and squeezed his hands around her waist and clung to her as if he never wanted to let her go! They flew through the evening sky with ease. The wind blew past their ears and tickled on their little bodies. The great eagle swooped and circled bringing them to the entrance on the mountain that was hidden from view.

They climbed down from her back with shaky legs. She pushed back the stone and the children walked inside the home of the 'outsiders.'

The first part was just the entrance that was still camouflaged with twigs and sticks and looked like an old birds nest. The outsiders called it the hall. Then further on was the living quarter. A large room inside a cave lit with glowing candles and lanterns was cosy and warm with cushions and wooden carved out tree trunks to sit in. It was like a little den for all shapes and sizes and creature alike.

They were greeted by a strange group- Gobber, Jee Hanna, Jax, Samlit and Keto. Each head popped up. Some were sat others appeared out of cracks in the cave to see who had arrived with their 'mother-bird' Falentona. Dexy was minutes away.

Soon the mountain was a home of activity and buzzing chatter. Everyone was pleased to see the children safe and alive! And all of them had so many questions. It had been such a triumph to make it to the cave that Luca could not stop smiling and Ettie was weepy from her experience but smiled too so thankful to be alive. She had happy tears running down her cheeks most of that night. Falentona introduced them,

"Luca and Ettie!" she exclaimed.

The group cheered with delight. Jee Hanna smiled with glee and her little fairy heart leapt to see Luca again.

"So you made it to the mountains!" Gobber cried happily, whilst munching on some chicken wings.

"Only just," added Dexy.

"You hungry?" Gobber thought only of food in all times.

"Of course they must be starving, I will do some soup!" added Falentona.

"So how are you feeling?" asked Keto wisely.

"Ok" said the two children both tongue tied and a bit shy of the strange creatures.

"We weren't expecting you," teased Gobber. "I would have tidied up had I known!"

"You tidy up? Don't make me laugh," chuckled Jax. Their jovial quips made the children relax quickly as they warmed by a healthy fire in the middle of the room.

"Let them get warm and stop teasing," said Falentona, calling order. "Jax and Jee Hanna go and look for some clothes they can borrow, these ones are frozen and wet. You are both they same sizes. Ettie let's clean up those legs." Ettie looked down to see her legs gushing with blood from the scrapes on the mountain. She held back her tears, the shock had stopped her from feeling any pain till now but her cuts stung now like smarting ants bites and the sticky blood felt warm.

"I have some black jumpers and skirts. Do you want tights too?" she asked Ettie, feeling sorry for the state of her cuts legs, though she was already a bit jealous of knowing she was Luca best friend.

"Yes please," said Ettie quietly but pleased.

"Come with me," said the spider fairy keen to show her new friend her bedroom cave, she was so proud of.

"Keto will have some ointment for them," added Jax. Ettie blushed at this seeing a young man offering her kindness. He was cute she thought to herself and hoped her cheeks didn't show her up.

Jax had Dexy's charm and good looks, he was seventeen and confident. He sat comfortable on a stool by the fire with a mug of nutmeg milk, a favourite drink of the outsiders, after beer. He smiled at the two children and felt keen to get to know them, it was good to have new people around he often got lonely in the mountains.

"Don't be long, the soup will be warmed through very soon," added Falentona wanting to get the children warm and fed as quickly as possible to help their recovery.

"So you're the lost king everyone has been talking of," said Gobber.

Luca didn't answer, his hands and feet tingled thawing from the cold and he didn't understand what the creature was saying to him.

"Let the boy settle in," said Keto quickly, realising that Luca might not know who he was yet.

"We should wait till Dexy gets here then we can talk, till then let them be," agreed Falentona seeing the boy had no idea.

"Was only saying," apologised Gobber.

"Shall I sing a song?" said Samlit helpfully it was his answer to everything. His ears twitched with excitement at the excuse for some music.

"No!" cried Keto, Gobber, Jax and Falentona all together.

"The children need rest, not music," she reprimanded.

"Always time for a song," Samlit whispered to Luca and went back to playing a pretend guitar on his comfortable cushion in the corner of the cave.

"Don't we know it," quipped Gobber who overheard.

The group calmed down and carried on eating and warming. Luca eased a bit as he felt better for being safe. He wondered what Gobber had meant but thought it best to keep quiet for now. He would wait for Dexy to arrive as they had said. He didn't have to wait long as twenty minutes later Dexy appeared at the cave.

"Hello again Luca," he said. "Where's young Ettie? Is she ok after her fall, I saw it from the bottom of the mountain, nasty?"

"She's fine, just getting some warm clothes on with Jee Hanna," said Falentona, with that the girls came out, Ettie appeared looking much better and colour back in her face at last, the feeling in her fingers had returned too.

"So you two you found us you did well, it can't have been easy getting here," he praised them.

"They have my mother," Luca burst out he couldn't help it.

"And we shall get her back Luca," assured Dexy.

"But tonight the children must rest," added Keto who knew they would be needing their strength in the next coming days.

"Yes," said Falentona handing them both a bowl of soup and two spoons. "You eating now?" she asked Dexy.

"Course," he answered was starving. He sat next to Luca on a wooden chair that was fit for him he had made it himself.

The children tucked in, they were on cushions nearest the fire, sat inside the circle of outsiders. It was a homely group. Jee Hanna moved her cushion closer to Luca and stared at him a bit too much, Luca didn't notice but the older ones did, recognising a crush when they saw it.

"Ah so they get to eat, what about they rest of us?" joked Gobber.

"You never stop eating," piped up Samlit.

"I need my strength," he replied unoffended.

"So Gerrado came for you?" said Dexy changing to a serious tone.

"He was looking for a boy like me," said Luca confused. "He must want someone else."

"He came through the village with his sluggett army they had a picture of Luca with them," added Ettie helpfully through her soup slurps.

"Luca he was looking for you... You are the boy he wanted," said Dexy slowly knowing it would be a shock for Luca to hear.

Luca stopped eating as his stomach churned upside down. He was the boy they were after? It didn't make any sense.

"You have heard of the Great War, yes? Before the Slug Pit ruled there was a king and queen who ruled, King Marcus and Queen Amber- they were your mother and father. Your mother, Ava...she took you to safety when the battle reached the city walls and hid in the village under another identity. You are their child and would have been the next king. You are the lost King," explained Dexy.

The silence hit the room with Dexy's word ringing through the cave. They knew his words would hit Luca like an arrow through his heart. Luca felt his body go limp and the words hung in the air like a vapour of mist that would not disappear. His lips dried as he tried to speak,

"...and my father?" he said slowly.

"Your father...he...he..." Dexy didn't know what to say. The group waited for Dexy to answer but he could not.

"...he was lost in battle," said Falentona softly.

Dexy held his breath. He should have said more but he couldn't not at this time. (He had only just learned of Luca' father being alive and the state he was in, he wasn't ready to tell Luca the truth though he knew he should have.)

Ettie gasped and gulped down her last spoonful of soup. She felt for her friend. How would his mind take all this in? Luca could not focus the news was too much, but he still thought of his mother in the hands of the Slug King and knew that her capture was more dangerous than he had imagined, he thought it was all a mistake, but these words, they were real, this was real.

"So the slug king will kill my mother?" asked Luca.

"No, he will keep her alive. She is still useful to him. We won't leave her with him we will go and get her, try not to worry we will do everything we can to get her back again," Dexy added.

"We already have plans to storm the Slug Pit," said Gobber.

"We will do all it takes," said Dexy, trying to reassure a confused and tired Luca.

Dexy hoped the Slug King would keep her alive, he knew once he had the boy she would not be spared, so he felt so much comfort from having Luca with him now and he was determined to help them. It was what Marcus would have wanted.

"So that's why you gave my mother the map so we could get to the mountains if they came for me?" quizzed Luca.

"That's right. I gave her the map. I recognised you on the day we saved you, you look just like your father and when you told me about the bracelet I had no reason doubt,"

"Why didn't she tell me?" Luca asked.

"I don't know," said Dexy.

"She wanted to protect you," said Falentona.

"She did what she thought best," added Keto.

The group let these moments sink in. Luca and Ettie could not believe the truth it was too much to understand.

"Ettie you look so tired. Would you like to go to bed? Jee Hanna she can share with you," said Falentona.

"I guess I am beat," she agreed though she thought she might not sleep after the news, but her body was weak and weary so she knew it was a good idea.

"The children should sleep it is late and rest is needed. Tomorrow we shall make plans! Don't worry about your mum, Luca she will be pleased that you are here with us," Falentona concluded.

Luca smiled but his stomach was in cramps at the thought of his mother a prisoner. He could only feel blank at her not being with them and unable to do anything. It was horrible. His body kept shaking, he hoped no one could see. He too was turning cold with his body in shock and traumatised.

The children went to their beds, too stunned and exhausted to ask any more questions. Their minds were full but they needed rest, sleep seemed impossible but wasn't far away.

Dexy, Falentona, Gobber, Samlit, Jax and Keto sat up longer. Their plans could not wait. They plotted how to save Luca' mum from the Slug Pit. Dexy told them of Marcus and the state that their old king was in. Falentona agreed to fly to get news to Roper and his wife about their daughter, in the night.

They slept very little, it was not a time when sleep was easy; for each of them knew that their plans tonight might make their dreams of the future settle into fate's heart and turn their future into freedom...

It was a chance for the Freedom Warriors. They had waited a long time. It was their time to move, but there was so much resting on the next few days!

Chapter 22. A New Dawn

The day begins at dawn, but who knows how the day will end.

Luca woke up and remembered the day before. His amazement was still making his head spin. Was he really a lost king? Had he lived with his mother, a queen, now a village woman in the village for ten years?

He heard the creatures in the other rooms speaking in muffled voices he could hear plans being made. He looked over and saw Jax's bed was empty. He wondered if he had slept late, it didn't seem so. After he stretched and shook himself he crept into the next room. His stomach was grumbling, Falentona greeted him with a plate of toasted pumpkin bread. He felt sick with worry but knew he must eat, as it had been so long since his last meal. The bustle of breakfast felt safe. He felt safe here.

Jee Hanna and Ettie were also waking. Ettie's legs ached from the climb but she was glad to be alive and safe. They got dressed and wandered through to the busy room where breakfast was being devoured by all the dwellers. Dexy was talking carefully to Gobber in a corner, for all his jokes Dexy knew he would be a fine asset today and wanted to make sure he knew what to do when they stormed the pit. They were talking of taking the castle on the left side where the Slug Pit was placed. It was the easiest way not to be seen. It was the beginning of their plan to save Ava. They knew she would be there. It was where all prisoners of the king were sent.

"Morning Luca!" cried Samlit as he walked in trying not to be seen.

"Did you sleep well?" asked Keto.

"Yes thanks," lied Luca sitting down on a cushion as Falentona handed him a mug of parsnip juice that was sweet and cold on his teeth.

"This will give you strength," she added. "Ettie, I spoke to your father, he knows you are here."

He had woken many times in the night and worried until he drifted again and then woke again.

Jee Hanna poured her own juice and handed some to Ettie. She again sat herself next to Luca and Ettie found a small seat by the fire. Dexy and Gobber stopped their plan making for a bit to join the morning breakfast gathering.

"How did you sleep?" said Gobber kindly to Ettie and Luca.

They nodded shyly.

"Ok thanks," said Luca lying again to be polite.

"Ok," answered Ettie looking shyly over at Jax and then to Luca to see if he had slept.

Falentona continued to churn out toasted buckwheat flats, all buttered with honey and the kettle kept warm for continuous raspberry tea or parsnip juice. She knew her breakfast would come later when she went hunting over in the fields, though she drank a warm raspberry tea. Dexy watched Luca carefully. He could see the boy was still stunned. He let the boy eat and waited till after breakfast before he spoke with the children and the group...

Everyone listened intently as he spoke. They knew these were important words.

"I want to head to the castle this evening to make a go of getting Ava out of the prison. I am assuming she is there. The pit is easy to reach from the East and if we can get close enough without being seen we stand a good chance of getting in. The first job will be to reach the main guard with the keys. He will be stood at the door to the pit and will be the largest sluggett. Gobber will be in charge of getting the keys,"

"No problem," said Gobber knowing his role clearly. Glad his muscle would be of use.

"Me, Gobber, Jax, Samlit will be enough, with Bevan if he can make it," he added.

Jee Hanna looked disappointed but she knew Dexy was right, as she was no use to them, in the pit she would only be a liability. Luca and Ettie sat listening. Ettie was wondering about her family too and how she could tell them where she was, but she didn't have to wait long as they moved through their plans with a solution for each problem.

"Falentona will head off now to Roper's and drop a letter to Ettie's parents so they know our plans. It is early so she won't be seen," he asked.

"Of course," she had expected him to send her there. "And then I shall come back and check on these three," she nodded over at Jee Hanna, Luca and Ettie.

"We will go to the castle this evening, it will be easier at night," said Dexy.

"Falentona make sure you are not seen, though I doubt anyone will suspect you of anything other than a bird of prey looking for food," He added.

"I know. The village will be asleep and the sluggetts will hide from an old bird like me," she laughed.

Dexy laughed and tied the letter he had written to her leg. He knew she would scare a sluggett half to death as she would make a tasty meal of them if she could.

And so Falentona left the cave entrance, spread her magnificent wings ready to fly into action. She flew over the mountain range and onward to the village. She could see for miles. It was only dawn and her early flight meant she could be undetected. She spotted Roper's house. Luca' house next door had two guards at the door. It was being watched. She landed silently on the roof of Roper. The letter was attached to her foot. She knew a sluggett would fear a falconette and would not give her any hassle. The two guards had seen her flying around and headed inside to Luca' for cover till she was gone. A sluggett would make a healthy meal for a falconette. They did not want to be eaten and did not suspect the bird, they thought she was eyeing them up for a meal and didn't hesitate to move inside for a bit till she had gone. She waited until they were out of sight and dropped down to the door. She unattached the letter and pushed it under the door with her claws. Roper was not sleeping and heard the noise outside. He ran to the door thinking it might be the children. Opening the door, he saw the falconette.

"It's you?" he said in surprise.

"I have news," she whispered quickly. "Let me in." She added as she ducked inside, looking huge on their small village house. Her feather cold from the morning air stuck up making her even larger.

"How is Ettie?" Roper's wife, Garla cried.

"It's news," he whispered, aware that the village was under watch. Garla gasped.

"She is safe!" he hugged her.

"I must come with you," he said.

"It's too dangerous!" replied Falconette. "You will be seen if you fly with me,"
"Then I shall come alone on foot," he answered.

"You must stay here. The children are safe. I promise you," she was clear and would not move.

"Roper you are getting too old to climb mountains. I don't want you missing too," added his wife.

"I cannot stay here and leave them," he was getting cross.

"But it is for the best. The children are fine. Ettie is well. We will take good care of her," she said trying to reassure them.

"I don't understand, what do they want with the Luca and Ava?" he was confused and wanted answers. "You know he has Ava?"

"They are wanted by the king because they are the heirs to the throne. It's too much to explain now. Luca is the baby born to the Queen Amber years ago. They have been living undiscovered for years," she said.

Roper sat down. It was too much to take in. It also meant that his daughter and friends were in more danger than he had imagined.

"The lost king?" said his wife. "Isn't that just a myth?"

"It is true. Dexy and the outsiders are off to the castle tonight to get Ava from that prison pit. When they return with the queen will shall send more news. That is all I can tell you for now," she said sympathetically.

"Please I can't do nothing!" he pleaded.

"We have been sick with worry," added Garla.

"But there is nothing you can do. If you follow them to the mountains you are only putting them in more danger. Please Roper. You have my word we shall keep them safe!" she said hoping he would not argue.

"Tell her we love her…and Luca too," said Garla seeing it was for the best, they had to stay out and go on as normal for the sake of the children. She squeezed her husband's hand as she spoke; she knew he would have to accept this too.

"Tell her…" he took his time. "I love her too…the moment you have news…"

Falentona interrupted, "We will let you know."

She turned to leave. Roper opened the door and checked for sluggetts.

"It's clear," he said.

She ducked through the doorway and flew up into the air as quickly as she could away from the house, glad of her mission complete. The mountain range looked steamy in the morning dew and she returned to the cave once again to guard her newfound youngsters with her life. And she would.

And so the plans in the tall mountains continued for the rest of the day. Luca and Ettie settled into mountain life getting to know their new companions and home. Ettie felt better from news of her parents. She was glad that they knew she was in the mountains. It was good to hear news of them and know they might worry a little less knowing where she was. They felt their wounds healing with Keto's medicine. He gave them creams for their cuts and juice for their wellbeing. Their strength returned with each passing hour and their scratches from the day before seemed to disappear into nothing. Dexy and the others collected their backpacks and filled them with bits for the journey ahead. They needed salt bags and weapons to prepare for any resistance. They had a busy day and night in front of them.

Chapter 23. The King's Wrath

Ava was restless in the Slug Pit. She had slept very little and was wondering how her son had got on. As she tried to get comfortable on a stone cold floor, she hoped he was in the mountains and consoled herself with the fact that if they had found him, she would have seen him brought there, so he must be safe for now. The floor was a constant battle to master any sort of comfort on. It made her body ache like it was ninety years old. Sleeping here was a skill in itself!

The pit was always noisy with moaning and terrible cries in the darkness. It was a place where madness would take over if you let it in. The weeping was the worst, as it seemed to be so helpless and lost. The prisoners were fed simple porridge type slop it was not a healthy meal. The bowls were filthy and the rations were cold and lumpy, as grey as stone and gritty as the dirt on the ground. Ava had eaten nothing since she had arrived, but knew at some point she would have to find substance from somewhere. Aviras slept mostly or lay staring into the walls. He was quiet. Ava tried to talk with him, she felt so sorry for him.

"Have you managed to eat this stuff?" she asked laughing.

"No, I'd rather die," he answered crossly.

"I guess. They say anything is tolerable once you get used to it," she added helpfully.

"I wouldn't let my dog eat that," he said.

"Yes it looks very...old, doesn't it?" she smiled, pleased to be getting some sentences from the sullen boy.

"I bet the guards can get food in. You know for bribes," she continued with her small talk.

"Do you think?" he seemed to liven up at the thought of this.

"Yeah course. I would be very surprised if that doesn't happen here," she was a wise woman of the world and knew how things worked, even in prisons.

"I have some money," he offered dipping into his pockets to pull out some roonies.

"Keep it quiet though. Don't flash that around," she warned him.

"Sorry, yes I guess, but it could come in useful. I should have thought of that. I think my brain has stopped working since I have been here. Why didn't I think of that?" he said starting to return to his usual self again.

"It's the shock. Your body's way of coping," she answered him.

"Survival, I guess," he added.

"We'll you and me, we are survivors," she felt a motherly kindness towards him, it was nice to feel this in the absence of her son.

Guards could be heard moving around. It was hard to see why but there was definitely new creatures entering the pit. Ava heard Gerrado's voice and shuddered. Was it her son? Had he found him so soon? Her heart almost stopped and she stopped breathing to hear more. The cell railings were being hit by other inmates, they always clanged when visitors arrived. Ava could see Gerrado up ahead. She could not see any boy with him, just other sluggetts. Two were cowering low and on their knees. Another guard was hitting them across their heads and asking questions.

"Silence!" roared Gerrado, his voice ringing out in the pit and everything stopped to a deadly silence. "Listen to these lazy insolent sluggetts. They are not worthy of a role in my army. They shall be punished for not following orders. Returning without the boy was not an option. You have lied and cheated Gerrado? You now pay!" he screeched, waving his arms above his head with fury.

"Sir we did not see the boy, you must be mistaken," one tried to explain in vain.

"I have it on good authority that you let those children run for the woods and made no attempt to chase them. Lazy imbecceles!"

"Please your honour of holiness," cried the other. But they both knew what was coming.

"I 've heard enough lies! In the pit with you both! Throw them in," he ordered two other guards. "...and leave them to rot!"

Ava and Aviras watched and listened hardly breathing. They could both see what was happening over in the other corner of the pit, though it was hard to watch. They other prisoners were also watching from their cells. Everyone watched. Those who had been there long enough knew full well what was coming next. The guards picked up the two trembling sluggetts, scraping them off the floor and dragging them over to the edge of the slurping black tar pit. The first was clasping his hands together and muttering a garbled prayer to himself. The other looked round at the king for a last chance of reprisal. The two were kicked from behind and were somersaulting forwards into the pit. On head first, the other slower and knocking on the wall sides as he went down banging every bit of his body on the side. The pit bubbled and they disappeared quickly into its murky depths, sliding down quickly with ease. Their voices soon silent as the mud slush gushed into their mouths. The drowning sludge quickly eating them up. They were no more. Gerrado yelled, "You'll all end up in there one day! Be glad you're still here!" as he stormed out leaving the pit again. "Hate getting my hands dirty," he muttered to himself in disgust.

Ava and Aviras shuddered. It was a reminder of the king's unmerciless wrath. A harsh reminder of what he did to his enemies. They tried not to dwell on these moments but it was hard and nightmares were never far away from them. They slept uncomfortably in short sessions. The fear was not easily overcome in either of them.

"You ok?" Ava asked when she was awake and saw Aviras staring blankly into the dark coved ceiling.

Aviras nodded but his quietness had returned. His voice was becoming harder to find with every minute he spent there. Ava didn't push him. She understood. She missed her son and her heart ached for him every second, sometimes she thought it would break if she couldn't see him or speak to him again, but she kept bad thoughts down. She knew she had to think only of hope to survive!

Chapter 24. An Enemy Approaches

Bevan arrived. They were expecting him. As ever he was late, but Dexy knew him well enough to anticipate it...

He had finished his duties at the Queen Narla's for the day and headed over to the meeting Dexy had called with urgency.

Bevan was no bigger than a tree stump. He wore round glasses which rested far out on the end of a small wet black nose, his eyes were tiny black coals round and dusty smudges on his fur on the outsides of his eyeholes. His clothes were smart, a little velvet waistcoat and green trousers with a leather belt to hold in his rounded tummy. Bevan appearance did not outwardly show his skill and the brilliant brain he possessed. He pretended to be clumsy. His enemies would always underestimate him and his had been a useful spy for the freedom warriors for years.

He brought with him a map of the palace he had made from memory of his time their working for Gerrado. He knew ways in and out of the Slug Pit. He was here to talk the group through the way in and out of the Pit. He knew how to fight and trick any sluggett. He would be of great use to them now. His knowledge of the castle and his planning skills made him valuable as ever to their plans.

He had been a freedom warrior from the start. Again, his family wiped away in the war, apart from his distant aunt. He was left on his own until he found others. The story of each freedom warrior always started with loss of the loved ones and how they survived.

Dexy, Jax, Gobber, Bevan and Samilt collected their weapons and put on various types of armour for their journey to the castle. Dexy had leather cuffs and belts he wore to protect him. Gobber had his own gear made of thick leaves sewn together. He had always worn this during his time in the forest as a troll. He used it now as a second skin. Jax copied his older brother, they had similar belts and leather ties which protected elbows, shins and their leather waistcoats they always wore.

Bevan prepared rope, tape and salt bags to help with any frisky sluggett; the salt would sting and burn slug skin buying them time when confronted in the pit. They spoke little as their thoughts were on the task ahead. Each had their role to think about in the daunting task ahead.

Luca sat watching them get ready. He thought of his mother. Had they hurt her? How bad was the Pit where she was? He didn't want to imagine. He had only heard stories of the Slug Pit and Gerrado. He remembered he was a king with a reputation for being charming and intelligent but cruel; throwing prisoners and servants into the pit if they displeased him. It terrified Luca to think of his mother at his mercy.

When the final packing was done, Dexy and the group sat down to a hearty meal.

The fire crackled tunes and sent smoky splinters up the chimney like on any other night, but it seemed to know their plight, as it roared with an extra warm glow, with high pitched cackles that were mesmerising. There was tension on each face. They ate, some sat on the floor close to the fire, others sat back on the stools and carves benches in the cave wall. Keto lay in his long seat, which was part of the wall of the cave. It was perfect for his body to lie back in.

The soup was warm for their bellies, hearty energy for what lay ahead. Gobber ate quickly whilst the others were slower. Everyone was quiet and little words were said other than compliments to Keto and Jee Hanna for their cooking. Samlit could hardly eat. He was too jittery with nerves. He pushed his food around his plate for the whole of the meal. Falentona noticed but said nothing, the others were too preoccupied to notice. Luca and Ettie ate quietly still feeling lost and far away from their homes. They knew the outsiders had a big task ahead. It was for them.

When the supper was over they knew it was time to leave. Dexy showed them how to cover themselves in thick leather bandages wrapped around their body, including arms and legs, which acted as protection. They picked up their bags checking the weight was manageable and said their good byes.

"Good luck!" kissed Falentona to each of them with a motherly squeeze.

"We will be and we shall return with Ava!" exclaimed Gobber in a jubilant voice. He was ready for this.

"Good luck," said Luca and Ettie. Luca shook their hands one by one. Bevan winked as he left. Ettie smiled and whispered her 'good lucks'. Jax gave her a small wave, which she cherished and her heart bubbled at his eyes meeting hers. Jee Hanna flew around their heads and kissed each one, leaving some fairy dust over them for luck.

Keto rose from his curved stone seat, which was sculpted into the rock, where he always sat and from his purple robe in his pocket, he handed Dexy a pot, "For wounds if necessary, stops infection; made it fresh today."

Dexy thanked him and put it in his rucksack.

"Keep watch on the children," said Dexy to Falentona. It was never far from his mind that there would be many looking for Luca.

"I shall," she read his fears and took his hand tightly. "We will wait for news. I will keep guard and Keto is here too," she added. (Luca wanted to go with them, he felt man enough but he knew he would have to stay behind, too much if a risk to take. He felt frustrated by it.)

"Bye!" they shouted and began their journey to the castle, ducking through the cave doorway and into the moonlight night.

The air was cold, with the sun gone it hit their ears like stinging bees and they pulled their scarves up to stop the freezing air flowing down their throats, their brisk pace kept their bodies warm. Gobber, Jax and Dexy carried the most. They were the fittest. Samlit and Bevan were smaller so they had smaller backpacks.

Jax waved at Ettie one last time. She had run out to watch from the cave entrance, peering into the night and wondering what it would bring. Jax saw and waved back. He wondered when he would see her again. She was pretty he thought, as he turned back to tread carefully further down the mountain. She smiled back and looking at the stars in the night's sky wished him well.

"You'll be back in no time," said Dexy, noticing his brother's longing looks to Ettie. Jax went red and turned back to hide his embarrassment. The rest of them smiled, remembering young love and how it starts...

"How long to the castle, Dexy?" asked Bevan, getting back to practicalities.

"Four hours if we ride steady," he answered.

"The horses and waiting at the field. We can be there by twelve." He had worked out the journey carefully.

The salt bags weighed them down but they went swiftly and reached the bottom of the mountain in no time. The forest was spooky in the black night. The stars twinkled through the tall leafy trees and a fat blotchy moon smiled on them. They headed north. The forest noises were loud and awake. Owlets wooed and bat birds flew around. They swooped low above their heads. The group were used to them apart from Samlit who was nervous of these creatures and ducked every time one flew by. Birds twitched and hummed their night tunes. The night was full of life!

Under the trees at the edge of the forest the horses were ready. They had been fed in the day. The group unravelled the horses' reigns from the fence where they had been left by Dexy earlier. The five of them were all experienced riders and were glad to be moving forward on their way. They galloped through the night following the trees lined their way. Dexy rode at the front leading. Jax and Bevan were next and Samlit and Gobber rode at the back. The darkness seemed to fade with each gallop and their eyes focussed on the rider in front. They rode on adjusting to the night.

The hour passed quickly. The horses were steady and went briskly through the woodland. They continued North from the mountain to the edge of the Darcorrian boundary till it met the Saccorian swamps where the sluggetts used to live. Now abanndoned and bare. They lived peacefully there for centuries, till the uprising, when Gerrado had led them to war. Most sluggetts enjoyed the swamplands. Some had gone back even after the war. They preferred it to the city life and courtiers were seen as a different breed of sluggett. They were harsher and more like humans. The sluggetts living in the swampland were peace-loving and stayed away from the castle and new life Gerrado had built for them.

Dexy turned and rode back to the group.

"Drink stop?" he asked. It was gladly received.

The group dismounted in the cover of the trees gathering together giving their horses needed water. They were in good spirits and they knew within the hour they would be within the palace boundaries. They all had water bottles and drank enough to stay hydrated for the rest of the journey. It was a chance to check everyone was ok.

"We ride another hour till the path bends into a fork, then we will walk the rest. We are covered by the trees while we ride, after that we are exposed so must keep low," he instructed. "All ok?"

"Sweating like a pig," said Gobber wiping himself with a cloth.

"Yep," said Bevan as he stretched his legs and arms.

"I'm good. Needed that drink," replied Jax.

"Glad of the drink, been a while since I've been on a horse," said Samlit who had stayed at the back and was the least athletic of the group.

"Back on it?" Dexy asked as he finished his drink and climbed back on his horse.

The other followed and prepared for the next stretch. Suddenly a twig broke! It's noise echoed through the quiet forest making them jump.

"What was that?" cried Samlit, swinging round still on the ground, holding tight to his horse.

"Take cover," whispered Dexy, listening intently.

Everyone moved back behind a tree. They bent low and crouched, daring not to move, each pulling their horses tight and turning around to see where the noise had come from. A snapping twig could mean someone was following. Had someone been following them? Their ears listened again for more noise, but nothing came. It unnerved them. The silence grew louder.

"Shall we go on?" whispered Jax to his brother who was close by on alert.

"Wait. Give it a minute," he said keeping his voice low.

The group waited nervously as they peered behind them, ready for an ambush or another sound. The moments passed and nothing more came. Had someone stopped, or had they imagined it? The night quiet again felt wrong.

"You move on. I'm gonna go back along the path just check it out. I'll catch you up," said Dexy.

"You going alone?" asked Bevan cautiously.

"I'll cover you," added Gobber, following behind him.

"I just want to check it out. It could have been a small animal," he replied.

"Be careful. Use the warning sound if you need back up," reminded Jax, not happy for his brother to investigate on his own.

As they talked another twig broke. This time louder. There was definitely someone there.

"We're being followed!" cried Gobber with his hand close to his sword ready for action. He and Dexy were both fine swordsmen and both sensing danger had their hands hovered over their swords, if needed they would pull them out in a second. Dexy continued walking forwards. His eyes bulged wide attempting to see into the dark wooded path in front of him. His hand still hovered, his sword still hanging by the side of his leg.

A figure approached in the distance heading straight towards them. They strained their eyes and held their breath trying to see in the dark.

Gobber had had enough of waiting,

"Show yourself!" he shouted, the shadow kept moving towards them.

Gobber reached for his sword and waved it into the air in front of him, warning of his strength and commitment to use it.

"Who's there?" asked Bevan.

A heavily built man approached. He walked on towards them. They stood frozen waiting for a reply. They could make out a villager.

"It's Roper! Roper Stern, Ettie's dad," came the reply from the dark.

The man walked over and smiled reaching out his hand to shake with Dexy.

"Its ok!" cried Dexy. "I know him."

The sighs of relief were heavy. There nerves rested once more.

"For god's sake man!" murmured Gobber. "Gave us a fright!"

"Sorry. I had to come and find Ettie. I know Falentona said she was safe, but I couldn't sleep and had to try. I saw you a while back and followed until I was sure it was safe. Are you going to the castle?" he asked.

"Yes, to get Ava," said Dexy.

"Need help?" he laughed and looked slightly ashamed that he had given them all a fright.

"We'll you're here now. I guess one more will be useful. Man you gave us a scare!" laughed Dexy with relief.

The others smiled pleased that it was an ally.

"Everyone- Roper Stern, Ettie's dad. Saved our little Jee Hanna from drowning the other night. You can ride with Samilt," he said pointing at the harefoot.

The others greeted him with various hellos.

Relief hung in the night air. It was a friendly face they hadn't expected. Smiling, he shook each one's hand. He was no enemy. He climbed on the back of the horse with Samlit holding the reigns. Roper a much larger being than the small rabbit man, the sturdy horse could take his extra weight for the rest of the journey.

"I couldn't sit at home doing nothing," he added.

They understood. He wanted to help and they were happy to let him join them. They knew he only had his daughter's safety in his mind.

After mounting their horses, they turned back to the path for the castle. Dexy again led at the front, trotting along the path once more. The others followed and the ride continued briskly into the night, the path now less shaded than before as the trees grew sparse and the riders became more exposed, but the stars stayed bright seemed to goad them onwards. It was hard to see far ahead with only moonshine and starry lights guiding them on.

On reaching the forest edge the view of the elegant castle came into sight. They breathed heavily as they rode on sweat dripping under their clothes and sticking to their skin. Suddenly Dexy stopped.

"We dismount here. The horses will be safe here," he explained as the tied them to some fencing. It was time to go on foot.

The horses were tied and grazing in a field till they returned. Marshy fields led up to the castle. Then the grassy castle grounds were ahead. The marshes were thick with mud. Then the drier grass evened out into thicker well kept lawns. Below the castle wall, a stone path curved around for walking in the day. Gerrado kept it neat with his gardeners from the village to trim and tidy. Most sluggetts had some job to do which involved the upkeep of the castle. Gerrado was a proud slug.

Dexy looked ahead at the castle. It loomed like a haunted city behind the large stonewall that protected it. *The last time he had been this close was on the day of the war.* It was only a whisker away now, and his heart thumped harder as he remembered everything it stood for. It always left a sinking feeling in his stomach that rose when he thought of the past…ten years had healed some wounds but not all and not those that were so deep!

The Slug Pit was to the back of the castle. They kept on the western side of it. Bevan had told them of the sluggett working entrance which they would go through, less obvious than the large double wooden doors leading to the Pit. Samlit's legs like jelly but he said nothing, he knew the others would feel it too being this close. Roper was pleased to have something to focus his mind away from his missing daughter. Dexy and Bevan led. The darkness soaked through their skin like a blanket wrapped around them, keeping them safe like an opaque invisible cloak. The torches of light from the large castle walls cast hardly any shadow in the darkness.

"We walk till we get to the back surrounding wall. Then we climb out of view of sluggett guards and we walk down to the pit."

"Sounds easy when you say it like that," laughed Gobber, as he thought it was an impossible task looking at the height of the wall.

"We all know it's not," replied Dexy.

"They won't be expecting us so soon. This is our best chance," said Bevan who knew there was no other safe way in and news of Luca being with them in the mountains would soon filter through to Gerrado and his advisors.

"The sluggetts won't be looking for us. There may be some on the wall, no more than ten for the whole circumference of the castle, so probably only one slug looking in this direction at most. At night the lookouts usually doze off, its common practice and nothing is said," said Bevan.

He had been to the castle many times on errands and knew how it worked. He knew they were a small group and could be in quickly. It was the best chance to storm the pit, maybe their only chance, he thought.

"If we are seen, lights will be lit and we will hear them shouting warnings to the others in the castle. We do not want to see any new lights. I think if we're careful we will get to the walls without being seen," he added.

The half a mile of steep hill to walk up to the wall was done quickly. It was mostly mud and grass underfoot, as they made their way forward keeping low in crouched down shapes, not wanting to draw any unwanted attention.

"Keep together," Dexy instructed as he ran along.

Onwards to the castle, with each step they felt more alert and excited at the prospect of reaching the wall. The danger was more intense. The group moved swiftly. They knew this was the time to be quick. The hill hurt their legs as it unforgiving steepness increased. Their bags got heavier. All had wet backs from the sweat that dripped down their moving bodies. Gobber struggled the most. He was heavy and his breathing the same. Roper was used to it and coped well being the eldest as a fit man all his life working in the village. Dexy and Jax took the hill easily and Samlit jumped up the tufts with the most ease. Bevan's little legs throbbed with the climb but he didn't show it.

Now they could see the castle...no longer a dark shadow as it had been in the woods. Its' stone wall, as real as their hands in front of them all ten times as high as any of them.

Bevan could see one tower on the right with no sluggett in the turrets. He continued to check for torchlight but it never came. He hoped that any guard would be looking out over the eastward city and not over to the west where they came from. The west was really the quieter side of the castle with the city in the east; it had much more to offer. The guards were there to watch over the city, for thieves or looters in market stalls, or grand houses, rather than the woodlands and marshes of the west. Maybe it was even unmanned tonight Bevan thought. He saw no figures in it. He had to assume they were safe.

They continued further and further into the castle grounds.

The castle was quiet. It seemed empty, but they knew it held a court of eighty sluggett servants and over one hundred sluggett guards, at night most would be sleeping, some in the pit, only ten or so, as the pit was quiet at night. Bevan had given them an idea of numbers before they left they had planned their route back in the safety of their cave.

The Slug King lived on the East side furthest away from the pit. He would visit the pit only when he had to and left most of its management to his guards. The head prison guard, a fearsome creature, Tully, would check the key swap overs and day-to-day prison duties, such as feeding prisoners. The prison was a forgotten place used only on the serious occasions, when punishments were being dished out or new prisoners being passed in. More sluggetts were thrown into the Pit than villagers and it was rare though the stories of it happening were always told with great gusto.

Once at the outer castle wall they stayed close in to the edge. They bent low. Glad to reach the wall they moved closer together and packed themselves up against it. It protected them from being seen. All relieved to be at the bottom of the castle.

"Made it," whispered Bevan with a raised and gleeful eyebrow.

Dexy nodded back smiling. He wasted no time. He took off his rucksack to retrieve a large wide rope with a hook tied on the end. Gobber, with the strongest arms threw it over the top of the wall for them to climb up. Dexy passed him the rope. He threw it high and it bumped against the wall. The hook clanged against the masonry. It made them duck again as the it failed to hook over the top boulder and came bouncing back down towards them. The others held their breath. The noise of it rang in their ears. The hook reached the ground and Dexy picked it up from its grassy resting place.

"And again, Gobber," Bevan encouraged him quietly.

Gobber tried again this time it swung over the wall and latched onto the other side. He pulled it taught to check it was tight.

"Ready?" he asked.

Dexy swung his feet up and he grabbed the rope. He started to climb. His legs moved swiftly. He pushed himself up. He moved skilfully. He was used to climbing in the mountains. The wall was no problem for him. The others watched in awe. They followed in turn. They looked like small ants following one by one and the huge grey wall. It took them over ten minutes to reach the top. Dexy reached the top and jumped over and crouched low checking the tower on his right once again. His arms ached violently and his legs pulsed with blood pumping through his body. It was quiet. The others close behind. Everyone felt the strain of the physicality of the climb. Roper's legs had gone to jelly and Bevan wasn't getting any younger. Jax and Samlit were young and fit, so coped better. He wasn't one for heights and had a lot of weight to pull up. He clung to the rope with gritted strength. His hands raw from the pulling and shoulders feeling pulled from each socket. He willed himself onwards. At the top the others saw his weakness was gone and helped to pull him over the last part. All were over the wall. Once inside the wall, Dexy pulled up the rope and wound it back placing it on his shoulder for later. He didn't want to risk it falling or being taken and it was the only rope they had that was long enough.

"Bevan you lead from here," he announced.

Bevan knew the way to the pit along the top galley, which laced the castle wall. Then ducked inside the curved archway of a turret. It gave them shelter from view and a moment to catch their breath. The huddled together and took a moment to inhale before the steps which led to the pit.

"At the bottom we reach the corridor, which leads to the pit entrance. It has two large steel gates. They will have the two guards on the door. There is a sharp bend, so we can sneak up. Gobber is taking one. Dexy and Jax take the other. They carry the keys on their belts we will need a set of keys," explained Bevan who was their knowledge to what lay ahead. The listened carefully to his words and nodded to show understanding. No one spoke after that. They concentrated on the task ahead.

"Have your salt ready to throw to distract them. The salt will sting them and buy us time if we need it," Dexy added.

Bevan continued," We will wait at the entrance while Dexy, Jax and Gobber walk around the pit looking for the cells for Ava. They will use the keys from the guards belts."

Roper was listening intently, catching up. He would help where he could, taking on any sluggetts in the way in the pit. They hoped as Bevan had predicted than numbers would be low.

There was no more time to talk. They moved forwards, conscious of the time they had, staying close to each other in a line as the pathway was narrow and began again towards the steps, with Dexy, Jax and Gobber at the front.

The steps in front of them twisted narrowly round, they were thin stone stairs. It was much narrower than Jax was expecting. He felt trapped in this space. The walls seemed to get thinner and nearer with each step. Their descent was steep. The winding made him dizzy. There were many steps. The darkness made each one lethal.

They kept tight, close to each other, quietly moving to ensure footsteps were unheard. Roper scrapped his sides several times, as he was a large man in the small area. Round and round as the steps twisted. The last turn came before the steps ended and they stopped in a deadly silence to hear for noise and movement of the guards were further along, still out of sight. Bevan still bent low and peered around the corridor wall to see the guard's position.

Two sluggett guards stood on each side of the doorway into the pit, carrying out their night duty as they always did. This was the smaller of the two entrances to the pit. Bevan had chosen this one as the other would have been too obvious and they would have caused too much attention to themselves opening the huge double of the main Pit entrance.

It was not an exciting job and most nights they fought off sleep and stood day-dreaming and leaning. They both were clad in armour and helmets, with swords and keys visible on their belts. One guard was large and stocky, he looked older, the other thin and tall. They looked straight ahead.

Bevan beaconed to Gobber, "We do what we planned, I'll create a distraction while you take out the one nearest, I will go for the one furthest away. We go on my nod," he said quietly but clearly.

Gobber nodded.

Bevan put his hand in his pocket and took out some pebbles. He threw one straight along the corridor towards the guards. The noise of the pebbles made them peer into the grey corridor.

"Rats again?" said Tully the larger of the two.

"Probably," said the other looking at the ground and getting an overhead torchlight from the wall beside him to spread light around where the noise had come from.

The shadow from the light caught the heads of the group and they ducked down silently with breaths held.

"Keep back!" whispered Dexy, desperate for them to remain unseen.

Taking their chance with the stocky guard busy peering into the floor, Dexy, Jax and Gobber rushed out from the darkness, leaping forwards and taking them both to the floor. They reached for their mouths and arms to stop the guards' cries and swiftly took their tape to each guard's mouth and held each arm firmly behind their backs to tie together with strong rope. The guards kicking and screaming but their mouths could not raise an alarm. The tape held their lips together tightly, so no more sounds were heard. They were voiceless.

Bevan ran along to help the binding of the guards. It took a few of them.

"You got him, Jax?" asked Dexy as the wrapped their ropes and taped around the guards.

"Yep, ok" he replied, as the guard tried to kick his feet out, booting Jax in the mouth as blood burst out.

"I got him," added Gobber helpfully.

They all took many blows from the fists of the guards, but held strong with Jax, Dexy and Gobber binding them like clever spiders might to flies caught in their webs. They bound them until their arms and legs were still.

"Good work," said Dexy.

"They're secure," said Gobber checking over the tape on both sluggetts.

"Good work," added Bevan as the others smiled and knew it was the first of many parts of their plan completed.

"Take their helmets," said Bevan. "Dexy and Jax are first in, so they should wear them," he added.

So, as the tightly held sluggetts they were tied and placed both sitting on the damp stone floor, Dexy and Jax removed their helmets and placed them on their heads, to make them look more like the guards, to buy precious seconds when entering the pit. The guards wriggling like wormy cocoons on the floor but bound tightly by the rope, they struggled in vain. Gobber took their swords and handing one to Jax and keeping the other. The noise each of them made with a whimper through the tape was minimal. Dexy whipped the keys from the belt of the older one and moved over to unlock the gates at the entrance to the pit. His heart beating faster again, he wondered what would greet him on the other side. The smell rose as he covered his mouth and nose and entered in.

Chapter 25. Freedom's Choice

In a pit of darkness always look up to the light!

Dexy pushed the wooden gate open. The smell hit. Torches on the walls fought the darkness but lost their battle to shed light. He peered looking for evidence of bodies. The only sound was the ooze from the hungry pit, in the middle of the prison oozing bubbling threatening gulps. Guards in the shadows mostly slumped and sleeping kept a sort of watch. The prison cells were dark and damp, small and bare. Life had shrivelled to dust. Only forgotten souls lived here.

Shivering from the change in temperature, surrounded by stone and mud, Dexy, with Jax following, entered the pit. The shadow of cells curved in front of them. Waves of dust hung in the air. The dusty breath of each prisoner- a reminder of lost hope. The smell of rot lingered. Prisoners scuffled in the Pit bent over, twisted, turning into creatures themselves shadows of hopelessness. Most died within two years' life expectancy in the Pit was short.

Dexy and Jax hoped to be quick. They moved with speed in their shoes. The guard's stolen helmets were heavy as they dashed, shaking fingers unlocking each cell they came to with the keys they had taken earlier. Seventy or more cells lay ahead of them, prisoners in each. Sluggett guards with two torches either side of their holding points spread out along the circular pit. There were thirty guards on duty tonight Dexy estimated. He checked cells and guards and prisoners as he continued to turn the cold keys in the locks and leave doors open for prisoners to move outside. Jax walked beside him, helping with every door, speaking quietly to sleepy prisoners urging them to get up and leave. Cries of confusion sent his blood cold along with the fat tailed rats that scurried over their feet. Some were asleep and hardly stirred as Dexy and Jax whispered to usher them out.

None of the guards raised an eyebrow to see Jax and Dexy moving around. Some slept, some played cards. No one took much notice of what was happening as nothing ever happened in the pit at night. They assumed it was other sluggett guards on duty looking in on prisoners for the night. The helmets hid their faces. The guards weren't looking. It was night as any other with the cries and moans of night, like the last.

In order to breathe Dexy covered his mouth with his elbow. The smell of putrid mud from the pit felt unbearable like a giant bath of death. It bubbled, a fountain of disease. A jagged mountain covered in lifeless rot. Suffocating mud took most victims who fell into its deep belly. The stomach of the Pit belched with the heat rising in steaming glory from its surface and spreading its rank death tones. Prisoners had seen many a friend or rotten sluggett hurled into it with one word from Gerrado.

As they moved round the cells looking for Ava, other prisoners left their cells as the freeing continued. Dexy and Jax whispered to them to get up and leave. The system was working. They kept moving. They went to more and more, in seconds more prisoners were emptying their cells. The tension eased with every release but Dexy was tight with apprehension at finding Ava. Jax was a good companion, he rounded them up and grabbed their frail bony arms towards the doors, disbelief which slowed them momentarily from the realisation of freedom which brought life back to them. Rushing out of their cells as fast as their skinny legs would take them. Skin and bone knew freedom too.

"Go, go, go!" cried Jax behind them. He shadowed them and kept so low. It was hard to pick him out at all.

Roper and the others watched and waited from the safe distance by the entrance, knowing it would be too dangerous for them all to go in at once.

"Leave, you're free to go," Dexy whispered quietly as he beckoned the prisoners out of their cells. Jax shook the sleeping ones awake.

Prisoners woke and left their cells, dazzled. It was quiet at first and looked nothing beyond normal. But more and more started walking out into the path around the pit, towards the wooden gated exit. Jax and Dexy continued to move as fast as they could.

Guards who had taken little notice at first, started to look now to see what was happening slowly realised something was amiss. They could see prisoners getting up and leaving their cells, but they didn't know why. The crowd of walking escapees became bigger as more were set free. Dexy continued to unlock cells one by one, in the disguise of a sluggett guard. His calm manner had helped the illusion. It seemed nothing was wrong, yet something was wrong. Tannot one of the guards felt it. He looked over at prisoners walking out and suddenly he knew this was not right.

"Did Flutts mention anything about prisoners being let out tonight?" asked one of the sluggetts from a turret in the North side.

"No, nothing was said...why?" said Moxan.

"Just I can see Marrot opening cells. I wondered what it was for?"

"Bit late to be opening cells at this time of night?" said Moxan.

"Yes it is," paused the other sluggett.

Worried, the sluggetts got up and fixed themselves ready to investigate the untimely releasing of prisoners. Tannot wondered to himself who would have authorized such a thing. He had heard nothing. Was there to be an evacuation of prisoners? Gerrardo would have sent orders to everyone.

Starting to worry he hurried the others, "Go and see what's going on!" he cried.

The guards found their way over nearer to the escapees. They realised it was unauthorized and their negligence hit them in the gut. The only thing to do was to try to push prisoners back into their cells. It was difficult. Many prisoners, though weak, outnumbered the few guards. They tried to keep back prisoners and get them into their cells again.

"Stop! Stop there! Who let them out?" cried Moxon to another.

"Get back in your cell!" Flutts cried as they tried to win order.

"Back! Get back!" Five more joined in.

Sluggetts voices could be heard, Jax and Dexy continued undisturbed by the confusion and not wanting to waste a moment. The prisoners seized their chance. They may have been weak but they had waited years for this and they were ready to fight with everything they had, for a chance of escape.

Freed prisoners headed to the large wooden doors on the other side of the Pit. It was the bigger of the two entrances. The doors were locked with a huge plank across. Three of the stronger prisoners lifted up the plank. The door now pushed open by another ten prisoners working together as a team. The sluggetts could do little but watch in horror to see the doors being opened at night leaving prisoners free to run. They knew Gerrado would not spare any of them who had let such a thing happen. But what could they do with tens of prisoners heading past them?

In the confusion, Dexy, Jax and Bevan quickly made their way further, sweating in the heat. Most guards were headed for the door with most of the prisoners. Dripping, Dexy suffered the most as his concentration to open cell doors with his keys had to be fast. His nerves jangled in his fingers and his hands sweated with the keys. Jax helped when he could, trying to ignore the gulping slurping pit to the side of them. It spat up muddy bubbles and gases with venom. Remembering to keep close to Dexy, he swung cell doors open as Dexy unlocked and helped Bevan, who cried to each prisoner to get up and get out! The steam rose and putrefied the air. The smell from it like rotting rat bones and dead mice tails. Their legs pulsed on with purpose as they continued through the Pit to open more and more cells.

Dexy shook the keys. They were getting round the pit at a fast pace. He was looking for Ava, hoping they would see her soon as he unlocked each cell door one after the other. His hot clammy hands clumsy as the keys slipped in them.

When sluggetts approached Bevan and Jax batted they away. Most seems to be preoccupied with getting prisoners back into their cells, but it was useless. Jax was pushing each metal bar door open wide and ushering out prisoners, pointing to the exit, for those too unsure to know.

"Go! Go!" he cried to them, pushing them out into the path towards to way out.

Some prisoners who slept were shaken awake by fellow prisoners-

"Wake up! We're free! Run! Come on!"

Prisoners stared with incredulous doubt as they reached their bars and found their cell open. They moved out with looks of amazement.

Dexy could see that all this confusion was helping them get further. He was so sure that Ava must be here. He had heard she had been taken into the Pit, so where was she? The sluggetts still could not work out who was freeing prisoners.

"Go! Move! You're free!" he cried at them, as they grabbed at him to say words of thanks for a split moment before moving onwards to their freedom.

"That way!" pointed Jax to help the more disorientated sleepy ones, still moving quickly round with every second.

The small trio worked well together.

The prisoners piled out of their cells, some disorientated at first, but then heading for the exit of the gates.

Falling over each other, sluggetts tried to push them back, with little success. Some fought hand to hand with prisoners to keep them from escaping, but this took energy and more prisoners were running past than being held back.

The pit duty for a sluggett usually meant endless hours of sleep and giving food to prisoners. But today they were wrestling and fighting. None of them knew who was freeing prisoners and why?

Each had their own section, a small turret inside the large caved pit walls. Their turrets were bigger than some cells. The higher up the guard in rank, the bigger his turret. It was cosy and a guard had a comfortable night in his own little place. Now all turrets had been abandoned and the sluggetts were running around the cells and the pit in bewilderment. They began to move down to the pit level on the path. They could see something was wrong. Disorder was growing. Prisoners ran from every direction. The watched at first in shock, as they saw prisoners seep out of their cells, like moving ants.

More prisoners began to run into the circular corridor and towards the double gates that had held them in with no hope for so long. They thought nothing of the sluggetts behind them, who might try and stop them. These prisoners were prepared to fight to the death for their chance of freedom. This was hope, more than they had had in years!

"We're free!" some said to each other.

"Run!" others instructed.

It was becoming more chaotic by the minute.

They moved quickly to the gates, causing the sluggetts confusion as to what to do for the best- pull in the prisoners or find the rebels? They couldn't see what had happened to free the prisoners, but the more prisoners who entered the walkway, the less chance they had of stopping them escape.

Roper, Samlit and Gobber came through running against the tide of freed prisoners who were taking their first steps towards freedom. Samlit took his position behind a rock. He shot arrows at anyone getting too close to Dexy. He could do this well from the small indent in the wall and the rock gave him more protection. The other two ran on.

Others prisoners seeing cells being unlocked were banging and shaking their cell gates crying for Dexy to come with his keys. He was opening as many as he could faster and faster but where was Ava?

He abandoned opening and ran fast looking into every cell, peering to see who the prisoners were.

"Ava!" Ava!" he called out.

"Let us out! Let us out!" cried prisoners.

It was cruel to stop unlocking doors but he worried that time was running out. The screams from the next set of locked prisoners rang in his ears like screeching birds. It was horrible, but Dexy moved around the pit frantically looking for Ava, peering into each cell. He knew there was only a small amount of time before the Slug King would hear of the invasion send reinforcements. He couldn't afford to waste time. Ava had to be found and everything else was secondary till then. The rest of the prisoners moaned and banged on the bars of their cells as Dexy fled past looking in for the queen.

Gobber caught up with Dexy. He spat blood from his mouth, he had bitten his cheek. He batted sluggetts off with his sword, keeping Dexy free from attack and free to look for Ava. Dexy's freedom to move quickly was paramount to the success of their mission. They were to protect him at all times so that he could unlock Ava's cell. Sluggetts moved in. Some fierce and fast, Gobber wasted no time in batting them to the side like flies into the air! Some fell so far they rolled down into the pit itself. Others cried high- pitched screams as they were prodded out of the way.

Jax fought back too. His skill with a sword from hours of practice with Dexy and used now with athletic precision to slice through any sluggett who got too close.

Their bodies gooey and soft on the inside, once the epidermis of their grey skin had been sliced. They fell and oozed with clear liquid.

"Arghhh!" cried wounded sluggetts.

Ava was awake. She had heard the commotion and seen prisoners emptying from their cells on the other side of the pit. Stood at the bars she tried to see more, but it was still too far away to see. She was on the furthest side from the entrance. It was hard to tell who had arrived and what they were doing, why they were freeing prisoners, even when she tried to look as far out as the bars on her cell would let her.

She looked over to Aviras who was sleeping and shouted,

"Wake up Aviras something is happening. Wake up!"

The lump of prisoners was growing a battle struck up between guards and prisoners. The noise become louder as the cries of prisoners increased with every second. The sluggetts were in chaos, away from their posts and running in every direction to try and put a stop to the escaping mass. It was hard to tell who was winning or what exactly was happening.

Roper and Samlit were lost in the crowd. Dexy was up ahead the furthest and Jax had kept up with him covering him.

Dexy was making his way closer to her.

Ava squinted and pushed her head as far as it would go her cheeks pressed against the bars. She still had no idea what was causing all the madness. But as he ran nearer his outline became clearer and she saw Dexy heading towards her. She waved out of the bar, just as all the other prisoners were doing, grabbing and scratching at his arms and legs as he ran past. She called him over till he was in hearing distance. Dexy saw! It was! It was Ava! At last! He called her and ran to her.

"Ava!" he shouted in disbelief.

"Dexy! Here! Here!" she just kept calling.

"Ava!" he cried as he rubbed his eyes for more clarity.

"In here!" she yelled again.

With all the noise Aviras was stirring too. Ava looked back to see him waking and went to shake him further to get him up.

"Wake up! Wake up! We are getting out!" she cried to him with tears welling in her eyes.

His grey eyelids opened to see what was so urgent.

"Get up!" she continued yelling as she went back and forward from the bars and checking Dexy's progress.

"Get ready to run!" she cried grabbing his face and making sure he had heard.

"We head for the entrance, don't stop till you're out!" Dexy instructed them as he unlocked their cell, his hands shaking with excitement as he pulled them out.

Aviras looked stunned and didn't speak, but he ran with them. They wasted not a second and felt their legs wobbling as they moved into the crowd, jumping past some as they fell to the floor, pelting over the bodies and bedlam.

"Come on!" yelled Dexy at Aviras.

As they ran along Dexy pulled Ava at times, dragging her out of harm's way. Aviras kept up only just. He ran and ran, his sleep from moments earlier a distant memory. His heart pumped and he pushed anyone out of the way who blocked his escape.

Roper, Bevan and Jax also pushed and ran past. They would strike any nearby sluggett and making a clear path for the others behind. They led the battle. They cleared the way.

Samlit was still hidden crouched down in an empty turret. He had a bow and arrow that he used to target dangerous sluggetts who got too close to his friends. With his ears back, he kept out of sight and close to the wall. He shot arrows with great accuracy. He could fire safely if anyone got too close. He did it well. Arrow after arrow hitting the target. The unsuspecting sluggetts fell like broken birds with their wings clipped. No one got close to Dexy and the queen while he was here.

Dexy, Jax, Ava and Aviras carried on running, heading for the exit. The gates were back on the other side of the pit. They had to keep running. Sluggetts appeared from nowhere, there seemed more than ever. Ava threw them off as they launched at her whilst Dexy batted them away with his sword. Samlit kept his aim. He placed an arrow in the thigh of one who had grabbed Ava's shoulder. He let go again clutching his leg and crying in pain. It helped them, now closer to the exit.

"Gotcha!" he said, congratulating himself, as the sluggett stumbled in pain. Samlit fired again. Sluggetts fell in front and behind. They all went down.

Dexy watched for Ava. He couldn't let her out of his sight. Samlit's arrows would help to protect them to a point. Up ahead there was a large clump of sluggetts and prisoners fighting. The only way to avoid them was to move closer to the bubbling pit. The edge of it nearer than ever now. It spat out like an angry dragon. Its muddy bubbles splattered on anyone too close, burning skin and hair. The smell was unbearable.

As they moved nearer, Ava felt the heat of it and her skirt was sprayed with hot mud as it piped out more heated gloop. She sweated from the heat. They all did. Dexy's shirt was ringing wet, he could feel the sweat running down his legs and arms. The heat an enemy too. Ava made sure her footing was not too close to the edge. Aviras went with them. He was wide awake now and moved quickly. Dexy guided them around the bottle-neck of prisoners. He didn't like being so close to the pit's edge but it was necessary to stay away from the crowd of fighters. The pit closer as it oozed it's steamy warning.

They kept on. The fear of falling ever close as they ran.

Roper, Bevan and Gobber fought up ahead near to the exit. Most of the prisoners and sluggetts were here. They had become a mash of bodies. The sluggetts were gathered near to the exit gates. It was a way of stopping the escaping prisoners. They swung their swords at anyone who got too close. They took out several prisoners at a time. Those who got close to the exit threw themselves at the gates to get past. Many did. Others were cut down. The sluggetts did not move. Some were injured but six or so stood strong with their weapons. The prisoners were powerless to fight back with no equipment. They fought with bare hands and grabbed anything they could to throw at guards, rocks and stones. Some hurling themselves over the gateway and into the castle grounds ahead.

Samlit helped many of them with his arrows. He could pick out a sluggett and aim. More prisoners pushed forwards. More sluggetts arrived from the other side of the pit to help. A dust ball appeared above them, a mark of the fight to escape.

Gobber looked back to see how far away Dexy, Jax and Ava were from the doors, having gone to the open doors where prisoners were running out. Here he waited for the others and helped topple sluggetts, sweeping their feet from under them, swiping with his baton. Many of them had been injured and had stopped fighting to look at their wounds. There were less and less to worry about and the prisoners were getting free. He could see Jax was closest. He ran ahead to clear the way for them all. He made sure frisky sluggetts were taken out.

"We all here?" he called to him.

"Yes, they're behind!" Jax called as he met his friend.

He helped him slice down sluggett enemies. The two waited eagerly for Dexy to appear with Ava.

"Over there," shouted Jax as he saw Dexy in the distance from the corner of his eye, still swinging his sword fiercely to warn a guard who got too close.

"Can't see!" shouted Gobber who was busy with two sluggetts banging their helmets together.

"By the pit! I guess it will take them a few more minutes to get round," he added.

"I'll go and help them," cried Bevan.

"No! We need you here!" shouted Gobber, he was worried about holding off the sluggetts it was getting harder and they were tiring.

"Ok, what about Samilt? He could go?" he asked, trusting Gobber's opinion.

"Yep we can spare him for now. I just need man power here!" he added.

"Yep you're right!" replied Bevan.

"Samilt!" cried Jax, knowing he was closest to the harefoot creature.

"Samilt! Go help Dexy with Ava. They're over by the pit! They need to come in closer. They're being held back and are too close in!" he bellowed.

Samilt's big ears heard him.

The harefoot jumped up, springing and leaping over the crowds with his long rabbit legs. He could get to places quickly like this. Jax waved his arms rapidly pointing in the right direction. Samlit hurdled past, like a large jumping flea. Dexy saw him heading towards them, frustrated at being stuck by the pit held back by two sluggetts who were trying to push them back.

A weak Ava ran on but slower than before. She had eaten very little since arriving in the pit. She tried to move faster but hadn't much strength. Samlit took Ava's arm and pushed her forwards. Aviras now ahead of them. Dexy cleared the way, keeping guards at bay he slashed at anyone who got near.

"We're nearly there! Keep going!" he hollered at them both to encourage the weary two.

They both nodded. Samlit swung punches out at any sluggett who got near to Ava. Aviras ran ahead. He hadn't seen two sluggetts turn and run towards him. They flew into him knocking him to the ground. Stones embedded into his knees as he fell. Crawling around he tried to stand up but they knocked him down again. Samlit let go of Ava to help the boy; he could see he wasn't strong enough to defend himself against the two sluggetts. Dexy turned and came back to help. The two of them pulled on the backs of the sluggetts flinging them off the boy. They tossed them away from him. Only meters away the two maddened sluggetts scrambled up and launched back at the boy. In seconds the meaner sluggett swung his sword at Aviras. Stunned, he jumped backwards out of the way, but it was too far... the ground beneath his feet gave way, stones rushed down into the pit below and Aviras had been flung backwards with them. He looked like a leaf floating in the air as his body fell into the pit!

"Grab him!" cried Dexy lunging forwards to grab the boy.

"Noooo!" Ava could see him fall rushing to him towards the edge of the bubbling mud pit.

"He's gone!" said the sluggett with certainty turning to find another victim.

Samlit jumped into the air with great power in his legs. He caught the boy's arm and pulled him in, though he was too far down to pull out of the Pit. Aviras held on and they both fell, scrambling for the edge of the pit to hold onto. Aviras grabbed onto a lower ledge and climbed up the rocks that provided some footing on the sheer muddy walls of the pit. They had fallen a many feet down, but Samlit clung onto Aviras, till his grip was tight on the wall. Clumps of soil came away in their hands as they climbed, but they held on to what they could with the pit spitting beneath them, ready to take them.

Ava called down to them,

"Hang on!"

"We're gonna climb back up!" called Samlit pulling Aviras up the wall of the Pit with all his arm strength with renewed determination.

The sluggetts couldn't believe the boy had been saved. Each of their mouths dropped open to see the boy saved. They were sure he was gone to the Pit. Dexy looked at them in fury. He swung his sword back and forwards with clean brisk sweeps. They inched backwards and moved out of the swords way. Dexy bit his lip as he swung, keeping them away as Samilt pulled Aviras to safety and they climbed up to a small ledge in the pit's wall.

The two sluggetts lunged forwards, Dexy took one clean swipe and his sword wiped right through them both. They collapsed on the floor and goo oozed out onto the ground by Dexy's feet. He had no remorse for either of them.

Ava bent over and called. There was so much hot steam it was hard to see. Her face dripped with melting heat as she peered into the chasm below. Aviras grabbed at a soil, which made the wall. He was pulling himself up. It was hard to grip. There was nothing to hold onto. His body dripped with sweat and tears rolled like bits of hot water down his cheeks. The boy was strong and he got himself onto the floor of a higher ledge, with Samlit still holding onto him. It was still too far for Dexy or Ava to climb down and help them.

Dexy had joined Ava at the Pit's edge.

"Where is he?" Dexy asked.

"He's on a ledge bit further down," answered Ava.

"Can we reach him? What d'you think Samlit?" asked Dexy, knowing the harefoot's ability.

"I can hold him," said Samlit feeling his paw slipping away from Aviras hand with every second. He knew it was going to push him to his limit, but what choice was left.

"Do you want the rope around you?"

"No time," said Samlit as he leapt down into the pitted bath of hot muddy bubbling sludge, joining Avira on the ledge.

Samlit caught the edge. He was next to Aviras now.

"Hold onto me. I will jump up. If you grab on we can reach the ledge," he instructed.

In the meantime, Dexy turned to Ava.

"The minute they reach the top, we get out of here, ok? You run to the gates, don't stop till you're out," he said sweat polishing his teeth now.

She nodded, knowing she had to move and standing still was costing them valuable time.

Samlit leapt up, with Aviras on his back. Aviras was pushed into the air. In front of him the top of the pit was close enough to grab out and reach the ledge. Bending over carefully Ava held onto his wrists and began to pull him out. As soon as he was halfway out, the harefoot clung onto him and Dexy and Ava pulled continued to pull. It took seconds for Aviras to be dragged out. His leg came over the top and he pulled himself up and onto the ground. As he did, Samlit had lost his grip and let go of as the boy had risen over the edge. Samlit fell back.

"Noooo!" cried Dexy watching with complete dismay, as he threw his hands behind his head in frustration, then crouched back down to shout more instruction to his friend.

"No! I'll get Samlit!" he reassured.

"You two run now!" he ordered Ava and Aviras. Dexy was fearful of time and reinforcements arriving.

Samlit scrambled up the sidewall of the pit. His large hare feet clawing into the sidewall mud giving him grip with his claws, as the mud flew away from the wall unable to hold the hare.

"Samlit, I can pull you from here," cried Dexy as he reached into the pit, his finger stretching down to the little hare.

"Thanks man!" cried Samlit reaching up, sweat pouring from his large floppy ears as the ground fell away from him.

Fresh with a surge of adrenalin, Dexy pulled using only his arm. His veins pumped out with the strain as the hare was pulled up through the air.

Finally, he clasped the top of the pit, and held on with his face down in the mud he knew he was safe again. Feeling the cold flakes of dirt on his face he rejoiced that he was on solid ground. His insides felt like they had been stretched to here and eternity, but he ignored the pain as his eyes filled with tears of joy. Dexy reached for him and pulled him to his feet and hugged his furry friend.
"Let's get out of here," he said handing Samilt a small knife and taking his own sword ready for what lay ahead. "Go everyone go!' he cried.

As soon as they were back at the top of the pit, they ran out towards the main doors following the rest of the prisoners. All of the others were ahead now they were heading through the castle. The steps lead up to the main hall. It was dark as prisoners ran through banging into tables and chairs around the edge of the hall. From the main hall they could escape into the courtyard and through the castle walls into the city. Everyone ran towards the city; it was their way out of the castle.

An arrow flew through the air hitting Roper in his shoulder. He yelped in pain. Blood poured down his arm but he kept running.

Everyone ran. Roper and Bevan kept together and running through the main hall and onwards to the market stalls keeping low and unseen. Jax and Aviras were well ahead of Dexy. Roper had slowed down with his shoulder pouring blood. Bevan pulled him forward giving him momentum.

Dexy had been looking out for Ava but she had been lost in the crowds. It was impossible. She was nowhere to be seen. She had run on with the others but separated. Two guards had spotted her and grabbed her into a corner. Her screams muffled by their hands over her mouth as she was whisked away out of sight.

The night was long and the stars led the prisoners and Dexy through the city market stalls. Sluggetts flowed but didn't stop many as they surged forward with determination. They wanted their freedom more than sluggetts could stop them. The city was crawling with prisoners escaping like ants down into the city and down beyond to the freedom of the villages and fields where their families lived. It was a dash to the end. Roper was losing strength fast but he kept going. Dexy caught him and Bevan up and helped carry him forward.

The freedom warriors continued. Samlit aching but legs pumped on. Aviras and Jax were the youngest and fittest and escaped far ahead of the other. They stuck together, but they had lost Ava. The prisoners and Aviras were free and making their way out of the castle view and into the safety of the city and away to wherever they had one had a home. The freedom warriors surged on, but knew their mission had failed and they would be going back to the mountains, they called home, empty handed.

Ava scraped her fingers down the face of her attacker but it wasn't enough to save her. They two guards pulled her round into the side, out of the way of the surging prisoners who were escaping forwards. She was led back to the cells and placed under guard. Four sluggetts watched her cell.

Gerrado would be pleased with those who had saved her and there was no shortage of volunteers to guard her cell and claim some reward in the fiasco of the Slug Pit prisoner escape.

"We could get a commendation for this," said Jutta with glee as they watched Ava in back in her cell.

"Maybe, or still thrown into that pit when Gerrado sees what's happened. Reckon he's lost about a hundred prisoners tonight. He won't be happy!" said Flan.

"Were all for it! Saving the queen could save us, if we're lucky!" said Marl.

"Surley not hundred gone?" replied Jutte.

"Flaxon thought so!" replied Marlon.

"No idea what happened?" Amac looked dismayed.

"It was that freedom warrior gang, gotta be," answered Jutte.

"Never thought they were real," said Amac.

"Oh there real alright. Real as you and I," finished Jutte.

"Well at least we got the queen back." Said Amac.

"Fristly don't let Gerrado hear you calling her a queen, or you'll be in that pit faster than you can say it. And secondly, let's see, knowing Gerrado, he's gonna be livid. I've seen him flung us sluggetts in the pit for as much as a sneeze out of place, do you think he's gonna let us off on tonight's fiasco? Don't count on it." said Jutte.

"He's right. Do you think we should run for it back to the slug swampland outside the city? You know, not take the chance?" said Marlon.

"He'd sniff us out," answered Jutte. "If we stay, we got some chance of living. If we go we're definitely dead sluggetts!"

Gerrado was in his bed chamber having a sleepless night. His twiddled and turned. His grey toes flexing as he tied to sleep. Maybe he knew something was amiss. He tossed and turned and wondered if he could hear noises more than other nights when the wind howled through the castle walls. He tossed and turned and threw bedsheets on and off in annoyance.

~~

Weeks passed by as warmer nights set in. The villagers thought less frequently about the boy and the mother who were no longer lived in the village. Luca and Ettie became used to the routines of mountain life, the fetching and carrying of food. They would race up the mountain as their fitness increased. Jee Hanna would watch Luca like a wide-eyed bear, taking in his every move. Jax and Ettie grew closer. Each enjoying being together more every day. Aviras tried to fit in, but knew he found it hard to be friendly and was always jealous of the way the others got along. He scowled most days and hardly cracked any smiles, except maybe for Gobber jokes at times.

Ava endured the pit, hoping one day for another attempt at rescue. Pleased that her son was free but missing him daily. She grew thinner and thinner as time crawled by. The dirt ingrained into her skin and hair making her scratch till she bled.

Dexy visited Marcus every three days. He watched him slowly getting used to him. He sat with his friend for hours while Marcus whittled his carvings. Dexy would talk about the old times hoping it would help Marcus in some way. He studied his face for signs of improvement or recognition, but they never came.

Gerrado continued to dine with Queen Narla. His regular visits becoming more and more of a drain on her patience, but he expected her attention.

Life continued... sun down, moon on, sunrise, moon glow.

The nights and days fell and rose with the patience and passing of time.
It gave hearts of all time to heal and wake, or break and die,
but life never stopped not for one, or a thousand broken hearts.

And so, their lives became their own journey,
Each with their own thoughts,
but all had the same dream, and that alone held them together.

Chapter 26. A Favour from a Queen

Dexy walked up the steps to the Queen's large castle. He hands clammy and top lip sweated. He knew he had come to her door with a favour to ask. If she refused, he put Ava in more danger. The risk was worth it he hoped.

Narla had no idea Dexy was on his way to her. She had not seen Dexy for years. He was an outsider and their paths never crossed. Her thoughts of him were never far away. She knew he was in the mountains living as he must. The days when they would meet in the woods and share hours were long gone, of course, she still remembered. Things had changed after the war. Nothing was the same and everyone changed. Too much had happened. His future no longer involved her. She had accepted this, their days together seemed from another life.

Bevan answered the door.

He knew of the plan. He was expecting Dexy. His clumsy butler role served him well at the castle, but to Dexy he was a Freedom Warrior of the finest calibre. Bevan showed little sign of knowing Dexy and continued to led him into the hall. He told him to wait while he went for the Queen. She would be surprised to see Dexy but would always accept his visit. He counted on it.

"I will announce you. Wait here," said Bevan, hoping the Queen was in a good

mood. It was Dexy who assured him she would see him so he asked no questions.
"My lady, you have a visitor. A woodsman calls himself Dexy," Bevan sounded as nonchalant as he could.

The queen turned to him as if she had misheard. Her stomach turned a somersault it was not what she had been expecting. Her heart felt a blade of ice slice into it, as it always did when she heard his name. Dexy was the past she did not expect him. She said quietly,
"Tell him to wait in the drawing room."
"As you wish, my Lady," Bevan knew this was a good sign for she had not turned him away.

With thoughts racing as to why he was here, she rushed to the dressing table and brushed her hair, ruffled at the news of him. She knew he would not come to see her if it wasn't important. She could not think why he would see her, it was business that was all, just business. He must need her help in some way. She would help him. She knew before he asked.

As she walked down the beautiful wooden staircase in the hallway she imagined how he would look. It was five long years since she had seen him. She walked slowly her legs trembled. The drawing room door was open slightly, she could see his strong back and tall figure. She took a moment to breath and took in the sight of her true love for the first time in years. She looked outwardly calm inside she was not.

"Hello," she said quietly and smiled. Her eyes welled with a tear but she blinked it away. He would not appreciate tears from her.
"Narla," he replied.

Some moments passed as they looked at each other hardly daring, for fear of what it might tell them. His green eyes were as they had been but he looked older and tired, not the carefree man she had known. The moment went by.

"What do you want?" she asked.

"I know this is a surprise,"

"You are always welcome, you know that," she smiled. "How are the mountains?" she added.

"They are comfortable enough for my simple needs," he laughed.

"A man of simple needs. You don't change," she replied.

"And you? Are you well?" he asked nervously.

"I am, well.".

"That is good. You look well." He paused. "I need your help," Dexy clenched his hands knowing she might not appreciate his question.

"Please sit down," she sensed his nerves.

She sat on the chair and looked towards the window at the green mountains which she often watched and thought of him.

"I need to ask you to do something for me," he said.

"You can always have my help you know that," she unsure of what help she could be to him.

"It is help with… our cause…the freedom warriors. I will understand if you don't want to help us," he added.

"I have no allegiances to anyone but myself. If I can help you I will," she said.

"It could be dangerous," he warned.

"Tell me and then I will decide if I can help. You always were a dangerous man to know," she smiled again.

"I need you to speak to Gerrado, to persuade him to give one of his prisoners to you. You could have the queen, his prisoner here," he said cautiously.

"I don't understand. Why would he do that?" she asked.

"I want you to speak to him. I want you to tell him, you have heard that we will be back to find her at the pit. Make him see it will be safer for him to give you the prisoner. Convince him, we will be looking for her at the Slug Pit and if she is with you out of the way, she is safer. It will be useful for him if he can keep her here. It will make him think she is safer here with you. We need to get her out of the pit. We tried once already and failed. I need to get her out."

The queen listened. She had heard the news that the old queen had been captured and an attempted rescue had failed. She knew what he was asking her.

"So you want me to persuade him to give the Queen to me?" she nodded. "I see."

"I know," he stopped and looked into her eyes.

"You know you are asking a lot?" she filled in his silence.

"You were the only one I could ask," he pleaded wondering if she would ever agree to him after what he had done.

"You are asking me to betray Gerrado. What do I tell him when the queen is rescued? You don't think he will be suspicious? He may consider me an ally, but he'll have no qualms about killing me if he thinks I've betrayed him," she added.

"You can say it was leaked by the sluggetts that she was there. We can protect you. I will protect you. I wouldn't ask if there was any other way," he said.

"...and you knew I would help," she finished his sentence.

He had only hoped she would, but as she spoke he saw how much she was prepared to do for him and he found himself back in a moment when they were alone years ago he wondered how he had ever given her up; her kindness and her strength were as strong as ever.

"I will help you. I have put up with Gerrado and his visits for a long time. It will be good to help. I will persuade Gerrado to give the Queen to me. I will play the curious Queen who wants to get to know another queen."

She understood he had come for the cause not for her but she would help him.

Bevan appeared. He had listened at the door, his timing as always impeccable.

"Bevan Hislop at your service, Freedom Warrior 10," he added.

"Bevan will help you in any way he can. He will protect you. He is one of our best," said Dexy.

"So I see," she said. "Not the clumsy butler you would have me believe?" she laughed as she saw him differently.

"Only when required," laughed Bevan.

And so Dexy's had his plan to get the Queen out to safety another way. Only the three of them knew about it. That was how it would stay for now.

"I will be in touch," he said as he went to touch her arm. Her hand wavered. He brushed rather than clasped it.

"Good day."

Dexy left with new hope.

Gerrado could be beaten with her help.

Chapter 27. Visit from a Queen.

Narla sat on her dressing chair and put a necklace of emerald clusters. Her velvet dress fitted her curves perfectly. She was ready for her visit, though her thoughts were of Dexy. She had remembered how much she had missed him. His hands, his tall frame near her, his voice.

The weather looked cloudy but dry and the mountains threatened no rain. The servants had been up early preparing and saddling the horses, the journey was a two-hour ride, galloping most of the way until the last part where she could walk through the town and up to the castle. She wore a cloak to give her warmth on the journey. It fitted well and helped keep the wind from her legs. She was to ride over with Bevan and another servant to ensure she arrived safely.

Two hours of horse riding were fine on a clear dry day and she enjoyed the exercise. Gerrado was spraying himself head to toe in expensive oil. He threw clothes on and off trying each one carefully and looking at himself from all angles in the mirror. Visits from Narla he always took seriously. His mood was good and he swept around his bedroom dancing with a pretend partner in his arms.

He had no idea of what Narla would ask him and he would be willing to please her. If she could catch him off guard, all the better.

A medley of food was brought out as the two unusual friends sat down to dinner. Silverware and glassware were on show. Fruits and vegetables, accompanied the many courses of meats and cheese. Goose and pigeon were both included.

Gerrado was on form tonight,

"You look radiant," he admired. "such a beautiful neck garment."

"Oh, my necklace...? Thank you," Narla was used to his compliments, but blushed all the same.

The candle lights flickered in approval as the night went on.

Gerrado discussed the politics of the day: handling sluggets, and the city he had inherited. He was a shrewd operator and he wanted Narla to hear of his dealings. The

Slug Pit was not on his mind, so when he mentions his army and guards, Narla took her chance.

"You say your guards are many? Did you lose many in the prisoner break out was it two months ago?" she asked.

Gerrado tone lowered, "Yes, we lost a few, about a dozen, but they're easily replaced my dear, you know, there are many more, why do you ask?"

"Oh I just heard about it and was imagining the danger."

Gerrado mistook her question for fear, "My dear, there are no prisoners who could harm you. They are as weak as fleas down there. They have little food of any substance, it's a wonder they can move at all."

"Did many escape?" she continued while she could.

"Erm, no no, well... yes... erm... a few. It was a shock. We just weren't expecting an attack," he admitted.

"And now?"

"And now what?"

"Are you expecting an another attack?"

"We'll be ready!" Gerrardo replied slightly taken aback at the Queen's questioning him on the matter.

"What if you're taken by surprise again? What did they want?"

"They wanted a prisoner, Ava, claims she is a queen," he replied laughing in doubt.

"A queen? A Queen like me?"

"Not like you at all," he replied. "A village woman at best."

"Then why does she claim to be a Queen?"

"She claims to be Queen Amber, wife of King Marcus. She claims she escaped in the Great War and has lived with her son in the village for the last eleven years. She's a mad woman, that's all. These things have to be dealt with unfortunately. It's the nature of the beast."

"That's incredibly odd," answered Narla.

"Indeed! The woman is a fantasist. I've locked her up till she knows what truth means. It will hit her on the head one day. Till then she is an enemy of the sluggett state and she will be kept locked away."

"The people who rescued her? What of them? Will they not return?" asked Narla.

"If they do they will all die. We're ready. I've doubled sluggett power and they are alert and ready at all times," assured Gerrado.

The conversation was going exactly as Narla had hoped.

She watched Gerrado sip his fruity wine and topped him up with a smile at every chance. She played dumb.

"This Queen, is she like me?" she laughed.

"She is not like you. She is no Queen."

"I would like to meet this woman who claims she is a Queen."

"You must not trouble yourself."

"No, I'm not troubled, I'm genuinely curious. What is she like?"

"She is a village simpleton. Nothing for you to worry about."

Narla continued, she wasn't about to let up and let Gerrado patronise her.

"What if I could meet her?"

"You mustn't trouble yourself with these things."

"But you know me, Gerrado, I like a good experiment. I would like to study and see what she is like," she instated.

"But you can't be going into the Pit,"

"No, I suppose not," she paused and seemed to give up. "...but, what if she came to me." It seemed as if Narla had made this up on the spot, of course she had planned it to the last detail.

She added, "...What if, she came to my castle. To live for a while, so I could study her. She what she is like. I'm fascinated by such a woman. I want to know her story. The Warriors will be coming back to save her an if she isn't in the Pit, they will fail and I will have my little experiment. What if they next time they came to save her, she was here with me. I could keep her miles away where they wouldn't know to look. I want to see what she is like. I'm so fascinated!" Narla exclaimed it as if Gerrado had already agreed, making it harder for him not to agree.

Gerrado was a bit taken aback, he sat quietly taking in what she had said. He could not see the appeal. But he was not a man of sympathy with other people's pleasures. He thought. Narla stared intently at him. Her stare clouding his judgement and mind.

"It would make you happy?" he asked curiously.

"It would make me so happy and grateful. I get so bored here sometimes, this would be fascinating and it would be helping you!" she added.

"Quite," Gerrado wasn't sure. He took a gulp of wine. "She would have to come with guards?"

"Of course," said Narla.

"And I would have to check in on you more often?" he said adding more rules.

"It would be a pleasure." She replied, hardly daring to breathe with his agreement so close.

"No one could know she had been moved."

"It will be our secret. She will be safer at mine as no one will know where she is.

Think of it as our plan." She assured him. "Let's celebrate!" she clinked their glasses and sealed the deal further.

Gerrado had been ambushed so quickly, it would be hard to back down, so it was agreed.

The night continued. Narla remained attentive and she happily rejoiced, she had just got the deal she wanted. Dexy would be happy and she had been of help to him. She felt a wave of excitement throughout her body. Gerrado had never seen her so excited. He was confused, but it was having a most unexpected effect on her. He thought what harm can it do, if it made her happy

Chapter 28. Strength

Ava was moved three days later. She had three sluggett guards with her at all times. Narla had her room ready. It was luxury compared to the pit. Bevan sent word through Falconetta, who flew to the castle most days. It was an easy way for Bevan to communicate with the outsiders in the mountains. Luca was so happy to hear news of his mother. Dexy found himself smiling uncontrollably at having his plan work. It felt like a miracle.

Ava was frail. On arrival, she needed to rest. Her body so weak from the weeks in The Pit. Narla took her straight to her bedroom. She had a large bed with furniture and all the refinements of a guest's room. The carpet felt soft on Ava's feet. Narla was shocked at her frame, so small and thin. She looked ill, the dirt ingrained in her skin and nails. Bevan came up with soup. She had a few sips and went to sleep as the journey had tired her.

They let her sleep. Narla looked in on her almost every hour. She was fascinated by her. She felt she had saved her life. She knew she had stepped in just in time. The sluggetts stayed outside the room by the door taking turns to sleep, with two awake at all times. They had been instructed to be alert, something sluggetts found difficult at the best of times. They were happy with the soup and food Bevan brought them though, better than their Pit food, by miles.

Days passed and Ava's strength returned. The outsiders stayed away, not wanting to draw attention to their plan. Luca asked about his mother every day and falconetta said she had seen her through the bedroom window, getting stronger. Dexy spoke with Freedom Warriors, they had to plan their next steps. He gave Ava a week of rest and then set a day to see her. From there they could plan the next steps. For now gaining her strength was more important. Bevan's food was the best. Some days Narla would sit in with her and eat. They smiled and ate and then Narla would leave. Their eyes would meet, but little was said apart from pleasantries. Ava's strength was returning.

Falconetta told Narla and Bevan that Dexy would come the next night. He would visit Ava late on and travel alone. Bevan had some sleep inducing berries he could place in the sluggets evening drinks. They would sleep for a few extra hours, none the wiser. Everything was planned carefully, but Dexy knew he only had hours and they had a lot to discuss.

As night fell, the darkness guided Dexy through the woods he knew so well. His feet snapped on branches under foot with step he felt excitement. His duty as a Freedom Warrior had led him to this moment. With the new Queen and her son free, they might be able to gather and rise up to overthrow Gerrado. His mind raced onwards, as his journey continued. At the edge of the forest, his horse waited for him. He jumped on and rode quickly to the castle.

Bevan greeted him. He had watched from the windows and seen him approach. He walked down the large stairway, sluggets were snoring outside the room Ava was in. He opened the door and greeted Dexy, with a look of hope in his eyes, as their moment so wonderful, to have the old queen here and safe.

"How is she?" asked Dexy.

"She is stronger. She is well. Come and see," he replied.

They walked up the stairs. Narla waited at the top to the side by her bedroom. She smiled as they approached. They nodded to her. She peered over as they headed to the queen's room and followed. They were quiet, aware of snoring sluggets by the doorway. Bevan hoped he hadn't put too strong a dose in their drinks. They were out for the count.

The queen, Ava was sat up in her bed, she had been resting a week and felt well.

"Hello," she smiled as her rescuers walked in.

"You are well," confirmed Dexy to himself.

"I am," they all laughed.

"How's Luca?" she hardly could think of much else.

"Luca is well and settled into mountain life. Ettie is with him too, they ask about you ten times a day," said Dexy.

"He asks to see you every day," added Bevan.

"Yes," said Dexy.

"I am so happy to hear he is safe," Ava answered.

"He is safe." Assured Dexy.

"What next? When can I see him?" said Ava.

"First things first. Now you are well. I have other news. I feel I must tell you," said Dexy seriously.

Ava listened intently, no news could be more important than news of her son.

Bevan and Dexy drew up seats and sat beside the bed, and Narla sat on the opposite side, resting sideways and listening too.

Ava felt her heart beat faster. She felt the tension in their looks.

Dexy continued, "There is no easy way to tell you, but your husband, Marcus, is alive. He is living in the Ancient Burial grounds, being cared for by the Loban Masters."

"Wh..? Alive? I don't understand? Ho..? Being cared for...?" said Ava sitting upright with her questions falling from her lips all at once.

"He is being cared for, his memory is... it's well, he is not as he was," Dexy didn't know how to say it.

"Alive? But he's alive? How is that possible? He died...?" she couldn't comprehend what they had said.

"He was thought dead," Dexy added.

"Oh," Ava caught her breath.

"He is changed... unwell," added Dexy.

"Unwell?" she repeated.

"He cannot remember much. His memory is not good. He doesn't know me. He might not know you. He doesn't remember his old life as the king. He doesn't speak much. He has help, but he is not how he was." Added Bevan.

"His mind...you must be prepared. He is changed," Dexy tried to explain.

"I see, well I must see him." She said.

"Yes, we agree. You must," they agreed.

Nothing could prepare Ava for this change in her husband. He wasn't the same man. Her husband, the king, his mind, were all that of an old man. He was hardly there at all at times. It was not the man she knew, she had loved.

Dexy and the others talked with her and made their plans to get her to him. The only thing to do next was to see Marcus. She had to see him for herself. She would see Luca in a few days, but she begged for Dexy to take her to her husband. Dexy and Bevan had anticipated she would and were not going to argue as they knew they had to let her see him. They talked of her seeing him on the Friday, as it was the night when most sluggets including Gerrado would party into the early hours. They could travel by horse, Dexy and Ava and visit him, alone, at the Ancient burial grounds. It would be a long horse ride but Ava insisted she had the strength. Falconetta was to send a safe message to the Loban Masters and it would be arranged.

She had two days to wait.

Dexy had given her such news, it was mind blowing. Her mind raced and she could hardly believe what they had just told her. The next two days would be the longest wait for this queen.

Chapter 29. A Shoemaker

The Loban Masters were intimidating creatures. Their formidable shells on their backs gave their shadows such rounded shoulders of clout and honour. They walked slowly, and their shells heavy and protective gave them an ancient demeanour like no other in the Daccorian region. Their burial grounds, protected but over run with sluggett guards in the week, taking ancient gold back to Gerrado. It was an occupancy they had had for ten years. Their numbers were diminished down to forty odd, and they had no choice but to live like this. They adapted and got some pieces away to their vaults, but some had paid with their lives if caught no handing burial pieces over. They had housed Marcus for years. Thought to be dead. It was their biggest secret and though they had the king with them, they knew his illness left him no use to them or their cause. They kept him safe and cared for as best they could.

Dexy was used to the journey as he had visited Marcus so much in the last few weeks. Ava had made it. She was sore, not used to the riding, but ready to see Marcus and nothing would stop that. Wrapped in furs and layers of clothing to keep her warm on the way. Her scarf wrapped around her head for warmth and also disguise.

Sedgefield was expecting them. He ushered them in as soon as they arrived. There was a back entrance to the burial grounds for their purposes. No sluggett knew of it. The pitch black made their eyes wince. They could not risk and light. They walked along the garden pathway and down into the monastic building. It was an underground maze as well as a ground floor building. Marcus was way down in the basement. He was protected and far away from peering eyes and noise. Ava's stomach was so tense she thought she might be ill. She held her breath and carried on behind Dexy. Sedgefield kept them close, checking they were behind him. He walked with purpose down each corridor. The light of his shelled back kept their path lit. The torches on the walls of the basement grounds helped their eyes adjust. At last, Sedgefield stopped and with large keys opened a huge wooden door. He left it ajar and presented the room to them. He stepped away,

"I will leave you. I will return in an hour." He instructed.

"Thank you," the whispered. Ava's voice was so dry it stuck in her throat as she croaked.

Dexy knew what awaited her. Her husband, dishevelled and changed. Nothing could prepare her for the moment. They walked in to the room. The light was dim, a man sat sewing. Leather sole in his hand and a large needle and thread. He rocked slowly humming to himself and unaware of visitors.

Ava gasped at the sight of him. An old man, long wiry hair, knuckles of an old man, skin and bone, and his eyes focussed on the shoe he sewed. His mind seemed gone, even from a glance. His eyes stayed down. He didn't acknowledge their presence. Ava's heart sank instantly. She knew he was ill, it was as clear as day. She walked slowly to him. Crouched low, she took his hand in hers. She knelt beside him, as he sat on the bed and watched as he stopped to look at her. She blinked a tear of joy and grief, she was so happy to see him. He looked down at her and stared, it was hard to know what his mind recognised. Did he know her? He let her stay. He let her keep hold of his hand. It was more than some. It was a moment the shared, it wasn't clear what he could tell. But it was clear he was calm enough to let her stay by his side. She spoke gently,

"Marcus, it is Amber," she paused, her voice cracked.

He remained silent but still looked at her, his sewing was loose in his hands.

"Marcus, I'm here to talk with you. Would you like that?" she asked with care.

He stared and did not move. It was hard to tell his thoughts. It was hard to respond to so little.

Dexy stood back, for these moments. He eventually moved closer and too crouched lower so as not to alarm Marcus.

Ava couldn't think straight. She thought it would be easier. She gulped large choking words from her throat, only some came out. Her fingers trembled on his hand, as she remembered him so well, but ten years had taken forty from him. His mind too distant to remember her.

They sat and Dexy spoke to Marcus while he could see Ava struggling to recover from the shock.

"It's Dexy again. Ava has come to see you. We can sit with you. Do you know who she is? Do you remember Marcus? Do you remember your wife?" he spoke trying to be patient, but urgency was in his voice. He wanted so badly for Marcus to remember. Their time went slowly, their minutes ticked. Ava and Dexy took turns to speak. He sat quietly listening. He didn't move. He once looked at Ava as if to say something but words never came. The time went and Sedgefield returned to get them.

"Any joy?" he whispered, knowing the answer.

"Yes, thank you," said Ava refusing to give in.

"Thank you," Dexy added.

They got up to leave. Ava didn't want to leave him. She lingered as long as she could. Her eyes she could not take from him.

"Can we come again?" she asked, grabbing Dexy's arm.

"We will have to see. We must do what is best for everyone," he added.

Sedgefield interrupted, "Come let's get you back to the castle before those sluggetts wake up!"

They left together.

Dexy thanked Sedgefield and they walked to the grounds outside. Sedgefield checked it was clear. They walked quickly through the shadows.

Suddenly, Falconetta appeared in the sky. She flew down and went to Dexy.

"Gerrado, he's on his way to the castle!" She squaked. "He's minutes away, Dexy! You must return as fast as you can!"

Dexy and Ava climbed onto Falconetta's back. She was quicker than any horse.

"Speed and strength!" shouted Sedgefield as they left.

Their panic set in.

If Gerrado found Ava gone, he would want answers. Falconetta, Dexy and Ava flew off into the night sky.

Falconetta knew even with her wings carrying them quickly, they would still not make it back before Gerrado. She hoped Bevan and Narla could hold him off while they got back to the castle. If Gerrado discovered Ava gone, everything was lost.

Chapter 30. To the Castle!

Falconetta could see as far ahead as any eagle. She could see right into the castle door miles ahead and it was clearly open, she knew this meant Gerrado was inside. Her wings beat harder than ever. The cold night stung their faces, Ava and Dexy clung on for dear life as the bird carried them through the night. Ava's hands red raw and chapped she knew she must cling on and get back to the castle in time.

The falconette swooped down into the back garden of the castle grounds, they jumped free and ran. Ava followed Dexy. His instinct told him they were too late. He was to find Narla and Bevan. Ava ran faster behind him as they tucked into the side tunnel and through the back door, racing through the castle kitchen, on into the dining room and along to the bottom of the hallway and stairs. They could hear movement from upstairs. The downstairs doors were open bringing in a breeze and night air. Dexy pulled out his sword form his belt. He told Ava,

"I think we're too late. Gerrado's upstairs. Stay here. Keep back. Keep out of sight." He commanded.

"Are you sure, if I am there..." she asked.

"I think it's best," he replied, he was used to following his gut and it told him to keep the queen out of sight.

Walking up the wide staircase, he saw the bedroom door open, one of the sluggett slumped outside, lifeless. Attacked and badly injured, Gerrado's punishment for sleeping on the job, Dexy guessed. Dexy's legs continued sideways with his sword ready as he crept. He slowed down to listen.

Noise came from Narla's room. Muffled shouting and movement of furniture, the door open but not enough to see anything, he had to rely on what he heard. He crept, out of sight and ready. Behind the door his breath quickened and his heart thumped in his chest. He leaned in. Grabbing the door, he peered into the room. Gerrado's sword was over Bevan, he towered over the otter-man. Narla was by the large dressing room table and mirror, she was throwing brushes and vases at Gerrado in vain.

"Let him go!" she yelled.

"Where's my prisoner?" Gerrado demanded, tightening his grasp on Bevan's neck.

"She's not here! We don't know. She must have escaped."

"That's impossible!" Now where is she? Tell me where she is!" he yelled swinging over Bevan menacingly. A slice of skin bled with the edge of the knife melting into Bevan's neck.

Bevan remained as still as he could. He could feel the blood trickle down his neck to his shirt. He loosened the grasp as he pushed himself under Gerrado's arm and jumped up, swiping simultaneously at Gerrado's leg with his sword.

Gerrado yelped in pain, grabbing his leg. It oozed grey liquid.

"My sluggets drugged! My prisoner gone! I know you had something to do with it!"

he looked at Bevan and pointed his sword at him again, stabbing towards him. Bevan moved around out of the way of the blade. Dexy could see he was limping and injured, with blood pouring from his chest and leg.

Geraddo swiped again at the otter-man as he yelled questions at him.

"He's just the butler! We don't know anything Gerrado," cried Narla. "Please won't you listen?" she tried to calm him.

She ran over behind Gerrado and tugged at his arm, but he swiped her away. His elbow crunching against her throat.

The two sluggetts drowsily tried to catch the butler as he kept moving. They were slow but dangerous. Narla struck at them if they got too near to Bevan.

"Take her!" Gerrado cried to the sluggetts, pointing at Narla.

They moved to grab her as she threw herself out of their grasp. Both didn't co-ordinate with the other, their clumsy attempts were close but they couldn't stop her getting out of the way. Dexy took his chance. He flew into the bedroom, launching his sword over at the two sluggetts, swiping one down in a second, the other backed off into the corner as he saw his friend drop down to his knees and collapse, the fluid oozed form his body. Dexy threw a dagger to Narla. She caught is and looked for Bevan. Dexy moved quickly. He gave Narla some protection as Gerrado tried to swing his sword at her in anger. She stabbed the air with her dagger and kept him away.

Bevan was bleeding badly and moved more slowly. Dragging himself to a corner of safety across the floor. Blood smeared from his legs into the carpet and floor boards as he moved away. Gerrado noticed he was still near enough to reach for, with a few steps towards him, he grabbed him again. He put his sword on the otter man's chest and laughed cruelly. He was ready to strike. His face shone with glee. He had no mercy in him.

"Saved one, but not them all," he taunted Dexy as he pushed his sword into Bevan's chest.

The sword sliced through Bevan's tiny body fell onto the sword. He lay on the ground. His body lifeless, not moving. Narla screamed and ran to help him, but it was too late. She rushed to hold his body and pick him up to sitting.

Dexy roared and plunged his sword over at Gerrado. The two fought each other with pure rage. Their swords swooped and sliced into the other, as each moved right and left to win. Narla continued to hold Bevan. She watched as they fought and she watched her butler, her friend, breathe his last few breaths. The otter man closed his eyes and his body went limp in her arms. He took his final sigh. He knew she had him. Her hands felt warm as his body lost its fight and he felt the cold wash over him like a deathly blanket. It was peaceful as she held him. As silent as he had always imagined it.

Gerrado, still moving violently, sword swinging in every direction, saw his chance and grabbed the huge dressing mirror, flinging it down, and throwing it over the queen, as he jumped out of the way of Dexy's sword. Shards of glass flew at them. They both were covered in glass. The mirror smashed over her head, cutting into her arms and face as she tried to protect herself.

Dexy jumped forwards and as Gerrado's arms were high, ignoring the glass. Gerrado pounced on top of him, writhing over Dexy. He was on his back and Gerrado had momentum. With a heave forwards, Gerrado looked dangerous. He punched at Dexy on the floor. Something flickered from behind. It was a figure. The door opened further and running towards them both flew Luca. He grabbed Gerrado's head and pulled him away from Dexy, enough so that Dexy could pull up again and gain his balance.

"Get off him!" cried Luca. "Where's my mother!" he cried.

"Luca!" cried Dexy. "Your mother is safe!" he added to Luca, as the scuffle continued, both of them launching at Gerrado and tackled him to the ground. Dexy now had the chance he needed. Stood tall again and in front of Gerrado he was no match, "Stand back Luca!" he said as he launched himself forwards at the Slug King.

He plunged his sword into Gerrado's chest. The sluggett king let out a high pitched scream as his metal sword dug deep for one last time. Luca watched from the side as he saw the sluggett fall. Gerrrado's face stuck like terror did in one's eyes. His body wretched and the gooey liquid oozed from his grey chest. His heart was stopping and his life was going. Dexy held the sword upright. It sliced further through the sluggett's body. The other sluggetts dribbled and cowered in the corner, watching their king fade away. His sluggett hands clenched as the body sunk into a mound. Gerrado yelled more as his fight for life was ending. They watched as he fell. His final moment as his body gave in and slumped over. His eyes rolled up, his head to the side and his body twisted.

Gerrado was dead.

Dexy let go of his sword and ran to help Bevan.

"Help me!" he cried to Luca.

They grabbed the otter-man, but no life was left. Narla let them take him from her. They carried him over to the bed and laid him down. Dexy reached his hands to close his eyes. The otter-man looked proud and a smile rested on his face. Lucca felt his tiny legs in his hands as his placed them together. They stared at him so still and gave a moments thoughts to his honour.

Narla stood again, staggering and in shock. Her face was bleeding. Glass fell from her body as she stood up. He arms and legs shredded with cuts. Her face was red with blood and eyes were blinking it away. It blinded her vision and she stumbled further into the middle of the room. Dexy reached out his hand to hold her. She took his arm, feeling her way round as her vison was gone.

Dexy continued, "I've got you. It's ok!" he whispered.

"I'm ok," she said quietly, brushing herself down, feeling the glass and sticky blood in her fingers.

The two sluggets left stood frozen still as they watched.

Dexy turned to them,

"Sluggetts, go now. Save yourselves. Go back to the Slug Palace and tell them their king is dead. Tell them to head to their swamplands, to live in peace. Tell them to leave the city, their King is dead!"

The sluggetts moved quickly, falling over each other to leave. They knew they had been lucky to leave. Narla slumped onto the other side of the bed as she found her bearings. Dexy kept her hand, he would not let go. Luca watched as the sluggetts clambered to leave, falling over each other. He stared at Bevan and his eyes filled with tears for his friend.

Gerrado was dead. His body bent smaller than ever. Dexy looked at Narla. He could see her eyes were badly damaged. He reached for some bedding and ripped it, takin git to wipe her face, he brushed over, wiping the blood away.

"Luca, your mother is downstairs, go and find her," he instructed, but as he said it, a figure from the doorway walked through. It was Ava.

"Mother!" Luca cried rushing over and grabbing her so tightly she was nearly knocked over.

"My son!" she cried with joy.

Then seeing the body of Bevan on the bed and Gerrado dead on the floor, with Narla covered in blood.

"He's dead," assured Dexy looking at Gerrado.

"And Bevan too?" gasped Narla.

"A Freedom Warrior to the end. He died doing his duty," added Dexy.

"Luca are you hurt?" she asked.

"I'm fine," he added. They hugged momentarily, as they could see Narla needed help.

"Narla, let me see. Rip more bedding Luca," she instructed him and helped clear more blood from Narla's face. "We need to get word to the mountains, tell them," said Ava.

"Falconetta will already be there I'm sure by now," said Dexy.

"And probably sending a search party out for my son by now?"

"Yes, I'm sure they will be looking for you!" scolded Dexy.

"I had to come!" cried Luca.

"Your timing was impeccable as ever," laughed Dexy. "Your guts has all it's instincts like me." He added.

"Will we be safe now? Do we need to stay hidden? Will Luca be safe here or should we all go back to the mountains for cover?" asked Ava.

"We are all safe now Gerrado has gone. The sluggetts will leave the city, they never wanted to be here, they will return to their swamplands now he is dead." He replied.

"And no more wars?" said Ava.

"Gerrado lived for his power and war, but the sluggetts fought only from fear, not for their own truth. They will leave now," he knew they would not stay.

Chapter 31. The Villagers, a City and a Place.

News of freedom spreads quickly, as it should be.

From village home, to the city and far beyond that Gerrado was dead. Sedgefield smiled as he knew the occupation of their Ancient grounds was at an end. He watched the sluggetts leave. They had no reason to stay.

Villagers smiled as the thought of giving more money to The Slug Pit King faded into a distant memory. Their lives were free again. The city's market sellers danced on the hill up to the place, no longer overlooked by Gerrado and sluggett guards, as their market stalls glistened in the sun, and the new days set in.

In the mountains, the outsiders were preparing to leave. Gobber was hungry and therefore grumpy. Aviras was eager to get back home, though he hung around waiting to be told what to do. Jax and Ettie laughed at their food parcels they had made for each other for their journey to the village. Jee Hanna danced around happy that everyone was free. Luca packed his bedding and the things he had used during his time in the mountains. He hadn't much, but his pen knife and wooden carvings he would take.

Life under the Slug King seemed a distant memory. The mountains which had once been their home for so long now seemed a place where memories had been made.

Falconetta of course would be staying on her high mountain peak. They prepared for their journeys home, each one a very different place. Ettie back to the village, Jax too, in a nearby home.

Ava was at home packing her belongings. The sluggetts had been gone from the palace a good few weeks, and it was ready to be lived in again. Her heart nervous at returning after ten long years away. Her husband still being taken care of by the Loban Masters. He could move in when they had had time to visit him and see how his health was. Luca had a father to meet. Their lives were changing in front of their eyes.

Dexy decided he would move to be with Narla to help her with her recovery and be her eyes; her sight. He did everything. He rarely left her side, as he helped her regain her confidence and her sight improved but never fully returned. He was no longer an outsider, they had their freedom and his days of fighting were over. Jee Hanna went with him, spreading her glittery wings, making days filled with wishes, the castle was always busy. She saw Luca at every chance she got and went up to the place whenever she was allowed. Gobber lived with Ava and Luca at the palace. He was to help, give them a hand with anything they needed. Luca loved having him there. He was a dear friend and made them laugh at every meal time with his jokes.

And so it became that the freedom won was freedom they gave to each other...

The new queen, Ava ran the palace. She did not command over the villagers, or in the city; they had their own ways now. She had her household in the palace, and one day would pass it on to Luca. His home, and for now he had his own growing up to do. He would be King in his own time. A king of choice, and for the times. Their world had changed. Kings, queens were as any; a man, a woman, a freedom warrior, villager or forest creature.

That summer, plans for Marcus to return to the palace were made. As day by day his mind grew stronger, and his memories began to return bit by bit, not all, but some. Luca and Ava's daily visits to the burial grounds to see him had helped him gain more strength and his mind seemed to be coming returning slowly. He made his shoes and carved wood every day. He would smile and laugh with his son and wife. His eyes came back to life. He was returning to them. Keto had some medicine which he took too. Luca and Ava constantly found new ways to help him. Ava talked of their days gone by, and Luca brought talk of new days and the future too. Dexy, Narla and Sedgefield and his friends would also visit. Their friendships sustained him and his health grew. He would take daily walks in the ancient grounds amoung the Loban Masters. Some of his memory came back more than they had ever hoped for. Luca helped his father; he learnt to make shoes in the hours they spent together. The Loban Masters agreed when, it was time for him to leave their basement and return to the palace. He could live there again. Not as King, but as a father.

Their new lives began. They built their new days and nights as they wished and dreams became reality. They sometimes remembered the times when they had felt so far away and thanked the stars at night for their patience and light.

A dream is always a wish in the right direction. And so as it was in the beginning, it is now in the ending.

Luca now knew why his father had never shown himself to him in The White Lake. The White Lady never told of the living. His father was alive and his legacy would be there in history, a shoe maker and a king. A lost king, found by chance.

A story complete, and nothing is ever really lost forever if you want to find it. Look inside for truth and it will find you.

"When your dreams seem furthest away,
That is when they are the closest to you.

Time is important for dreams to prevail.
Dreams will follow patience.

Their lengthy-making is always underestimated.

But dreams will always find you,
Always know that."

In a distant swampland the son of Gerrado sat. He flicked the mud away from his leg. He was too proud to bathe in it like the other sluggetts who spent their days basking in the mud. His dreams were of laws and gold, and rings for his clumpy fingers. Worrom's hand reached out. He wore a silver bracelet on his wrist, a bracelet engraved-

'For a King.'

Printed in Great Britain
by Amazon